HOSTAGE to FORTUNE

HOSTAGE to FORTUNE

Elizabeth Chaplin

THE MYSTERIOUS PRESS
New York • Tokyo • Sweden
Published by Warner Books

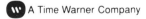 A Time Warner Company

First published in Great Britain in 1992 by Scribners, a Division of Macdonald and Co. (Publishers) Ltd., London and Sydney.

 Mysterious Press books are published by Warner Books, Inc., 1271 Avenue of the Americas, New York, NY 10020.

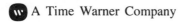 A Time Warner Company

The Mysterious Press name and logo are trademarks of Warner Books, Inc.

Printed in the United States of America

First U.S. printing: March 1993

10 9 8 7 6 5 4 3 2 1

Library of Congress Cataloging-in-Publication Data

Chaplin, Elizabeth.
     Hostage to fortune / Elizabeth Chaplin.
          p.   cm.
     ISBN 0-89296-504-5
     I. Title.
     PR6053.H3476H67   1992
     823'.914—dc20   92-53720
                                                             CIP

HOSTAGE to FORTUNE

Prologue

The grounds of the onetime farmhouse were semi-wild, bounded on one side by a tall wooden fence bleached almost white. The harsh light reflected off the faded wood; what scraps of varnish remained were curled and blistered, giving off a sharp, hot smell. On the other side, birds wheeled and circled, swooping down, calling. A border of parched earth had been dug beneath it, clay baked by the now expected sun which shone, as it had for the last seventeen improbable days, in an unclouded sky. It had been thirty-five days since it had rained.

The fence came to an abrupt end halfway down; whether there had ever been more of it was a matter for speculation. The soil there had been newly dug, dark against the rest of the pale, dry earth. The greenery backing onto it had been hacked back to allow vehicular access to the rear of the property; a dirt-track led onto the main road, just where it curved away down towards the town which lay beneath. An empty car, dusty from weeks of banned hosepipes, was parked there. Straight on, but rolling over hilly countryside, the road, on its way to link up with the motorway, bypassed a village whose church spire could just be seen in the hazy distance.

The other boundary was marked by a stream which ran almost unnoticed through a tangle of bracken and elder and tall grass; it had been reduced to a trickle now, and the vegetation grew pale and brittle in the unforgiving drought.

In between was an oasis; sunlight glinted on the clipped and rolled blades of grass of a turfed lawn, lush and green, illicitly watered every night. A joyful confusion of summer flowers, bright splashes of color in the washed-out landscape, spilled over the edges, and a bee hummed industriously as white butterflies swooped and dived.

Beyond that, under the shade of an oak, was a terrace of tiny pebbles, and a white-painted table at which three people sat. They weren't young; they weren't old. One of the men had certainly reached middle age. Sunlight glinted on the wine bottle as the younger of the men reached across the other to pour the last of its contents into the woman's glass, and she thanked him with mock prettiness.

She wore a sleeveless top loose over matching white shorts that accentuated the length and elegance of the brown legs at which the older man glanced appreciatively as he rose and wandered away from the table towards the road. He wore slacks and an open-neck shirt, thin summer socks and open sandals.

The other wore a T-shirt and shorts, and a baseball cap protected his ever more evident scalp. The gravel rustled under his tennis shoe as he tentatively moved his foot closer to the shapely ankle now that the obstruction had gone; he hurriedly withdrew it, creating a small cloud of dust. He reached for his glass to cover his slight embarrassment. She laughed, giving him encouragement; he leaned on the table as he shifted seats, the wood hot beneath his hand, despite the shade. At the other side where the empty bottles cast green mottled shadows, the sun was beating down unchecked,

2

and heat rose from the baking surface in a visible distortion of air. The smell of scorching paint mingled with the wine and the woman's perfume as he sat beside her.

The older man walked through the scrubby, mutilated grass, and took a pipe from his pocket, filling it slowly, contemplatively, from a worn leather pouch. He put the match back in the box once he had lit the pipe, and stood, arms folded, pipe jammed between his teeth, his eyebrows drawn into a frown of puzzled interest. Sexual cross-currents were always interesting, but these had an odd quality, as though the two were players in a drama.

He turned as a flash of sun on glass heralded a car making its way down from the distant village. For a moment, it disappeared in an invisible dip in the road, then emerged again, its ghostly image reflected in the heat haze. The mirage dissolved as the car swung down towards the town which sat under a misty veil of smoke and exhaust gases. The man grunted quietly, and turned his back on the road to watch the tableau once again.

Beside the house, the door of a newly built double garage sat open; inside could be seen the sleek lines of a Rolls, and outside on the garage forecourt, a sporty Mercedes and another, less upmarket car.

Inside the house, a third man, unseen by his guests, pressed a gloved fingertip down on the controls of the hi-fi; obediently, silently, the cassette began to run, taking up the leader tape. He turned the speakers towards the open patio window at the other end of the long room, and left, walking through the hallway and into the kitchen.

A sudden, deafening crack shattered the still air, disturbing the birds, but the people at the table didn't seem to notice. The woman touched the man's wine glass with her own, and took a sip as he stood the empty bottle beside another on the far side of the table, beyond the sharp, barely moving shadows of the leaves. A moment later, in a flurry of flapping wings, birds flew out of the tree, out of the tangled mass by the brook, out of the guttering of the house, and back over the fence. The silence which had followed the report was broken once again by birdsong, as they settled back down.

In the kitchen, the champagne bottle beaded with moisture as soon as the man removed it from the fridge, and he took a stainless-steel bucket from the lower shelf, placing the bottle inside. He reached into the freezer for the bag of ice, his hands growing numb as he packed it around the bottle.

He glanced into the garden, then smiled at the woman who was in the kitchen with him. She didn't smile back. He looked again from the darkness of the badly designed kitchen into the bright heat outside; he could see his guests, but they still couldn't see him.

Two sat at the table, and the third stood a little way back, watching them. They had been carefully chosen. There was the ex-police officer with whom he had had a fairly prickly relationship during the years of undistinguished legal practice in the town but which had turned to friendship since his enforced and untimely retirement from the legal profession; an old friend from childhood, just out of the army, ludicrously trying to pretend that he wasn't going bald by wearing a baseball cap, and predictably trying to seduce his third guest, the journalist whose luscious limbs were not up for grabs, despite the impression she was giving.

But this is really very nearly the end. The beginning was much earlier in the year...

January

Jeff Bentham caught a momentary glimpse of someone familiar in the crush of people around him. Graying hair, dark complexion, bored expression which broke into a smile when he realized it was his own reflection in a mirrored pillar. All around him, people made merry; balloons burst, music played, laughter and talk filled the room.

His wife had never had so much champagne in her life. Glass after glass, going down like water, and they still hadn't got to the presentation. She was looking forward to that; not just because they were going to give her a check for one million, four hundred and eighteen thousand, three hundred and twenty-one pounds and thirty-seven pence—the amount was engraved on his memory—but because Richard Price was going to present it. She had been irritated with him because he couldn't place Price at first; Jeff Bentham wasn't a man for soap operas. She had seemed more pleased about that than about the money.

He was sober, and waiting for all this nonsense to be over. Trust Susan not to put a cross for no publicity. They hadn't

5

had a moment to themselves from when she had made the phone call; there seemed to have been people surrounding them day and night. Advising them, instructing them, organizing them. He had had no idea that winning the pools was going to be such hard work. Susan was loving it all— every call, every visit, every reporter.

He closed his eyes and tried not to think about tomorrow morning's tabloids, or the faint contempt in which he had always held previous winners, grinning inanely, clutching outsized checks and saying that nothing would change. Now he was going to be one of them, for it was entirely true to say that he had no intention of giving up his job. He was a partner in a firm of solicitors, and he enjoyed the work. He liked seeing clients, and sorting out their affairs. He looked forward to Thursdays and his weekly appearance in the magistrates' court, when he would try to convince skeptical greengrocers and factory owners that his client had been more victim than villain. Perhaps, he thought, he had used that line rather too often of late. He'd work on a new one.

But then again, why shouldn't his life carry on as before? He wasn't a pools winner. He was married to a pools winner, and had still to work out whether that was better or worse. He had always faintly disapproved of Susan's slavish filling in of her coupon every week, but not enough to talk her out of it. Of course, it had never occurred to him that she would ever win. Now she *had* won, and for the moment, they were part of a circus that rolled on unstoppably. Sometimes he wondered if anyone would notice if he and Susan left, so little did they have to do with it. Publicity was all. Still, he supposed the temporary loss of normal life, the brief and soon forgotten public exposure, however embarrassing and tedious, was a small investment for such considerable financial gain. But it could all have been avoided if she had just asked for no publicity.

It had been a January Saturday not just like any other, but like every other. Cold, intermittent rain had streaked the windows, and a chilly breeze had stirred the neatly clipped

6

privet of the hedge as he had sat slumped on the sofa in front of the television. He couldn't work in the garden in the dead months, and he had been watching without much interest as the second half of a rugby league match had unfolded muddily before his eyes. He had bought Susan a little black and white portable for the kitchen, so that she could watch the Saturday afternoon film. The match had finished, the results of the day's sporting endeavors had been duly reported. He hadn't taken much notice; he was a summer games man.

Susan had come in from the kitchen, a piece of paper in her hand, her usually pale cheeks slightly pink.

"Jeff—I think I might have won something," she had said, rather as though she had been confessing a guilty secret.

He had made some remark about how much she had sent them over the years, words to the effect that she was still the net loser. She had gone quiet then, and he had thought no more about it.

But that night, she had barely slept. She had risen early, unusually so for a Sunday, and had seemed almost nervous, glancing out of the window at the cold gray morning every now and then. She had almost knocked him down in her rush to get to the papers first when the letter-box had finally clattered, indicating their arrival.

She had looked up from the paper, her cheeks pink again. "I think I've won a lot of money, Jeff," she had said, her voice quiet.

Now he took a glass of champagne from the young woman who circulated with a tray, and watched as the TV news cameras and the press photographers began to crowd around the little makeshift stage. At last it was happening. They were going to get the money.

He thoughtfully appraised the two girls who had come in, carrying a six-foot by three-foot piece of card up to the stage. They wore tight dresses which finished mid-thigh, and sashes bearing the name of the pools promoter fell from their shoulders across pert breasts. Not bad. Not bad at all.

7

People were still crowding around Susan, and he caught her eye. She rose, obviously a little startled to find that the movement hadn't been all that easy, and almost stumbled into one of the photographers. He had never seen her tipsy.

"How do you fancy having a rich wife?" someone asked him.

"I fancied her poor," he said, with a smile.

It was the truth; he had fancied her, once. Now the moments of shared pleasure had grown less frequent, but that was what happened after almost twenty-five years of marriage, he supposed. You couldn't fancy your wife. You could fancy scantily dressed would-be models like the two who stood on the stage ready for their big moment; you could fancy someone like Fiona, the streamlined journalist with the long dark hair and long shapely legs who was practically living with them. But not your wife. You got too used to one another; a great deal of the time was merely passed in one another's company.

He had fancied Susan when she had worn back-combed hair, pale make-up with even paler lipstick, and black mascara around her eyes. He smiled to himself as he looked at her now, infinitely more attractive with her brown hair straight and short, her eyes faintly powdered, her lips just pink, and wondered how the sixties warpaint had ever worked. But it had.

He had been an articled clerk then, with a short back and sides when other youths of his age were wearing their hair long, but he had had a profession, which was how come he had scored with Susan. He had been a catch in her eyes. Which meant that she had been prepared, after a couple of months' increasingly adventurous courtship, to come across. That, in the not-so-swinging sixties, had been enough to make her fanciable, and once had been enough to make her pregnant. Which was how come he had married her on the 31st of May 1966, when he was twenty-one, and she was seventeen.

*   *   *

Susan made her way carefully through the people and the tables and the chairs to where Jeff sat.

"They're almost ready," she said, and was surprised by the numbness. She couldn't really feel her lips, and that made talking really quite difficult.

Jeff smiled. "You're getting sozzled," he said.

She nodded slowly. She had always disliked alcohol; a shandy was about the nearest she had ever got to drinking. And the odd glass of wine at weddings and things. Never more than two. And she had lost count of how many she had had since they had arrived at the hotel; when she had at last been able to relax, knowing that it really was happening, it hadn't been a mistake. She had ridiculously found herself hoping that it *was* a mistake when she had checked her coupon with the football results, in case it upset Jeff. He hadn't liked her doing the football pools. The poor sending money every week to the rich, he had said, but she thought it was too working-class for him, really. But he hadn't been angry; far from it. He hadn't stopped smiling since last Thursday.

"Susan—Jeff?" Fiona, the girl who had been assigned to them by a Sunday newspaper to be a fly on the wall through the post pools-win period, appeared at her elbow. "They're just waiting for you, I think," she said, smiling at Susan. "The star of the show."

Susan felt stricken. "Where do I go?" she asked.

"Up onto the stage," Fiona laughed. "Follow me."

Jeff's eyes followed Fiona first, travelling down from her long, dark, shining hair past the trim waist and neat bottom to the colored tights she wore. Susan watched him as he watched Fiona, and he switched his attention back to her, smiling.

"Ready?" he asked.

She nodded, too petrified to move.

He stood up, putting his hand under her elbow. She was glad of the support, trembling as she was. They walked through the throng to the stage, and stood behind the microphones.

Everything became a little hazy, as her heart started to

beat faster and faster. Someone was speaking; the man from the pools was smiling at them. Two girls were off to the side, manhandling an outsized bit of cardboard. Then Richard Price appeared, and Susan's legs began to tremble. Jeff put his arm around her, and Richard Price started speaking.

She couldn't take in what he was saying. She could just see tanned skin, white teeth, and brown hair attractively graying at the temples. She found herself looking at the girls in the wings, envying them their figures. She had looked like that once, she thought. She wasn't that much overweight. If she lost a bit, perhaps she still could look like that . . .

"One million, four hundred and eighteen thousand, three hundred and twenty-one pounds . . ."

There was clapping, cheering, as the girls wiggled across the stage on their ultra high heels.

". . . and—of course—thirty-seven pence!" There was laughter.

Richard Price took the huge check from the girls with difficulty, and Susan and Jeff posed, holding it, holding one another, laughing, crying, as loudspeakers played tunes about money. Richard Price kissed her. Fiona kissed her. Jeff kissed her. Fiona kissed Jeff. Cameras flashed, and a huge bottle of champagne was opened with an explosion like gunfire. Another glass of champagne . . . hundreds of photographs, more kisses, more laughter.

"Richard—Richard! Put your arm around her!"

Richard Price's arm came around her shoulders, and she was squeezed against him as the flashbulbs popped. She could smell his aftershave as he pressed his face to hers, and the photographers crowded in.

"What are you going to do with all this money?" asked a reporter.

She had rehearsed this, but there had been too much champagne, too much excitement. Richard Price smiled at her. His arm went from her shoulders to around her waist. More photographs.

"I have to think about it," she said. She was answering the questions being thrown at her, but she wasn't really paying attention to them. Richard Price still held his arm around her waist, the little squeezes he gave her now and then apparently involuntary, in the crush of people on the stage.

"What about the old man? Is he getting any?"

Laughter greeted the deliberate *double entendre*. Jeff joined in, shaking his head, but he had no complaints in that department, and neither had she. It was a good marriage, basically. There weren't rows, not as with some of the couples they knew. He had seen enough of bad marriages in the course of his profession to know that theirs was all right. Susan was a wonderful cook, as his waistline could testify. She looked after the house, and him, and he looked after the garden and provided for her. The ever-rising mortgage rate had been a worry, but Susan got most of the things she asked for. All in all it was a satisfactory arrangement; a good marriage. Not exactly exciting, but he could always look elsewhere for that.

"He'll get the thirty-seven pee," said Richard Price, to more laughter.

He couldn't actually remember it ever having been exciting. It must have been, surely, to start with. Well . . . maybe before they were married, when he got her pregnant. There surely must have been some urgency, some passion then? But he couldn't, in all honesty, remember it. She had been very young; it had been more in the nature of coercion than passion.

She had got pregnant, so they had got married. Had he loved her? Probably not. She had been frightened to tell him about the baby; he remembered that. She had thought that he wouldn't want to marry someone like her. Her inflated idea of his importance in the social scheme of things had never diminished; she still thought of doctors and solicitors and other professionals as being somehow a cut above her, and spent her every waking hour living up to the image she had created. That was why she didn't normally drink, in his opinion. In case the façade slipped. She hadn't even joined

11

him in a celebration drink when the win had been confirmed. There had been a strange lack of excitement even then.

He had been excited about the baby, once he had stopped being appalled. Even before the hurriedly arranged wedding, he had had visions of handing out cigars, of changing nappies, of helping with homework, of school prize-givings and sports days. Even of setting up his own practice in the fullness of time, so that he would have something to pass on. Bentham and Son, solicitors. Susan would have loved that. But it wasn't to be. She had lost the baby, and they had remained childless. Now that he could set up on his own, now that they did have something to hand on, there was no one to hand it on to. Their son would have been twenty-four now, he thought.

So here they were, not a pools promoter's dream, but at least not a nightmare. They would have preferred newly-weds or old-age pensioners, but they were happy to settle for a reasonably attractive, forty-something couple whose lives had been blessed with God-knew-how-many first dividends. Better than a gay hairdresser, or an unemployed, tattooed brickie's laborer.

More questions, more champagne, more photographs. And Richard Price's arm around Susan's waist all the time. If you asked Jeff, Price fancied her. He didn't blame him; she was looking very good tonight. Inebriation suited her; it brought the color to her face, like the realization of the win had done.

The urbanely pleasant Mr. Price handed her on to Jeff as the photographers howled at them above the noise.

"Let's have you both together!"

* * *

Jeff's arm now, and more staged kisses for the cameras, until at last they had all got what they wanted, and melted away.

Richard Price took two glasses from a passing tray, and handed them one each. "Congratulations," he said. "I really am delighted for you both."

"Aren't you having a drink?" Susan asked.

He smiled again. "Better not," he said. "I'm onstage in a couple of hours."

"What are you in?" asked Jeff, in the easy way he had, as he set his glass down untouched. She wouldn't have dared ask, would have thought she ought to have known.

"Pretentious nonsense," said Richard. "I don't understand a word of it, but it keeps the wolf from the door for another week or two."

Susan laughed at the idea of his having to keep the wolf from the door.

"Well," said Richard Price. "How *did* you feel, when they told you? I know everyone's asked you already."

Susan smiled. Her reactions on winning the money had been a very definite sequence of emotions. Disbelief, followed by a feeling of elation which had turned into a stab of something very like fear in case it displeased Jeff. Which was odd, and unfair. She had no reason to be afraid of him. Bewilderment. All that money, and she had no idea what she wanted to do with it. Anger, for a while. She had almost made up her mind to walk out on her dead marriage, but the money changed things. What would people say, what would they think, if she went now? She couldn't go. The money was just another trap. Then . . . after all that, up there on the stage, a distinctly pleasurable feeling of power.

"I can't put it into words," she said.

"Have you thought of what you're going to do?" Price asked.

She smiled, and felt it again. "Oh, yes," she said. She didn't elaborate.

Richard Price looked a little surprised at her brief answer, but with the smooth fluency of someone used to making small talk, he steered the conversation comfortably around to himself, which suited Susan as much as it did him. It clearly bored Jeff.

"Er. . . Fiona?" he said diffidently, detaching himself from Susan as Fiona passed by, "Could I have a word, do you think?"

13

"Of course," she said brightly.

Susan watched as they walked through the smoky gloom of the room to a table at the far side, and turned back to Richard. "Tell me about the play you're in," she said.

* * *

"Seems like a pleasant man," Jeff said, with a jerk of his head back at Price.

"Yes," said Fiona, looking a little puzzled.

They sat down, and both shook their heads as the ever-circulating trays of champagne appeared.

"What did you want to talk to me about?" she asked.

Jeff cast around for something plausible. "The . . . the articles you'll be doing on us," he said. "Do we get to see them before they're published?"

"It's not usual," she said, her voice a little doubtful. "But I suppose if you insist . . ."

"No, no." He smiled. "Just wondered."

She frowned. "Sorry—wondered what, exactly?"

"If we would be seeing you again," said Jeff.

"I doubt it," she said. "My brief was to cover the winner from notification to presentation." She shrugged. "It's finished now." She smiled. "I don't suppose he wants to take any risks with what happens after you've got the money," she said. "The stories aren't always rosy."

"He" was the multimillionaire pools promoter who had just bought the Sunday paper.

"I haven't won any money," he reminded her.

"No," she said.

"So, I'm not your . . ." He searched for the right words. "Your professional concern," he said. "What I do afterwards is my business." He smiled. "I'd rather like it to be yours as well. But nothing to do with your boss." He glanced around at Susan. "Or mine," he said, looking back at Fiona.

She looked at him for a long time, her gray eyes a little wary.

14

He smiled again. He'd made body contact when everyone was kissing everyone else; it was no accident that Fiona had hung around, though technically her job was over. "Well," he said, lowering his voice. "For the past few days I've seen a great deal of you, and I like what I've seen. I flatter myself that maybe so have you."

Her mouth opened slightly, and he had the uncomfortable feeling that he had misjudged the situation.

"Tell me," she said, after some moments, "have you always expected women to come running, or is it just since the money?"

He laughed. "No harm in trying," he said. He didn't want this to become heavy; it was just a pass. If she was saying no, it certainly wouldn't be the first time.

"I think I'd better assume that you've been too liberal with the champagne too," she said.

He shook his head, and held up his index finger. "One glass," he said. "One of us had to stay sober."

She glanced across at Susan and Price. "That's your wife over there, Mr. Bentham," she said.

"What's with 'Mr. Bentham'? It's been Jeff up until now."

"Perhaps it shouldn't have been. And perhaps you should try staying faithful as well as sober."

He held up his hands. "I go home every night," he said "That's faithful, isn't it?"

"I see." She glanced across the room. "What about your wife?" she asked. "Is she faithful too?"

He smiled. "Oh, yes," he replied. "But Susan's properly faithful. No dalliance with the milkman."

"Perhaps you should be taking a little more notice of what she's doing now," she said.

Jeff twisted around to see Price and Susan sitting at a table, their heads close together as they agreed how wonderful he was. "Price?" he said, and laughed.

"Price," she said firmly. "Who has just come through a very messy and very costly divorce. Who has done nothing that has brought in more than rent money since the series ended two years ago. Who is very seriously chatting up your very attractive, seriously rich wife."

"He'll find out it isn't worth the hard work," he said.

Fiona raised her eyebrows. "A millionairess is always worth hard work," she said.

Jeff shook his head. "There is one thing that's important to Susan," he said, "and one thing only. The look of things. Right now she may be drunk enough even to lead him on, but I'm willing to bet the entire million and a half that he is not going to have his wicked way with either her body or her money." He leaned towards her, dropping his voice again. "Whereas," he said, "I have the great good fortune to be her husband. I'm entitled to a share of both. You could help me celebrate my luck." He twisted around again to look at Susan, just as Price sneaked a look at his watch, and he laughed, turning back to Fiona. "She is also very seriously dull," he said.

"Doesn't it bother you that I might put this conversation into my final article?"

He shook his head, still smiling.

A moment later, Price was at their table, apologizing for having to leave, shaking hands with him again, wishing him health and happiness. Susan still sat at the table, apparently lost in thought. Then she smiled across at Jeff, and stood up.

"Any chance of a phone number?" Jeff asked out of the corner of his mouth as Susan made her distinctly unsteady way towards them.

*   *   *

Susan walked slowly and carefully towards the table. Even at that distance, she could see that her husband was flirting with Fiona.

He was attractive, she supposed. Not terribly tall, but tall enough. Funny—she always thought of him as dark, but she could see now, looking at him for what seemed like the first time in years, that the curly, almost black hair was grizzled now, an effect that was perhaps even more attractive. Perhaps he was a little too fond of her cooking.

She was offered yet more champagne as she crossed the room. Even she waved it away this time.

Susan had met Jeff Bentham when she was working in a hotel, waiting on tables, earning some money before she went back to school to do her A levels again. Her mother had died a few months before she had sat them; her father had been convinced that she would get straight A's if she went back and took them again.

Jeff had flirted with her, just as he was doing now with Fiona. She had agreed to meet him, and it had developed from there. His parents had been less than pleased when he had declared his intention of doing the decent thing by her; they didn't care how pregnant he had got her. But marry her he had, and going back to school to re-take your A levels once married simply wasn't done in the sixties.

Fiona laughed as she joined them at the table. "Your husband's a terrible flirt, Susan," she said.

"I think I'm a jolly good flirt," he said, looking wounded.

Susan thought of Richard Price, and the book of matches from his hotel he had slipped into her hand as he left. "Drop by if you're passing," he had said. She had felt it again then: the power.

She stayed with the party for as long as she could, but she had never felt like this before. It was disorienting, unnatural; she didn't think she wanted to drink too much again.

*   *   *

There was a tiny dance floor, but Jeff had noticed that people seemed to be more into serious drinking, as Fiona would doubtless have said. She had excused herself after a suitable length of time, and wished Susan luck with whatever she decided to

17

do with the money. Susan had accepted a kiss on the cheek, and smiled. "I know what I'm going to do," she had said.

Dozens of people had joined them, some Jeff knew and some he didn't; they hadn't been alone all evening. Eventually, Susan had had enough.

"I'm a little tired," she said, in the euphemism of the year. "I think I'd like to go up now."

She had to catch the table as she got to her feet, and Jeff watched her make her carefully measured, would-be sober way to the lift. "Goodnight," he said, to whoever it was who had joined them. "And thank you." He wasn't sure what he was thanking them for. For coming to a free do? For claiming some sort of relationship with Susan?

He followed her to the lobby, a little puzzled still by her parting shot at Fiona. "What is this mysterious thing you want to do?" he asked, as the lift hummed its way up.

"It'll keep," she said.

In the honeymoon suite, they decided on black coffee for Susan and a whisky for him, and had no other communication until room service had delivered their order.

"What do you want to do tomorrow?" asked Jeff. "Stay in London or go back home?"

She sipped her coffee thoughtfully. "I . . . I think I'd like to stay," she said. "Do some shopping. But you won't like that."

"No," he said. "But that's all right—I don't mind amusing myself."

"Good," she said.

He had fancied Susan, once. He quite fancied her now, in her unaccustomed insobriety. Their marriage, reasonably successful though it was, had held very few surprises. Susan drunk was a pleasant one. Most had been unpleasant, like the miscarriage. That had been the only time in his adult life when he had cried. Perhaps if they had tried again . . . but Susan had steadfastly refused to contemplate another pregnancy.

Would he have married her if she hadn't been pregnant? Probably not. Or perhaps to spite his parents, who were so shocked at his having become involved with a *waitress*, of all things. Or perhaps—yes, perhaps because his friend Rob had fancied her. But Rob had been unemployed, thinking of joining the army as a private. No contest. He smiled. It was the only time in his life he had beaten Rob to the punch.

She had finished her coffee, and was undressing. He watched her, thinking about what Fiona had said.

It had taken him by surprise; he had never regarded himself as anything other than faithful. He was dependable, hard working. He was there when Susan needed him, to put up a shelf or change a plug. He hadn't run off with anyone, leaving her alone; he had never got emotionally involved with anyone else. He flirted with women; he always had, and now and again over the years, he had taken the opportunities that had come his way as a result. But in the main, he had cleaved only unto Susan.

She was still awake, even by the time he had finished his nightcap, though her side of the bed was in shadow. He stood up, but the effort involved in that simple movement made him suddenly aware that he was desperately tired. It was all such hard work; they had been up since dawn, and there had been precious little sleep for days before that.

He put out his light and walked to the window, looking out at the still-busy streets shiny with the rain which patterned the glass with glistening beads of light. He pushed it open, and listened to the rumble of traffic, felt the spots of cold rain fleck his face. He took a deep breath of chilly night air, and closed the window again.

He turned to look at Susan, his hand going to his pocket, checking that the shred of paper napkin was still there. He undressed in the dark and got into bed.

"Goodnight, love," he said.

*　　*　　*

He had watched her as she undressed; she couldn't remember the last time he had done that. Not since they were first married, and their silver wedding was less than six months away. Well, she didn't care what people would expect now that she had come into money; a big celebration was out. She had thought, when he had got to his feet, that he was coming to her, but he hadn't been. Not that it mattered.

Her head swam a little when she closed her eyes, so she opened them again, looking at the unfamiliar shapes and shadows thrown up by the street-lighting faintly illuminating the room.

She wasn't entirely sure when the idea had come to her; she wasn't sure it even qualified as an idea yet. She thought it was when the reporters asked her what she was going to do with the money. She and Jeff had rehearsed her reply. A joke reply. They weren't going to do anything rash straight away. They were going to wait a few months, and *then* do something rash.

She hadn't really forgotten what she had been going to say; it had been there, floating about at the back of her mind. She had blamed the champagne for not being able to get the words out, but she knew now that that wasn't it. She had known then, *because* of the rehearsed reply, what she wanted to do with the money.

And it wasn't something she could discuss.

*　　*　　*

Jeff saw it the following afternoon, when he left Fiona's flat. He was about to cross the road, when a gust of wind threw rain into his face, and turning, he caught a glimpse of it through the showroom window. He walked quickly, collar turned up as rain hit the back of his neck, down the side street to the entrance. Carpet. Carpet, in a car showroom. He wiped his shoes on the rubber mat, and walked in.

There it was, standing alone, a study in understated sensuality, a discreet notice indicating that it was available. It hadn't got a price on it, of course. He walked around it, running his hands gently over the smooth lines, reaching in through the open window to grasp the steering wheel. The smell of polished leather teased his nostrils, and he inhaled sheer luxury. There were a few miles on the clock; that just made it all the more desirable, in his opinion. He straightened up, standing back to admire the sleek body, beautifully put together, and quite irresistible. He let his fingers slide from the roof, over the bonnet, down to the Spirit of Ecstasy, which shrank from his touch, and disappeared.

He smiled. That was the only detail in which it had differed from Fiona.

"Trophy hunters, sir," said the salesman, sounding more like a gay Scottish butler. "She just goes into her bolthole if anyone tries to molest her."

He turned to see a portly man with rimless glasses and a toupee. "Can I . . . ?" he asked, indicating the driver's seat.

"Please do, sir," said the salesman, opening the door, ushering him into unheard-of opulence.

The door closed with a whisper.

"I'll leave you to get acquainted," he said, mincing off as the phone purred quietly in the office.

The softly polished wood of the fascia gleamed in the subdued showroom lighting. Outside, wind whipped rain along the pavement, and people scurried past, heads down, umbrellas threatening to turn inside out. Across the road, a dirty, mud-spattered red bus sucked up passengers, and moved on, leaving others to wait in the rain. He was sitting in a Rolls Royce.

His fingertips touched knobs and buttons, his heart beating a little faster. He wanted this car as surely as he had wanted Fiona. She wanted him too; she had asked him to come back. He wasn't too sure about that. That way lay involvement, and it was sometimes tricky to extricate yourself.

He got out, and sat in the back seat. You could hold a dance in the back. There was a drinks cabinet, and a TV. He touched a button and a glass partition slid silently across. A chauffeur might be a little over the top, he thought. Besides, he wanted to drive it.

"How does it fit, sir?"

He looked up at the salesman. "Perfectly," he said. "Can we talk money?"

The salesman had been indulging him, he knew that. Some poor sod who had come in out of the rain to idle away a few moments in a dream. Jeff watched with amusement as the man tried not to look surprised, or suspicious that his time might be wasted. He of all people must know that money came in all guises. He didn't know if he was talking to a millionaire or a minion. And he couldn't take any chances.

"Certainly sir. Would you care to come into the office?"

*   *   *

Richard Price smiled.

Waking up that morning sober—without the hangover that she had presumed would follow such unaccustomed merry-making—Susan had begun to wonder. Had he just been making fun of her? Would she be the butt of jokes in some bar? "And the bloody woman turned *up!*" Had she—the most horrifying thought of all—misunderstood?

The smile had reassured her. And Jeff, of all people, had reassured her. He had wanted her last night, though he hadn't done anything about it. Jeff made love to her from habit; he hardly noticed her before or during, and certainly not after. But she had seen him watch her last night, a look in his eyes that she faintly recalled from courtship. He had wanted her. So why shouldn't Richard Price? However famous, however handsome—he was a man, and she was a woman, and she had not misunderstood the invitation.

"I didn't think you'd come," he said. He smiled again; and closed the door. Then he laughed a little. "I feel a bit shy," he confessed.

She didn't. That's what one million, four hundred and eighteen thousand, three hundred and twenty-one pounds and thirty-seven pence did for you.

She still hadn't spoken; he was beginning to look a little uncomfortable.

"I . . . I just wanted to get to know you better," he said.

Her eyes went to the bed, which dominated the little room, and he looked embarrassed.

"Oh—no. Well, it's a hotel room. Hence the proximity of the bed. But that isn't why I . . ." His voice trailed off.

"Isn't it?" she asked, surprising herself with her directness.

"Not really," he said, defensively.

She looked around. It was a very modest hotel, even by her pre-win standards; she had laughed yesterday at the thought of his having to keep the wolf from the door, but looking at it from a sober perspective, it wasn't so unlikely.

"Do you want to stay here, or go for a walk, or something? Lunch perhaps?" he asked.

She looked at him. Handsome, famous Richard Price, asking her what she wanted to do. Being shy. Being hesitant. And thinking that his looks and his charm and his famous face would dazzle her. He was wrong. They pleased her, but they didn't dazzle her.

And he very probably did want to get to know her better; she was sure he wouldn't be averse to a relationship which might give him access to all that loot. He would want to show her how charming, how diffident, how gentlemanly he was. But she hadn't come here in order to go for a walk.

Her eyes went to the bed again. "Let's stay here," she said.

*　　*　　*

Jeff had been back in the hotel room for about half an hour when Susan came in. He had expected her to be festooned with Harrod's bags and dress boxes.

"You don't seem to have bought much," he said, pouring himself a drink. "Or are you having them delivered?"

She shook her head. "Funny thing about money," she said. "When you don't have any you see a million things you want that you can't afford. But when you can afford them . . ." She shrugged.

That wasn't his experience. "Do you want a drink?" he asked.

"I'll have a tonic water."

"One tonic water, coming up." He poured it, and smiled. "Wards off malaria," he said, handing it to her.

She took her drink, and smiled at him. "I wanted to buy something for you," she said. "But I didn't know what."

He had a fortifying sip of whisky, and sat on the arm of her chair. It was like magic. An opening like that—he couldn't fail. "Do you really want to buy me something?" he asked.

She looked up at him. "Yes, of course," she said. "Is there something you want?"

He smiled and shook his head. "No," he said. "It would make too much of a hole in even a million and a half quid. It was just a dream," he added, with a little soulful laugh. "Forget it."

"No, tell me!" she said.

He knew how to play Susan.

"Unless it's a golf course, I can probably afford it," she said.

He smiled. He had joined the golf club last year, in the mistaken belief that watching the televised game with avid interest meant that you were golfing material. He might take lessons now; so far, he had only made use of the bar.

"Jeff? Tell me."

The gay Scottish butler was most awfully pleased to see them. He had just known that Jeff and the car were made for one another, and Jeff went back on the train that evening knowing that within the city, waiting for him to return, were both Fiona and the Rolls. He would be picking the car up the following week, and he had made up his mind to see Fiona again. He dozed off as the train picked up speed, and awoke from a complex dream involving both of his new toys to a sudden, unforecast blizzard as they approached home.

The train pulled in, and Jeff pushed down the window to reach out and open the door, turning his head away from the flurry of snow that blew in. Heads down, they battled their way to the car park, to find the car looking like a snow sculpture from the rear bumper to the front doors. As fast as he brushed off the thin layer of snow, it settled again.

His hands were numb; he had to wait in the car, heater on, and suffer the agonies of pins and needles before he could begin the less than attractive drive home. Susan sat huddled in the passenger seat, her hands thrust in the pockets of her coat. They didn't speak; there really didn't seem to be much to say.

It was only long afterwards that it occurred to Jeff that they could have stayed at the Railway Hotel; somehow actually living in the town had made it seem obligatory to go home.

He finally set off in what he was already thinking of as the old car, though it had been bought the previous August, and was newer than the Rolls. The quickest route, normally, was to skirt the town by taking the A road around, and entering again from the roundabout. Automatically, that was the route he took, and it was a mistake. The constant traffic had cleared the snow as it fell, but the road was wet and slick and littered with traffic cones that he had forgotten were there to guard the work being done to dual two single-carriageway sections. The wind had sent the ones on the more exposed high ground spinning, and driving was a treacherous business.

It was then, peering through snow still dancing onto his windscreen, driving at fifteen miles an hour on the cone-littered road, his hands now hot and tingling and itchy while the rest of him froze because all the heat was being directed at the windscreen, that what the money really meant came home to him.

It didn't mean endless talks and discussions with pools

advisory services. It didn't mean parties and champagne, however interesting an effect it had on Susan. It meant that they could pay off the car loan. The mortgage. My God, the mortgage, which had gone up steadily every month for a year, squeezing his finances, making even a perfectly ordinary car seem like an unnecessary luxury that might have to go. He had already skipped a payment on the car when the quarterly bills came. But then a double payment had had to be found from somewhere the following month.

All that was over. His salary would be just that—his. No huge outgoings before he could see if he had enough money to stand his corner in the clubhouse; no more wondering if he could still afford to belong to the golf club at all. He had been released from being the provider; he could keep Fiona as sweet as he wanted her to be, for as long as he felt like it. And it was then, nosing through the swirling snow, feeling his tires slip on the road, avoiding cones which were being blown into his path by the bitter wind, that Jeff had begun to view his new life with pleasurable anticipation.

He had without realizing begun to whistle softly to himself, which must in retrospect have seemed a little odd, in the circumstances.

"You're happy all of a sudden," Susan said.

"And why not?" He smiled at her.

As he looked back at the road, he saw, a fraction too late, the diversion to the other side of the dual carriageway. He wrenched the wheel to the right, feeling the tires slide into a skid, but away, at least, from the six-foot drop into the foundations of the new road. His whole being was concentrated on driving into the skid, his soul on praying that nothing was coming, as the car slithered at right-angles across the road, straddling the two lanes, coming to rest with its front wheels biting into the snow-covered grass verge.

Headlights lit up the falling snow, pointing skyward like anti-aircraft search lights, as a car approached from the other side, laboring up the hill towards the curve in the road. His mouth was dry as he tried to start the engine. Get out, a voice was saying. Get out, Susan, get out. But he couldn't say it out loud. He turned the key again, and the engine fired. He threw the car into reverse, ramming the steering wheel further right still, shooting out backwards into his own lane. He spun the wheel back the other way, righting the car, and stopping. The other car's headlights, now resolved into two dipped beams of light, rounded the bend. The driver flashed his lights, irritated because Jeff was still on full beam.

He released the breath he had been holding, and looked at Susan, who was wide-eyed and silent, as she had been throughout. If your luck was in, it was in, obviously.

They made it home in the end, and let themselves into the warmth of the house, shutting out the black, snow-filled night. It was good to be back in his own house, and alone at last. No Fiona being a fly on the wall, a role to which she had not been entirely suited, because it was difficult to ignore Fiona. No anxious young men in suits, no telephone ringing.

He went to bed with Susan, exhilarated by the realization of how rich they were, of thoughts of Fiona, even by the near-miss on the way home.

Fiona had been different, of course, and he was looking forward to his next visit to her even as he made love to Susan, but there was something very soothing about a long-established relationship. He could relax, knowing what to expect and what was expected of him, and what it lacked in excitement it made up for in satisfaction. It was like having apple pie and custard after nouvelle cuisine.

He slept for twelve hours straight, waking to the smell of lunch being cooked. Perhaps he was the luckiest man in the world, he thought, as he bathed and shaved and dressed.

Downstairs, he poured them each a dry sherry. She took hers, rather to his surprise.

"I've got someone coming from a woman's magazine," she said. "She'd like to talk to you too."

"On a Sunday?" he said.

Susan shrugged. "It was the first day I was available."

She came in the middle of lunch, of course. She asked him how he felt. She wore glasses, no make-up and an earnest expression. She asked Susan what she was going to do with the money.

"I have plans," Susan said, with a smile.

What plans? It was beginning to bother Jeff a little.

*   *   *

Susan watched the young woman drive off, and waved in response to the hoot from the car.

The snow had gone now, except for a powdery coating on the high ground which skirted the town, where she and Jeff had so very nearly come to grief. She could still see Jeff's face, lit by the yellow glare of the other car's lights, as he had wrenched the car out of its path. She had frozen; she hadn't blinked, hadn't breathed.

She had gone to bed almost as soon as they had got home, exhausted by the weekend, still shaken up by what had happened. But it seemed to have put him on more of a high than ever; he had misconstrued her desire for an early night, and had joined her. She had thought briefly of exercising some power in that direction, but had decided against it.

It was hard to get worked up one way or the other about sex; if he wanted it, he could have it, as far as she was concerned. She didn't find it especially enjoyable, but it wasn't unpleasant either. He had rolled over and gone to sleep, snoring within minutes. She had lain awake, thinking about what might have been, on that treacherous road.

What if they had died? Where would all the money have gone? Her father had died four years ago; she had an aunt somewhere in Canada, but she didn't even know her married name. Someone she had never met would suddenly have become rich, because Jeff had taken his eyes off the road for an instant.

What if Jeff had lived a little longer than she had? His

mother was still very much in evidence, though she had retired to an old folks' home from choice. Letters arrived, visits were made. My God, that old witch would have got it. And where then, once she had gone?

She didn't like thinking of her own mortality, but she liked even less the thought of some second cousin twice removed of Jeff's mother suddenly becoming the sole heir to her money.

Yes, two things had come home to her in those frozen moments which she had thought might be her last. She would take driving lessons, and she would make a will.

*   *   *

Fiona couldn't have worked out better, really. Living in London, far away from anyone who knew Susan, there was very little risk. He could hardly have conducted any sort of clandestine relationship around here, not now.

Before, there had been the great and taken-for-granted blessing of anonymity. Now, if he were to be seen having a quiet drink with one of the nubile typists favored by his senior partner, it would get back to Susan in no time flat. People were, it seemed, keen to see him—or more accurately, Susan—come a cropper. It made sense, he supposed, if one thought of the glee with which newspapers reported the downfall of business tycoons and once-rich TV stars like Richard Price, whose most recent appearance had been in a bankruptcy hearing.

And they had worked for their money, whereas Susan had had a stroke of sheer good fortune, and that was even more difficult to forgive. It would have given a lot of people who didn't even know Susan great pleasure to let her know that her husband was being unfaithful. This way, they wouldn't get the chance.

Rather more kindly, but nonetheless odd, was the reaction of his friends and colleagues to the knowledge that he had come into a great deal of money. The teasing had an edge to it at times, but they seemed to have grown used to the Rolls outside the office, and the comments about his bank balance were growing fewer.

Comments on almost anything were growing fewer, though. He had noticed that. It didn't, in all honesty, worry him too greatly. He couldn't really work out whether it was that people didn't want to seem to be over-friendly in case their friendliness was misconstrued, or whether there was real resentment. He had grown a little weary of making jocular responses to the effect that the money *wasn't* in his bank account, and that he had not won anything.

It was true, of course. And eventually they would forget about it all, and things would be normal again. They would realize that there had been no fundamental change in him, or in his way of life.

No, he hadn't won the pools. What had happened to him was, in many ways, much better than that, and the new routine was blending pleasantly with the old, as they settled back down to normal life. He and Susan had always had different tastes; there was nothing unusual about his going off on his own on Saturdays, when he would visit garden centers, or vintage car sales, or bookshops—the sort of pursuits that had never interested Susan. Now, he visited Fiona. Nothing could be simpler.

There were drawbacks, still, but they could hardly last forever. He would go home to find Susan not in the kitchen, as she always used to be, watching an Australian soap with half an eye while making dinner, but being interviewed by one of the dozens of magazines whose readers were apparently panting to know just what it was *like*. He would find himself being involved, much against his will.

"How did you feel?"

How had he felt? His first thought had been that Susan must have got the results wrong. His own careful checking having revealed that this was not the case, he had assumed that she was under a misapprehension about how many of the draws she actually had. He had scrutinized her copy of her entry, and found that she wasn't mistaken. But the copy could be wrong. She could have misread the original, put a cross in the wrong place. The phone call had confirmed that Susan had done everything right, and had won in excess of one million pounds. How had he felt?

His stock answer was "Stunned." Hardly original, but the chances were that the reporter could spell it.

Every day, it seemed, yet another penny dreadful wanted a photograph of them, wanted to know how it felt. It seemed that *he* was the news value aspect of the story, which he had wrongly assumed would be a nine-day wonder. But it was his wife who had won the money, and when they asked him how he felt, it wasn't about becoming rich. It was about his wife becoming rich.

He smiled as he left the office, waving to the girls in reception as they pulled on anoraks and sheepskin coats to face the blustery wet weather.

How did he feel about his wife becoming rich? Wonderful. It had released him. It had made a new man of him. If he had won the money, he would have had to think about investments and shares; he would have had to think about starting up on his own, and all the hassle that self-employment brought with it. And, as far as he could recall from his partnership agreement, they would have had to move in order for him to do all that. As it was, he was going to have his salary every month to spend any way he pleased. Which, for the moment, was on Fiona. How did he feel? He felt wonderful.

But then, he didn't know that Fiona was going to be the last of his infidelities.

*   *   *

"There is a fairly standard clause to cover just such an eventuality."

Richard had been the first; the first time she had ever

31

been unfaithful, the first time she had ever gone to bed with anyone other than Jeff. And it had been Richard Price. That made her smile, every time she thought of it.

It had been more fun, more enjoyable than it was with Jeff, but that wouldn't have been difficult, given that the man was at least trying, if unsuccessfully, to please her as well as himself. But perhaps it always was a disappointment; perhaps sex could never live up to its publicity.

Susan dragged her thoughts back to her newly acquired solicitor. Marty Rogers, Jeff's senior partner.

She had met him now and again over the years at the odd function; she had never spoken to him much. He seemed never to get any older; his almost-handsome face never changed, his brown hair didn't recede, or grow gray. She didn't like him very much.

He had indicated that she might prefer to use another firm; she had smiled, and said no. She and Jeff didn't have secrets from one another.

She raised her eyebrows in a query.

"Your both being involved in some sort of accident," he explained.

"Good," she said.

"It allows for the eventuality of Jeff predeceasing you— that is, dying before you . . ." His voice trailed off as her look indicated that he had no need to translate. "Sorry," he said, smiling.

Marty had somehow just missed being truly handsome. A stronger jaw, perhaps. A more definite color of iris; his eyes weren't blue or green or gray. Either fairer or darker. It was difficult to pinpoint what it was about his regular features and youthful face that was somehow just wide of the mark. Perhaps it was the youthful look itself; he was ten years older than Jeff, and looked younger. He had an open, friendly smile, to which had been added an artless little-boy-lost look since his wife died.

He had spent most of Susan's time telling her his troubles;

he wanted to expand, but he needed capital. Banks couldn't see any further than the end of the cashcard queues. If he could open a branch in Bramcote, it would pay for itself within three years. He had the figures—bank managers were so blinkered. He had spoken to Jeff when he heard about the . . . er . . . uh, well, win . . . but he had said that it wasn't his money.

She rather imagined that she had been supposed to whip out her checkbook. When she hadn't, he had got around to discussing her will. And now he was explaining big words to her. Clearly, Marty had accepted Jeff's conception of her; he was having trouble adjusting to the real thing.

"Occupational hazard," he explained. "You get so used to having to reduce everything to two syllables at the most. Anyway, if Jeff predeceases you, or dies within thirty days— then he gets missed out altogether and the other bequests kick in, as it were." He smiled again. "It was devised to avoid paying double death duties, but it works just as well for your purposes, too."

Afterwards, Richard had held her in his arms, and told her how fascinating she was, how she had bewitched him. She had felt a little foolish, and more than a little skeptical. At least Jeff had never said anything like that. Not to her, at any rate.

"Fine," she said to Marty.

"Of course, in reality," Marty went on, "if Jeff were to die before you, you might well want to change the will. There could be someone else in your life."

She looked up quickly, annoyed with herself as soon as she realized that it had been a guilty reaction. Jeff would never have given himself away like that. She saw a flicker of interest in Marty's professionally bland gaze.

"And if you were to remarry, you would have to make a new will," Marty said.

Remarry? He must be joking. Men were not an essential to good living, and one was quite enough in a lifetime. Her experiment had shown her that there was little point in seeking another, now or later. She had independent means, and security was all they had to offer, as far as she was concerned. Men were not part of her plan, and if Richard Price had expected more than the slim gold cigarette lighter that she had jokingly sent him to replace his book of matches, then he too had been disappointed.

"But you, if I understand you, are more concerned about what happens if you die first," Marty said. "And there are ways of keeping tabs on your money from beyond the grave, you know."

She had just wanted to know what it would be like with someone else. And now she did. It was much the same; Richard had been more considerate, but it had still left her with a vague feeling of having been used for someone else's pleasure, and the pretty words afterwards had not dispelled that feeling.

"Sorry, Marty?" she said, realizing that he had been speaking for some time without an audience. "I . . . my mind was on something else. What were you saying?"

"It could be held in trust—Jeff would have access to it during his lifetime, but not beyond. When he died, it would still be your wishes that carried the day." He looked up from the pad on which he was jotting down notes. "He couldn't leave your money to anyone else, in other words," he said.

She could stop one of his bits on the side getting her hands on it. That was what he meant. It was an attractive thought, but she had no real desire to be vindictive for its own sake. She simply wanted to do as she had been done by.

"No," she said. "I just don't want it ending up with someone that neither of us has ever clapped eyes on."

"Fine," said Marty. "Then I think I've got everything I need. I'll get it drawn up for you, and you can come in and sign it."

He knew, of course, about Jeff's peccadilloes. That was why he had thought she might want to keep tabs on the money. But she didn't really care about that. If he wanted to sleep with other women, he was welcome. She had never seen any reason why they wanted to sleep with him, but there it was. The whole thing was wildly overrated in her opinion.

But of course, she believed that her brief time with the disappointing Richard Price was going to be her only infidelity.

And she was wrong.

February

Don't read them," Jeff said, looking up from his catalogue. "I have to," she said.

The begging letters had started after some damn fool had published their address; Susan insisted on dealing with them herself.

"Well, don't read them out loud."

She complied with that request at least, but she still made noises. Sympathetic, impatient, whatever. She tutted quietly to herself, and he was struck by a thought.

"You're not sending them any money, are you?"

She looked up. "No," she said. "Not yet."

"Susan—they are professional beggars. These stories are made up. Believe me."

"They won't all be," she said.

He sighed, and ticked a catalogue number. "I'm taking a run out to this nursery on Saturday," he said. "Do you want to come? It's a nice run."

It was a nice run. And he had thought that perhaps, if they were out in the country together, they could go to one of the little pubs on the way and have a meal. It had been a long time since they'd done anything like that.

"What?" She looked up again. "Oh—no. Thanks. I've got things to do on Saturday."

"More interviews?"

She smiled. "No," she said.

Jeff frowned. "Not some other lame dog charity wanting money?"

"No lame dogs," she said. "But the vicar of St. Mark's is doing a project with disabled children that I've promised to take a look at."

This wasn't like her. It wasn't like her at all, and it was worrying him. Was she giving all her money away to anyone who said they needed it? Was that why she wouldn't tell him what she was doing? Jeff closed the catalogue. "Susan—you can't involve yourself with every group of underprivileged people in the country. It isn't possible. Where is it you keep going to? You're never here when I get home from work anymore."

She smiled. "You can put up with a late meal now and then, can't you?"

He supposed he could. Though it was hardly now and then. And she had employed a daily to do the housework, so rarely was she at home. Still, so long as she didn't take to employing a cook, he'd be happy.

"How much is all this costing you?" he asked.

"I've put aside ten thousand," she said. "For local charities. When it's gone, I'll stop. Most of it's gone already."

Jeff breathed again. Only ten thousand. He smiled at himself. *Only.* This time last year, he'd have bitten someone's hand off for ten thousand. He abandoned the catalogue, and picked up the evening paper.

"There's a new restaurant out by Brackley Mill," he said. "It gets a good write-up in here."

"Yes," she said, putting a letter aside, and writing something at the foot. "I saw that."

Jeff smiled. "We should try it some time," he said.

"Mm." She shook her head as she read the next letter.

A night out. He wanted to do something. Something they could enjoy together, like they used to.

"Do you fancy going to see what it's like?" he asked. "I should be back by teatime."

She looked up, her eyes vague. "Sorry?" she said.

He lifted the paper. His voice didn't betray the sweep of intense irritation; he had learned long ago to disguise it. "The restaurant," he said. "On Saturday night. Dinner."

She shrugged. "I've promised the vicar," she said vaguely.

"I thought that was the afternoon," he said.

"No. The evening. It's some sort of party. I probably won't be back until late."

"Then why can't you come out with me in the afternoon?" he asked.

"Oh—that's something different."

As long as she was limiting herself to ten grand, it wasn't too bad, he supposed. He watched as she went back to the begging letters, marking the ones she wanted to know more about.

"I think you're mad," he said, and gave up, going to bed, leaving her with her correspondence and her newly discovered social conscience. He had tried.

He would phone Fiona in the morning.

*   *   *

Susan's life had never been so busy. Interviews all the time, as if she were some sort of pop star. People ringing up representing magazines she had never heard of, newspapers that she wouldn't have had in the house. And she was saying yes to all of them, because Jeff didn't like it. It stopped her being able to cook for him, for one thing.

She had booked the driving lessons for every afternoon; it hadn't been easy. Most of the instructors had other pupils, and couldn't give her all afternoon. But then she had found

Tom, just starting up, who had only got half a dozen customers. She would have a break while he went off for an hour to one of the others.

She had surprised herself when she discovered how quickly she had picked up the basics. She still couldn't maneuver terribly well, but she didn't crash the gears and the car didn't lurch forward when she started, as it had the first time. She could start on a hill without slipping backwards, and she had stopped being frightened of roundabouts and traffic lights.

Tom was in his fifties, stockily built, and quiet. Slightly shy even. His face was rounded, and bore the marks of what had probably been teenage acne, but which now gave it a comfortable, lived-in look. His fair, wavy hair was receding fast; he had bushy fair eyebrows and blue eyes.

He picked her up, as usual, three streets away. He had accepted her desire for secrecy, and hadn't questioned it.

"You know," he said, as she arrived, crooked, at an angle across a side street, "you could perhaps do with some evening lessons."

Tom's brief was to get her through her test in the quickest possible time, and that was what he was trying to do. But she had seen the way he looked at her sometimes, and she wasn't sure about this.

"Why?" she asked.

"Because I've been notified of a cancellation," he said. "If we can get you ready for your test in three weeks, you've got a place."

She stared at him. "Three *weeks?*" she repeated, her voice rising to a squeak.

"Why not? If you'd been having one lesson a week like most people, you wouldn't think it was so odd."

"But other people are driving cars in between lessons," she said.

"Not at all. It's worth a try. But you might need the extra tuition."

She might. She laughed at herself for thinking that Tom had had any ulterior motive. "Right," she said. "Extra tuition it is."

Tom smiled. "First gear," he said. "Check for traffic, signal, check again..."

*   *   *

Perhaps it wasn't so much Fiona's attractions as the excuse it afforded him to glide up the motorway in the Rolls. Not for Jeff doing 110 mph in a Porsche and getting done for speeding. He savored every luxurious moment at the wheel, and kept her purring at a steady seventy on the good stretches. But even being stuck behind a convoy of lorries was good in this beautiful creature.

He drove across London to Fiona's flat, happily aware that he was probably the only man in the city who was actually enjoying driving through the Saturday shoppers; he didn't care if he was cruising at seventy or stopping and starting alongside buses and taxis, just as long as he was in the Rolls.

The car had been waiting for him on the forecourt the day he had gone to collect it. They had said they would deliver it, but it was his as soon as Susan had written the check, and no one was ever going to drive it but him. Besides, he had wanted to see Fiona again.

The street had been full of traffic and noise and the inevitable rain. He had turned the ignition key, and nothing had happened. Trust me, he had thought, to buy the only Rolls Royce in the country that doesn't start. But it *had* started. It just didn't make a noise. If he had never been in love before, he was from that moment on.

He pulled into the private car park of Fiona's block of flats, and opened the glove compartment, taking out a jeweler's box. The panther brooch with the emerald eyes winked at him, promising him that she would never guess. They had somehow evolved a game on his second visit whereby she had to guess what he had brought her. It was harmless and fun, and the sort of game that Susan would never have countenanced.

*   *   *

It was about half past ten when she got home that night, after a quite mind-bogglingly boring evening at the church hall. At the end of the evening, she had waited with the vicar's wife while the Reverend Phil Houseman ferried children home, two at a time, which was as many as he could manage, with the wheelchairs to accommodate.

"What we need," he said as he drove her home through the sleet that had fallen miserably all evening, "is a teacher."

Phil Houseman was thin and fair and earnest.

"A teacher?" she queried.

"Oh yes. A public address system, advertising agency and labor force organizer rolled into one," he said. "Do you know any?"

"Sorry," she said.

"We need drivers," he said. "A teacher could drum some up. Colleagues, parents—even pupils, these days."

"There really was no need to drive me home," she said. "I could have got a taxi." Her suggestion that she should ring for one had been regarded as positively offensive by the Housemans.

"Not at all," he said again. "It's the least I can do. Don't you drive, Mrs. Bentham?" he asked.

She shook her head, not prepared to tell even him that she was learning. No one was to know.

Jeff had always been the driver, from when they had been able to afford a car. Jeff loved cars. She had thought about taking lessons once, but Jeff had just laughed. It was too expensive to go to a driving school, and he certainly wasn't risking life and limb by teaching her. Besides, he could take

41

her wherever she wanted to go. Of course he could. Unless he was elsewhere.

"Oh, I couldn't manage without the car," the vicar said.

He was a very kind man, a very dedicated man. She had already told him that he was getting the money. But he did have a tendency to go on a little, and she stopped listening as he went through a typical day in the parish, to show how essential a car was to him. But with the Relief for Carers project, what he could really do with was one of these big seven-seater ones, for ferrying the disabled children about. Or a teacher.

"And your money is going to be a Godsend," he said. "It is expensive—we try to have something going on most weeks." He slowed down as she indicated the house. "It gives the rest of the family a break," he said. "It's important."

He pulled up, keeping the engine running, clearly hoping not to be asked in. He looked tired; she could see that all he wanted to do was go home and go to bed.

"It was kind of you to bring me home," she said. "I'd ask you in to meet my husband, but I think you'd rather get off."

He smiled. "I am a little tired," he said.

"About the money," she said. "You should get an annual sum—the theory is that it increases each year, but that's assuming the investments go up."

"You have been more than generous. It's good of you to consider us."

She looked at him. No, it wasn't. She was doing it to worry Jeff. It was good of him to be there in order to be considered. "Look," she said, on impulse. "Pick out whatever kind of vehicle you need for the disabled group, and I'll pay for it."

His mouth fell open. "You can't do that," he said. "I couldn't let you do that! You're already contributing more than anyone expected, and—"

She sighed. "You don't need a bigger car," she said. "Not for that sort of thing. You need a minibus. One with wheelchair access and all the rest of it."

He switched off the engine. "But, Mrs. Bentham—do you have any idea how much that sort of thing costs? They have to be specially adapted . . ."

"If it makes you feel better, get an estimate," she said. "But whatever it is, I'll OK it, so you'd be better just getting it under way as soon as possible."

He was speechless. She took advantage of that to get out of the car. "Goodnight," she said.

Her first honestly generous impulse; it made her feel good.

He wound down the window as she passed. "You should learn," he said.

"Sorry?"

"To drive. It gives you independence. Changes your whole outlook on life."

She thought about that, and smiled. Twenty-five years. *You don't need to drive, Susan, I'll drive you where you want to go.* Twenty-five years of looking at four walls as the nation became motorized, and public transport became virtually nonexistent. Twenty-five years of being home when Jeff got home—whenever he got home—because she didn't have the means to be anywhere else. Perhaps vicars did have a hotline to your soul.

"Yes," she said. "I think perhaps I should."

She waved, and waited at the gate until he had driven off, then walked slowly up the path.

Jeff wasn't home, of course. She had known that when she had half invited the vicar in to meet him. It wasn't too difficult to work out where he was; he had been checking out the talent during their entire weekend in London. But she wasn't certain which one it was. There were a number of candidates, but on the whole she favored Fiona, with her long hair and her long legs and her slim hips.

She went to bed, and lay awake, thinking. There were a lot of surprises in store for Jeff; the idea had begun to take real shape now. There would be incidental things, like the driving lessons, and the giving to charity, which had occurred to her along the way. But irritating him, alarming him, was hardly all she had in mind. If she was to do exactly what she wanted to do, then there was one very big hurdle, and it was hard to see how to clear it.

But after an hour or so's intense thinking, a way had presented itself to her. It was wicked, deliciously wicked. Much more wicked than her visit to Richard Price.

*   *   *

The panther brooch had kept its promise; it was after ten as he emerged from the warmth of Fiona's flat to the chilly, damp night. She had fed him; her cooking wasn't a patch on Susan's.

On how Susan's used to be, he amended, as he made his way down to the car park. She hadn't cooked for him for a long time, and he was missing it. He was missing *her,* come to that. He wanted his wife back. He wanted to come home from work to a predinner drink, and the kind of meal that she used to cook. He wanted to see her hoovering and dusting. He wanted to be slumped, bored, in front of the TV, while she watched a film in the kitchen. She had said the money earmarked for charity was almost finished; perhaps things would get back to normal soon.

He stopped as he walked up to the car, admiring it, as he always did. It alone was worth any inconvenience that the money had brought in its wake, and things would settle down; they were bound to. He glanced up at Fiona's flat, expecting to see her wave to him, but it was in darkness already.

He enjoyed his northbound journey as he fantasized about dull, boring, normal married life. It wasn't until he was back in the town that he realized how very late it was, and he began to work on his alibi. He had got into a conversation with the man, he decided.

"The man" had come to the rescue quite often in the past. That would do. He had got into a conversation, and before he knew it, it was ten o'clock, and he had a two-hour journey

44

ahead of him. She had no idea where the nursery was, and she would believe him.

There were a number of things that Susan didn't know about him, but perhaps the oddest one of all was that he didn't like gardening. She thought he loved it; she would buy him secateurs and pruning shears as presents. Gardening was something he had done from necessity twelve years ago when they had moved into the newly built semi; he had discovered that it helped prevent boredom, but he had never actively liked it. It had, however, provided perfect excuses before, and his well-known passion for things horticultural explained any number of hours whiled away in the alluring presence of a nurseryman.

It was almost midnight when he got home; Susan didn't stir as he undressed and got into bed.

She snapped on the bedside light. "I saw the vicar," she said.

"I thought you were asleep," he complained.

"No." She smiled again. "I gave him the rest of the money," she said. "He's working himself ragged."

Jeff frowned. So? Presumably she would get to the point.

"That's it," she said. "This year's ten thousand."

He sat up alarmed. "*This* year's?" he repeated.

"Yes. I put money into one of those unit trust things, you see. And it should yield at least . . ."

He let the facts and figures wash over him. She hadn't used all that much of the capital, he supposed. Her basic investment, and this year's ten thousand. He wasn't interested in how the rest of it worked, just so long as the capital was still there. All the same . . . the house, the car, the unit trust, the daily . . . it was adding up. But perhaps now, now that she had got the Lady Bountiful bit out of her system, they could get back to normal.

"So," she finished, her fingertip tracing the line of his jaw, "I've done that now. I'm sorry I've been so busy. I've been neglecting you."

Oh my God. Even nouvelle cuisine was filling if you had enough of it.

But she just smiled, turned off the light, and lay down, her back to him, the quilt pulled up to her neck. "Goodnight," she said.

He sat for a moment, looking down at the bump in the quilt, unable to believe his luck. She had been too full of her own activities to be worried by his lateness, and hadn't after all had any expectations of him. That would, now he came to think of it, have been a bit out of character.

He gave a little sigh of sheer relief, and lay down himself. "Goodnight," he said.

Definitely the luckiest man in the world.

*   *   *

She had seen the look of near panic; she had almost been able to see him trying to summon up the energy. And she lay awake, long after he had gone to sleep.

He was so transparent, it was almost pathetic. She could almost feel sorry for him. But not quite. She only had to look at the range of designer leisurewear and the tailored suits; the hairstyle which he had suddenly acquired, having "stopped off at a barber" on the way back from some fictitious trip; the tasteful tie-studs and the elegant shoes. Jeff Bentham hadn't purchased these things without the benefit of some woman's advice. He didn't have that sort of eye for fashion.

Oh, he could take a piece of builders' debris and turn it into a garden, but only because he was minutely thorough, and almost obsessively keen to master anything for which he had some aptitude; he had bought a book that showed him how, step by step, to do just that. It told him what to plant when and where and which shrub went with which. If there was such a book for the fashion novice, he didn't have it. At least she had good taste, whoever she was.

She pushed her husband gently onto his side as he started

snoring, and he became momentarily conscious, patting her hand as it rested on his arm before he went back to sleep with a final, snuffling little snore. Poor Jeff. He thought he had it made, and he was quite, quite wrong.

That thought filled her with a warm glow.

*   *   *

The hate mail started then. The pools people had warned them from the outset that if people discovered their whereabouts they would get letters from every lunatic in the country, and they had been right. Why did they use green ink? Jeff felt that some psychologist ought to be addressing himself to this.

He tried to persuade her to let the pools people deal with it, but she wouldn't. She had a compulsion to read everything addressed to her; she always had had. Junk mail was always carefully slit open and read before being consigned to the bin. Every begging letter had to be read. But these really upset her. More perhaps than the unlovely sentiments, the fact that these apologies for people actually thought that money would alter their miserable lives depressed her.

So now his life, which had just been getting back into its comfortably boring groove, with some added bonuses, was upside down again, and he would find her reading a letter that called her every name the writer could think of, though very rarely spell, instead of waiting for his key to turn in the lock, calling hello. Once again, meals became haphazard affairs. At least she couldn't answer these letters, which were of course anonymous. But she read them. She even bought a metal detector, just in case one of them was tapped enough to send a letter bomb.

But metal detectors didn't detect everything, and it was after one such package that she declared her intention of selling the house, and moving.

Her intention. It was his house. True, the pools money

had paid the bulk of it, but it was in his name, and he really ought to be the one who said whether or not it was to be sold. Still, if he had thought for a moment that she would have agreed, he would have suggested a move himself, so there was little point in getting into a stew over the validity of her decision.

He came home one day to find her in conversation with yet another young woman, and assumed that some obscure magazine had only just found out about her. But no. This was the estate agent, apparently. The house had gone on the market.

"Elsa's going to help us find a new house," she said. "She'll do the negotiation—everything will be in her firm's name. And she thinks we should wait a few months before we actually sell this one, so that there's no connection."

He nodded. "Good idea," he said. "But we won't keep it secret for long, you know. Our name will still have to go on the deeds." He turned to Elsa, discovering with pleasure that she was very attractive. "And with all due respect," he said, "you will obviously keep your own counsel, but you do have colleagues and employees."

"I've thought of that," said Susan.

Jeff was surprised. She never used to think beyond the next meal.

"We'll use my maiden name," she said.

*   *   *

Lights loomed in her driving mirror, and she dithered.

Tom laughed, as the car shot past them. "Pull in," he said. "There's a lay-by ahead."

She didn't enjoy the lessons so much now. Yes, she was getting better at the actual driving; but now she had realized that there was a possibility that someone would test her on it one day. She still felt herself tense up at the mere mention of a three-point turn. And while learning to drive had seemed a good idea in theory, it was chipping away a little at her win-induced confidence. Jeff had never felt like this, she was sure.

"What you have to remember," said Tom, "is that you have just as much right to be on the road as he has. And what you want to do is just as important as what he wants to do. You are in front of him, and you check your mirror. He is way, way behind. You signal—and you maneuver. You don't dither about so that the other driver doesn't know what the hell you're going to do."

"I wasn't sure how far away he was," she said. "He got really close."

Tom smiled. "You had been indicating your intention to turn right all the time," he said. "He knew you were turning right. You were slowing down—of course he was closer to you than he had been. He was waiting for you to turn. He expected you to turn. What he didn't expect you to do was switch off the indicator, pull into the left and have a nervous breakdown."

She laughed. "How can you bear driving about with me?" she asked.

"Oh, you're all right," he said. "You just need some confidence. There are one or two homicidal maniacs driving about, but most drivers have no desire to hit you broadside, believe me. So providing you signal your intentions in good time, you are at liberty to turn right when you want to."

She nodded.

"Most learners never drive at night," he went on. "They don't panic until after they've got their licenses." He smiled again. "Do you want a break? There's a café up the road."

A cup of tea seemed like bliss, and she drove to the café almost without being aware that she was a learner. Obviously, all she needed was the incentive to get from A to B.

He bought the teas, and a couple of sandwiches, waving away her money.

"How long have you been a driving instructor?" she asked.

Tom swallowed his bite of sandwich. "Twenty years," he

said. "Then I saw how much the place I worked for was raking in every week, and I thought I'd set up my own school." He took a gulp of tea. "But it isn't as easy as it looks," he said.

"You're not losing customers because of me?" she asked.

He shook his head. "No," he said. "But that is the problem, by and large, if you've only got one car. You can only do so many lessons a day—and it may seem to you that I'm charging a fortune, but it only just covers my outgoings."

Here we go, thought Susan. Just like Marty.

"Not that it matters—I've only got myself to consider, financially. The wife went off with someone else." He shrugged.

"Oh—I'm sorry," said Susan.

"Unsociable hours, you see. She thought it was bad enough when I worked for someone else, but she wasn't putting up with me working for myself." He finished his sandwich. "But I wouldn't want to employ people. Too much grief, if you ask me."

"So you don't want another car?"

He shook his head. "I think," he said, "once I've got you through your test, I'll go back to working for someone else. It's much easier, really."

Susan nodded. "I expect it is," she said, for want of anything else to say.

He looked at her. "I'll . . . er . . . I'll miss you, when you do pass," he said.

My God. Worse than Marty. She smiled, and drank some tea.

"It gets a bit lonely, you know. Going back to an empty house. You've got a family, have you?"

"A husband," she said pointedly.

He wiped his mouth with the paper napkin. "Yes," he said. "I suppose you would have. I . . . I don't suppose you'd . . . well, I don't suppose you'd want to come out for a drink some time. Or something."

"No," she said, a little frostily. "Thank you, Tom." She stood up, and he hurriedly got to his feet, catching the table, knocking over his empty cup. He tried to right it, and knocked the sauce bottle with his sleeve.

They walked back out to the car.

"Can I ask you something?" he said as they got in.

Susan didn't answer.

"Why do you have to learn to drive so quickly? Is it a job or something? Do you have to be able to drive?"

"Why do you want to know?" she asked coldly.

"Because you shouldn't worry—you will pass, you know. The test won't be at night, and you're fine, really you are. Night driving's always a bit awkward the first time. I—" He looked down at his set of pedals. "You don't need extra tuition," he said. "I just thought that. . . ." He cleared his throat. "Anyway—I wasn't going to charge you. I just thought that if you were having to learn to drive quickly, maybe you were on your own too. Sorry."

He didn't know. He didn't know who she was. The run-down on his financial position had been Tom's honest introduction of himself as a possible suitor. He liked her; it was as simple as that. And Tom had done more for her confidence in that last twenty minutes than in all his hours of patient tuition. She smiled.

"Forget it," she said. "And of course I'll pay you for tonight."

She drove home like a veteran.

*   *   *

Jeff Kent sat in the back of Elsa's car, while she and Mrs. Kent discussed the pros and cons of the house they had just seen.

The name-change made sense, really. It was purely for their new house, so that they could escape the attention of the nutcases; as far as his colleagues were concerned, he was still Jeff Bentham. No one was to know that the people called Kent had ever been called anything else, and no one who didn't have to know was to discover that the people called

Bentham had changed their name. Mr. and Mrs. Bentham would simply have moved, as far as everyone else was concerned—if anyone was still interested. The letters would be returned marked "gone away," and the beggars and psychos could pick on someone else. It was sensible, he supposed. In the fullness of time, they could revert entirely to Bentham.

The only people in on the mild deception were those whose confidentiality could—he trusted—be counted on. Relatives, the bank, the pools people, the tax office, accountants.

Elsa would see the prospective vendors; if the house met the initial requirements, which were merely that it should be unoccupied and have parking space, they would go and look at it. If they were interested, Mr. and Mrs. Kent would make an offer. So far, however, they had made no offers— Susan was being rather more difficult to please than her brief list of requirements suggested.

Susan had no intention... *Susan*, he thought, with an inward sigh, had no intention of living in whatever house they finally did buy for any longer than she could help. She merely wanted to get lost for a year or so, until the last remnants of the fuss had died down. Then, it seemed, Mr. and Mrs. Kent would slip into the sunset, and Mr. and Mrs. Bentham, their anonymity restored, would buy a proper house.

This one could be anywhere. It could be enormous or tiny. It could be one of a row of cottages, or a mansion standing in its own grounds, just so long as Mr. and Mrs. Kent excited no speculation when they moved in there.

His thoughts on the matter hadn't really been sought. Not that that mattered. He'd live in a houseboat—had Susan *thought* of a houseboat, he wondered?—if it meant that his life could stop revolving around the postman. What bliss to live somewhere where no one wrote to you, where no one called on you, or telephoned you. How nice not to exist for a while at least.

He looked at the back of Elsa's head as she drove, her soft

brown hair pulled up in a loose knot. Feathery wisps escaped, and fell onto her slim, ballet-dancer's neck.

He was spending his evenings driving about in a car with an eminently fanciable woman, and his wife. Rolls on Saturday, and Fiona.

* * *

Jeff wasn't overly interested in the house-hunting, which was what Susan would have expected. But Elsa—that was another matter.

She sat in the passenger seat of Elsa's car, and glanced at her as she concentrated on driving through the darkening, wet night. She was a very pretty girl. But she hadn't seen the usual look in Jeff's eye; perhaps a mild recognition of her attractiveness, but no more. And that was odd.

He still went off at weekends to see whoever it was he had in London—Susan wondered if this time it had got serious. If it had, it would be the first time. Now that she came to think about it, she had never been aware of a long-term bit on the side before, serious or otherwise.

She glanced back at where he sat, eyes closed, in the back seat and wondered about that. She must be some girl, if he had lost all interest in the others who came his way. Or . . . yes, perhaps he was being careful. After all, she had the money, and he was very interested in that. Yes, that explained it. He was hoping to give no cause for concern.

She smiled, as the power that money imparted was once again made manifest.

"No good?" Elsa said, referring to the house they had just seen.

No good. Jeff hadn't seemed bothered one way or the other. She was looking for somewhere that Jeff loathed. But she could hardly tell Elsa that. "Not bad," she said. "But I think it's a bit too close to the house we've got. I don't want these people to find us if they start looking."

Elsa smiled. "You know, they'll probably forget all about you soon," she said. "I'm sure people like that find a new target every week."

"Hear, hear," said Jeff, from the back.

"I'd rather it was further away," said Susan. "I'd rather it didn't have neighbors, to be honest."

Elsa shrugged a little. "That might not be too easy," she said. "Not if you want to move as soon as possible."

It wouldn't be easy. Jeff took life very much as it came, and always had. Finding a house that he really didn't like might even be impossible. But one that he didn't *want*—that shouldn't be too difficult.

"We'll find something," she said.

*   *   *

Friday afternoon; Fiona tomorrow, thank God. Jeff looked out of his office window at the urban sprawl below him.

Elsa kept turning up houses, and there was always some reason why Susan didn't want them. Jeff had been dragged around every edifice in the town, he was sure, and it was a very large town, as he was finding out. He had suggested that they rent somewhere. Somewhere totally unobtrusive. A flat, a house—anything. Just rent somewhere, and look from there. What was the point, he had asked, in traipsing around houses they had no intention of making home?

He couldn't even drive the Rolls. That might have made it bearable; driving the Rolls filled him with well-being whenever and wherever he did it. But Susan thought it too obvious, of too much interest to the neighbors.

But he would be driving it once they lived wherever it was, he had pointed out.

She knew that, but that was different from driving around the town looking at empty houses. Elsa's was perfect.

So he would sit in the back seat of Elsa's car, looking at the back of Elsa's fetching neck, his interest in her increasing in inverse proportion to the decrease of his interest in house-hunting. And his interest in house-hunting had reached an all-time low.

He sighed, as he packed up his desk, and left the office. It was early, but what the hell? It was Friday.

She wasn't in again when he got home. This was happening all the time now; there was a note to the effect that there were frozen dinners in the freezer. They weren't even *her* dinners. They were packaged rubbish.

He had just put one of them in the oven when the phone rang.

"Mr. Kent?"

Jeff bristled. Elsa. Who had never called him anything else. He agreed, a touch reluctantly, that he was Mr. Kent.

"I think I might have found what your wife is looking for," she said. "Is she there?"

"No," he said. Was she ever?

"Oh—no matter. I'll give her a ring tomorrow. It's empty, it's secluded—it's even cheap, considering the size of the house and the amount of land that goes with it."

"Good," he said.

"Perhaps we could take a run up there tomorrow," said Elsa.

Perhaps, thought Jeff. Then he brightened slightly. "I could come and see it this evening," he said. "If you like." A run up to somewhere secluded with Elsa seemed like a less boring way to spend the evening than watching a centuries-old film on the TV.

"Not much point," she said briskly. "It'll be dark soon, and the electricity isn't connected. Susan will have to see it herself anyway."

No. Not much point. "I'll tell her," he said.

"Thank you." She hung up.

He wasn't particularly interested in Elsa; he wasn't about to rock any boats by taking up with anyone Susan actually knew, and Fiona had lost none of her attraction. He was perfectly used to being turned down. But what was worrying him was that she hadn't even seemed to notice the mild come-on; he must be losing his touch. Girls at least used to notice him.

He still had all the attributes that he had had before, which, while nothing to set the world on fire, were good enough, plus money to burn. And Susan's long and irritating absences had even caused him to lose a few of his surplus pounds.

He went up to the bedroom and looked at himself in the bedroom mirror. Made-to-measure suits, now. Shirts at a price he wouldn't have believed before. Slimmer, trimmer. Older than when he landed that girl at the bank, he thought, the memory of her making him smile, though her features had long since blurred, and her name escaped him. But maturity wasn't always a disadvantage. Hair graying quite rapidly, but cut and styled by experts.

No. It was her problem, not his.

The next day, Elsa took them to the house, the car climbing out of the town up to the high fields which had long been abandoned by farmers as wind and weather proved too formidable.

"We'll go in the back way," she said, indicating a right turn.

Jeff, who had been slumped, uninterested, in the back seat, sat up frowning. He had to forgo a visit to Fiona. This had better be good.

What had once been hedging towered into the air, swaying back and forth in the wind; there seemed to *be* no back way. But Elsa brought the car to a halt, and they got out into a gale that almost knocked them off their feet.

Jeff eyed the swaying, creaking branches and motioned to the two women to move away from them. His jacket ballooned out as he walked into the wind, towards a break in the mass of greenery.

"Is this it?" he bellowed.

Elsa nodded, the wind tugging at her blouse, and turned back to the car, reaching in for her jacket. Her loosely held hair was being pulled apart, and was falling around her shoulders by the time she got back to him and Susan.

She walked through the gap in the overgrown hedge, and he and Susan followed, a little apprehensively.

In the shelter of the twelve-foot-high privet, they could at least talk and walk like normal people. But what met them was not normal. Grass stood waist-high, shifting in the tempered wind; an old, weathered fence complained and groaned. A pathway of sorts, crazed and broken, almost overtaken by dandelion and couch-grass led to what had once been a farmhouse, and what was now an abandoned eyesore.

Elsa pushed her hair back up with careless elegance, and Susan walked carefully, stepping over rampant nettles and dock leaves as big as palm trees, towards the peeling, once-blue back door. Jeff just stood and watched as Elsa caught up with her, producing a key which worked, much to his surprise, opening the door into a dark passage.

She was going to *look* at it. He turned away from the house, and looked back, realizing just how far the wilderness stretched. In the middle of it all stood a magnificent oak tree, and he liked that.

He could see over the once close-boarded fence now, to a haven of neatness. Dug soil, awaiting whatever was to be planted. Grass paths between the beds, one of which led to a ramshackle but serviceable cottage.

Bracing himself, he turned back, and walked into the gloom of the passageway, which opened out into the only slightly less gloomy kitchen. A Belfast sink stuck out of one wall, the copper piping green and doubtless leaky, if the place still had any sort of plumbing to speak of. An old wooden kitchen table, big enough to seat the farmhands, sat in the middle of the quarry-tiled floor.

It smelled of damp and decay and neglect. The only window was on the side of the property, the light blocked by more sky-high hedging. A walk-in larder skulked under the stairs, which were presumably through the door off to the left. The door at the far end led to what could be turned into a dining room. He didn't go in there; he just looked, and crossed over the quarry tiling to the hallway.

At the bottom of the stairs, he could hear Elsa and Susan in the next room talking as though she were actually thinking of buying the place. The front door was big and solid; he tried to open it, but it was locked or stuck. The only light in the hallway came from a skylight at the top of the stairs, and that was opaque with the leaves of countless autumns, welded so firmly to the glass that even the gale wouldn't shift them.

It was cold; he shivered and walked towards the voices. They stood in what was presumably the sitting room, a long, thin room with windows at either end, which at least admitted some light. The view at the back he had already seen; he walked to the front, and looked out.

Nothing. Fields of some sort. Just fields, and in the far distance, a small group of water towers. Telegraph poles and electricity pylons marched across the green and brown landscape, and what seemed like a hundred miles away, a faintly discernible moving line, the traffic on the main road which bypassed the nearest village, and fell away down to the town as it skirted the rear of the property.

With difficulty, he pushed open the window; as soon as it was free of its bonds, it was caught by the gale, and was whipped out of his hand. It banged against the wall of the house, fortunately keeping its glass intact, and he leaned out to retrieve it.

The wind whined in the electricity cables, one of which at least was attached to the house, if only for the moment. It danced in the air, being jerked this way and that, and Jeff just knew that it was going to come adrift. It ought to be underground, he thought, up at this exposed height. He glanced at the nearest telegraph pole, but no reassuring line traveled from it to the house. God. It took forever to get a phone if you weren't already connected.

He needed both hands to pull the window back against its will, and closed it with a sigh of achievement.

Back out into the hall, and another room which turned out to be the bathroom. It was as big as their kitchen.

"Well?" said Susan. "Shall we go upstairs?"

He followed them up the curving stairway—dusty, graying wood, with dark varnish in a six-inch stripe down either side—to the landing, lit by the same beleaguered skylight.

"The electricity's been disconnected," said Elsa, helpfully, and opened one of the five doors off the landing.

A good-sized bedroom, except for a windowseat which he assumed was built in. Old-fashioned sash windows upstairs—he didn't attempt to open this one, but he knelt on the windowseat and looked out.

From this higher vantage point, he could see just how much land there was. He hadn't known that this place existed; as a solicitor who sometimes did conveyancing, he had a passing interest in the property that came up for sale in the town. It had obviously ceased to be a farm a generation ago, but either it had been lying empty, or it had been lived in by some eccentric who had now shuffled off.

He heard Susan's heels click out of the room, and eased himself off the windowseat.

Next door was a bedroom and a half. A smaller room opened off it; it was hard to tell what use it had been put to before, but it wasn't hard to see Susan's imagination fitting an *en suite* bathroom in there.

A third bedroom, on the other side of the landing. The two little rooms were presumably children's rooms, or possibly maids' rooms, depending on who had lived here and in what circumstances. It needed an incredible amount of work doing to it, but one could see that it did have possibilities.

"I could do something with this place," Susan said.

Jeff nodded. "But I thought the idea was to get somewhere we could move into straight away," he said, visions rising before him of months more of begging letters and hate mail and letters trying to sell them everything from Jaguars to Jacuzzis while Susan did something with this place.

"We can," said Susan.

Jeff swallowed. "What?"

"It's solid—no woodworm, no dry rot," said Elsa, to Susan. "It's sound. You would just need to rough it a bit."

They had won the pools and they would need to rough it a bit. That didn't sound right to Jeff. But Susan was nodding agreement.

"And here's the best bit," said Elsa.

She told them how much the estate wanted for it, and Jeff frowned. All right, it had been neglected. Yes, it needed modernizing and decorating, and of course the grounds had to be brought under control. But the price was laughable.

"How come it's so cheap?" he asked suspiciously.

"Technically, it has a sitting tenant," said Elsa. "The land next door belongs to the estate, but it's run as a small holding on a ninety-nine year lease which isn't up for another ninety years."

"But who's going to care about that? The estate could hang on to the sitting tenant and just sell the rest."

Susan smiled. "You must be the only house purchaser in the world who wants to offer more than the asking price," she said, and turned back to Elsa. "I'll take it," she said. "Subject to a survey."

March

I shall tap *here...*" He indicated exactly where. "... with my clipboard, and I want you to bring the vehicle to an emergency stop under control."

Susan swallowed, and licked dry lips, glancing in the mirror not so much in order to check what was behind her as to comply with Tom's instruction to look in the mirror, and be *seen* to look in the mirror at all times. Rain lashed down, and it was all she could do to see ahead of her, never mind behind her. He had had to tell her to pull in and put on her headlights because of the weather; she was sure that that would have failed her anyway.

"When you're ready," he said.

Why did people always say that when they meant hurry up, whether you're ready or not? She put her foot on the clutch and found first gear, eased off the handbrake, indicated that she was moving out, checked the mirror, checked over her shoulder, and moved off, gathering as little speed as she thought she could get away with.

The clipboard hit the appointed place; she braked hard,

and pulled on the handbrake, putting the gears in neutral. She didn't dare look at his face. The engine was still running, at least.

If only they would tell you whether what you had just done had blown your chances, then you could just go back to the test center and forget the rest of the torture.

"Take the next left, and pull in at the side of the road," he said, sounding for all the world like one of those recorded voices on telephone quizzes.

She did as she was told, sending rainwater splashing up the side of the car.

"I now want you to turn the car in the road without touching the curb . . ."

She wanted to die.

* * *

He had argued with Susan, but it had been a waste of breath. She was determined to move into the place practically as it stood—it was all he had been able to do to get her to wait until the electricity was reconnected. In the meantime, the real priority was to get the grass and hedges cut down before yet another spring, and the afternoon was becoming decidedly spring-like, now that the downpour had moved on.

He had been persuaded to go and see what could be done with the land, and had been startled to find a stream marked on the plans. Presumably there was one there, in amongst the bramble and the bracken.

Almost against his will, he pointed the Rolls up the hill, this time taking rather more notice of his surroundings. A pub, thank God, at the foot of the hill. A nice little detached pub built of gray stone with a dark gray slated roof. It had a friendly look, at least. The pub turned out to be the last sign of human habitation; at the top of the hill, the road curved around to the left, to bypass some village or other, and he stopped the car, unsure as to where Elsa had actually gone from here.

There didn't seem to be anywhere else to go. He shivered slightly, as though Elsa had taken them to some sort of enchanted house that could appear and disappear at will. He had been in the back of the car, eyes closed, Susan and Elsa's chat lulling him almost to sleep. There was a tiny dirt lane—no more than that—off to the right, going into what looked like dense woodland. That couldn't be it, but it had to be, because there wasn't any road going anywhere else.

He turned the car into the lane, branches brushing the sides as he drove. Two minutes later, he was at the gap in the hedge. He had just driven up the driveway to the house, and no one could possibly have known that it was there. It was two minutes from the main road, and it was invisible.

Well, he thought, as he scrutinized the silver paintwork, it might suit Susan, but that forest of greenery was going to go before anything else did. No damage, this time. He walked in through the gap, looking helplessly around. No wind today, and everything stood quiet and still, even less welcoming than before. He looked at the plans, and headed in the general direction of the brook.

*   *   *

She couldn't believe it. She sat at the wheel, just staring at it.

Tom stopped and spoke to the examiner, then came splashing through the puddles to the driver's side. "Move over," he said, smiling.

"I *passed*, Tom!" she said delightedly.

"I know. Move over—I'll drive you back."

"Oh, I can't go home yet."

He frowned. "Why not?"

"I'll tell him if I go home now." She moved over.

"All right," he said. "I've minded my own business up

until now. But I've got you through your test, so I'm going to ask. Why the secrecy?"

"Oh—I just wanted to surprise him," she said.

Tom started the engine. "I don't think that's all there is to it," he said.

She smiled. "Maybe not," she agreed. "But it's all I'm saying."

"Right, then," he said. "Where should I drop you?"

"You know the garage on Elmore Street?"

"The Mercedes-Benz place?"

She nodded, smiling. "I ordered a Mercedes from them the day I decided to take driving lessons," she said. "I want to see how fast they can get it to me."

Tom's face was a picture.

*   *   *

It was a long walk from the back entrance to the brook; Jeff turned, but he couldn't see the house through the woody tangle of bushes. A snap of branches made him whirl around, and he actually felt afraid as someone or something made its way out of the undergrowth where the brook was reputed to be.

It was John the Baptist, emerging from the wilderness. It had to be. Long-haired, long-bearded, ancient skin like leather, long flowing robe. Well, no, it wasn't a robe. It was a long white raincoat and he walked with his hands thrust into the pockets. "Who're you?" he asked Jeff suspiciously as he approached.

"My name is Ben—" He stopped himself. "Kent," he amended quickly. "I've just bought this place."

John the Baptist narrowed already small eyes. "You my new landlord then?" he demanded.

"I . . . I suppose I am," said Jeff. "You live . . ." He waved in the general direction of the old fence.

"You putting up my rent?"

Jeff shrugged. "I don't know much about that yet," he said. "Did you want something?"

The man slowly withdrew his hands from the deep pockets of the coat. There were three eggs in each hand.

Jeff frowned.

"My hens lay in there." He jerked his head back towards the bushes.

"In there?" Jeff couldn't see its attraction. "I'm probably going to cut all that down, you know," he warned.

"Then they'll have to find somewhere else," said John the Baptist, philosophically enough, and strode away back towards his smallholding.

Jeff stared after him for a moment, then walked in the direction of the house to try to get some sort of perspective with the plan of the property to refer to.

"Ben Kent!" roared his departing guest.

Ben? Why was he...? Jeff smiled as he realized, and turned. "Yes, John?" he called back.

"I won't pay a penny more rent. And you can't make me." He turned away, then turned back. "And my name isn't John," he added.

"Mine isn't Ben. Does it matter?"

John's face broke into a huge grin, and he went off making a sound that Jeff presumed was laughter.

He didn't know what Susan would make of him, but he rather liked their next-door neighbor.

*   *   *

The old man's relatives, almost heartbreakingly relieved at having finally got the property off their hands, had given Susan the keys and *carte blanche* to move in as soon as she was ready—the paperwork could get done any time.

Jeff was right, of course. There must be something wrong with the place, even if it did have a sitting tenant. It wasn't as though he was actually in the house—it would be easy enough to resell the house without the cottage next door. But there didn't seem to be anything wrong with it; the survey showed nothing wrong structurally, and nothing otherwise that couldn't be seen at a glance anyway. The surveyor said that it must have a ghost, because other than that, he could see no reason why they wanted such a ridiculous price for it.

Susan had bought it because Jeff didn't like it, but she had discovered the added bonus that she did. She was excited by the prospect of making improvements, of furnishing it, decorating it.

She was moving in, supervising the removal of their furniture, almost all of which she intended to replace, to the new house or to Oxfam, depending on its usefulness. She had sent Jeff to talk to landscape gardeners, rather against his will, because it smacked of permanence, and he didn't care for the farmhouse at all.

Which was absolutely perfect.

*   *   *

"It's too cheap. Much too cheap."

Fiona gave him the wine to uncork. "I must say I agree with Susan," she said. "Why complain?"

Jeff spoke in grunts, effort screwing up his face as he pulled. "Because the estate...isn't making...a..." The cork was released with a satisfying plop, and he put the bottle on the table. "...philanthropic gesture," he finished. "There's a catch. There has to be."

Jeff knew that there *must* be a catch, but his relief that the quest was over outweighed his dread at actually living in the place, and his disquiet at moving in before the contracts had been exchanged, which Susan was doing even now. Once again, he had felt a moment's rage at her naiveté; once again, he had suppressed it. It was her money, and at last, his time was his own again. Well—not exactly. He was supposed to be seeing landscape gardeners, after all. But that was only to get him out from under her feet, and he could do that on Monday. Marty wouldn't mind his sloping off for the morning.

"But you said you had it surveyed."

He shrugged. "Susan did—she says it's all right."

Fiona laughed. "Well, I don't suppose she'd be moving in this weekend if he'd said it had deathwatch beetles," she said.

He smiled, a little sheepishly. "No," he said. "But that business about the sitting tenant is nonsense—they are entirely separate parcels of land. You could sell what we've got for our use for half as much again. Well... almost," he said, admitting the exaggeration.

"Look," she said, sitting down. "Why don't we stop talking about your house, and eat?"

"Done," he said, joining her.

Her cooking might not measure up, but at least she fed him.

* * *

"Susan! This is a pleasant surprise. Do come in."

Marty Rogers looked over her shoulder at the girl in the outer office.

"Jenny—coffee, please."

Susan smiled. Once, she would have been quick to tell Jenny not to bother on her account. No more.

"Come in, come in." He held the door for her. "Take a seat, Susan, please. Do you want to change your will already?"

He hadn't mentioned that Jeff wasn't in the office that morning. Susan knew that he wasn't, knew that he had taken the morning off to go and talk to "more" landscaping people about what best to do with the wilderness she had just bought him. But Marty didn't know she knew where Jeff was; Marty, who knew nothing about the new house, didn't know where Jeff had gone. Marty was carefully not dropping him in it.

"I'm buying a house, Marty," she said.

"Ah. Wondered when you'd get around to that—I was beginning to think that you had settled for your semi."

She crossed her legs, aware once again of how shapely they were. Somehow twenty-five years with Jeff had made her overlook her natural assets. Marty's eyes flicked towards them, then up to her face.

"I might have," she lied. "But you know how it is."

Marty smiled, shaking his head. "Sadly," he said, "I have no idea how it is. Jeff did say that you had been getting some very peculiar mail."

Susan nodded shortly. "And some very peculiar callers," she said. "I don't want anyone at all to know where we live."

Marty sucked in his breath. "I'd say that that was impossible," he said. He shrugged a little. "Well, maybe. If you live like a pair of recluses—is that the plural?—don't put your name on the electoral register—don't register for poll tax . . ." He blew out his cheeks. "Even so," he said. "Bloody difficult."

"I don't intend breaking any laws," she said. "The poll tax will be paid. This house will be bought by a Mrs. Susan Kent."

"Kent? Oh, yes. That's your own name, isn't it?"

She nodded. "Yes. In effect," she said, slowly and carefully, as though he were a slightly dim child, "we will be living a double life. The people called Kent will live in the new house, and will have no connection with the people called Bentham who will simply have moved, and no one will be able to discover where."

Marty nodded as slowly as she was speaking. "Well," he said, "it's your best shot. But if someone wants to find you . . ." He finished with a shrug.

"I don't think that we're that interesting anymore," said Susan. "To anyone but the letter-writing loonies."

The coffee arrived. Marty stirred his thoughtfully until the girl had left, closing the door behind her. "I don't quite see where I fit in," he said.

"I'd like you to sort out all the legal ramifications," said Susan. "As I said, I don't want to break any laws. And I'd like you to handle the conveyance."

Marty thought about that. "The thing is," he said, putting his spoon in the saucer at last. "If you want as few people as possible to get involved in this, wouldn't it be simpler to have Jeff handle the legal side himself? I know he doesn't do much conveyancing, but he is perfectly capable of making sure the right searches are done. And he'll know what's what about who must know and who needn't just as well as I would."

Susan smiled. "I know," she said. "But I'm buying this house, Marty. Not Jeff. He bought the last one." She leaned across the desk a little. "Fair's fair, don't you think?" she asked.

Marty sat back in his seat, and looked at her over the rim of his coffee cup. She saw his sea-colored eyes change as he looked at her; change from puzzled surprise to understanding. The cup masked his mouth, but she knew he was smiling.

"Do I . . . er. . . do I *discuss* this with Jeff at all?" he asked.

"No," she said.

He drank some coffee, and set the cup and saucer down. "One more question," he said.

Susan waited.

"Why me? Why not another firm altogether? You are putting me in rather an invidious position, you know."

Susan knew. She intended putting him in an even more invidious position, but she had to know if he was as devious as she suspected. This was by way of a test. She smiled. "Because I don't mind your knowing that Mrs. Bentham and Mrs. Kent are one and the same person," she said. "I am aware of the position you will be in, and I am quite prepared to pay whatever fee is necessary for you to . . ." She looked up at him, ". . . feel comfortable," she finished. "I know you'll do your best for me."

He smiled back, and extended his hand. "It's a deal, Mrs. Kent," he said.

* * *

Jeff left copies of the plans with three landscape gardeners, and headed for what he had to start thinking of as home. Anything less like home would be hard to imagine, but it wasn't as bad as it might have been, he supposed. The electricity was on, the water was on. They even had a bottled gas water-heater, so they could have baths, and the bathroom wasn't too bad, considering. But food was supplied courtesy of the microwave; there was no gas that far out, and Susan wasn't prepared to buy any old electric cooker. The kitchen, it seemed, was to be transformed, and proper cooking facilities would have to wait until then.

Still, he rationalized, as he let the car soothe him, it was probably better than staying where they were.

* * *

Susan had employed a new daily, who had been told that she could bring as many hands as she required to get the place into some semblance of order. She had produced myriad nieces and daughters, all of whom seemed to have been born with a J-cloth in their hands.

Susan hadn't been. All her married life, she had resented it. She had been efficient; she had even taken a kind of pride in the finished result, but she knew now that she had resented it. Not so Mrs. Reeves and her family. They moved from room to room, making the place look almost as though it hadn't lain empty for three years. But then, being well paid for your endeavors did go a long way towards self-esteem, and all that these ladies were doing was work; when it was finished, they would go home. She had never had anywhere to go when she was finished.

And the man who came to see to the guttering and the skylight seemed actually to enjoy clearing dead leaves and God knew what else from the house's fiddly bits.

When the men came with chainsaws and scythes and rotovators, she hardly noticed the din, so immersed was she in brochures of fitted kitchens and luxury bathrooms.

"It takes a lot of organizing," she said to Jeff. "We have to get decorators and carpenters and electricians. Builders, if we want to get rid of that dark passageway. And we have to find a plumber who can put a new bathroom suite in the existing bathroom, and turn that little room off the master bedroom into an *en suite* shower and dressing room as soon as possible."

He turned from the window where he had been watching the grass fall to the scythe. "Susan—I keep telling you. We should not be doing all this before we've even exchanged contracts! As far as the law is concerned, we're squatters. The owners could still get a better offer—God knows, ours was hardly substantial for a place like this."

She smiled. "Don't you worry about that," she said, a favorite phrase of Jeff's.

He went away, looking puzzled. Perhaps a little worried. But Susan would swear that he hadn't noticed yet what was happening. Still, never mind. It was only half done.

The really big one was still to come.

He came back again. "Have you already exchanged contracts?" he asked, as it finally dawned on him.

"I've completed," she said. An action replay of twelve years ago:

"Well, what do you think of it?"

Susan looked at the unattractive, mass-produced semi-detached. "Not much," she said.

"Well, that's too bad. I completed this morning."

Too bad, Jeff, she thought. Too bad.

Her life was getting busy again; a lot of the charities to whom she had donated money had asked her if she would be interested in sitting on their committees; at first she had refused, but as the house became infested with tradesmen, it had seemed like a better idea. She had joined one or two, and was finding to her surprise that she actually enjoyed it. It was the first time she had *had* to be somewhere at a particular time, other than the dentist, and she liked that.

Going out more made her consider her image, and she didn't like it. She remembered Marty, thinking she wouldn't understand big words. She was brighter than he was, she would be prepared to bet. She just hadn't done anything about it. But she was going to now.

She was going to re-sit her A levels. A full-time course, starting in September. Well—you couldn't really call it re-sitting them. The subjects had changed. But there were enough with some passing reference to her O levels for it not to seem impossible.

And she was going to lose her extra pounds. She had decided that, too. She'd found a health farm, and it wasn't too long a drive. It wasn't just any health farm; it was sheer luxury, and the whole idea appealed to her.

She booked the first two weeks in April. She would have the car by the end of the month.

*   *   *

Jeff went to work, glad to get away from the army of workmen who descended on them from eight o'clock every morning until sometimes ten o'clock at night. Plasterers, bricklayers, flooring contractors, all calling him "guv" or "boss," which was at least an improvement on Mr. Kent. He got to sleep at night counting tradesmen.

Work was his only escape route. Work, and driving his lovely car, for which a double garage was even now being erected by a gang of the ever-present workmen. Why double? he had asked, but Susan had pointed out that if they did want to sell the place again—and after all, they might—whoever moved in would almost certainly be a two-car family.

He had polished the leather himself the evening before, and breathed in the smell again as he drove back to work, smiling happily to himself. Susan hadn't been able to do anything about lunch, there being no means by which cooked food could be produced since the electrician had turned the power off; he had had to make himself a sandwich, and eat it to the accompaniment of the fumes produced by something which resembled nothing more than a medieval instrument of torture, but which was apparently an essential piece of apparatus to the tiling contractor.

But none of that mattered when he was driving the Rolls, as it ghosted its way down the hill, past the pub that he would call into on his way home, through the town to the office. He only went home at lunchtime as an excuse to drive the car, anyway; he didn't really care what he ate in the middle of the day. It was in the evenings, going into a house still populated by various workmen, usually devoid of Susan—that was no fun. He would go and have a pie and a pint in the pub.

He pulled up outside his office, took one last sniff of polished leather, and went in, feeling at one with the world.

She had told him of her next project, prefacing it with a little speech on what she had always wanted to do; he had felt the familiar stomach lurch. At last, was this it? The mysterious project?

"I'm going to college," she had said. "I want to get my A levels. It's a full-time course, and it's for two years."

Relief had washed over him. Was that all? It didn't even start until September, and even if she had to pay the entire cost, it barely made a dent in the income.

He smiled as he sat at his desk, and opened the file on his

first client of the afternoon. She had made it sound like such a big deal.

There had been an odd moment, though, which made the smile waver a little as he thought of it.

"But this still isn't the biggie, is it?" he had asked.

She had looked puzzled. "The biggie?" she had repeated.

"You kept saying you knew what you were going to do with the money," he'd said. "It's not this college thing, is it?"

"Oh," she had said. "No."

"So . . . what is it?"

He didn't know why he had been pressing to know; there was something about this secret project that worried him, and usually he much preferred to ignore worrying matters.

But it worried him more that he *didn't* know, so he had tried to find out.

She smiled. "I'm already doing it," she'd said.

She had terminated the conversation then. Jeff didn't really know how she had, except that her tone of voice, her body language, her whole demeanor, come to that, precluded further discussion.

He absently pressed the intercom, and asked for his client to be shown in. Doing what? he wondered. The charity stuff? Was she giving away huge amounts that he didn't know about? It was decidedly worrying, but there wasn't much he could do, if she wouldn't tell him.

"Come in," he said, standing up as his would-be divorcee entered. "Take a seat."

His mind wasn't really on what he was doing. When Susan had spoken again, it had been on another topic.

"As to the more immediate future," she had said. "I'm going away for a week or two."

"When?" he had asked, startled.

"At the end of the month."

All this was very unsettling. Very unsettling indeed. It wasn't at all like her. "Where are you going?" he'd asked.

She had gone to the bureau, and taken out a leaflet, handing it to him. "A health farm."

He'd looked at the leaflet, which showed beautiful people swanning about in the height of luxury, and looked up at her. "Why?" he said.

"To lose a bit of weight, get toned up. To be pampered for a while."

Saunas, pools, Jacuzzis, gymnasium, massage, beauty treatment, four levels of calorie-counted menus, the highest one of which seemed hardly calculated to keep weight off. Aerobics, meditation . . . the list went on and on.

"How long for?"

"Two weeks."

Two weeks of eating rubbish. Two weeks of dealing with tradesmen. Two weeks of being alone, which he hated. He tried to tell her she didn't need to lose weight; he tried to talk her out of it. But she was determined.

Still—look on the bright side. Jeff was always able to look on the bright side. It was two weeks of being able to see as much of Fiona as he liked. He'd see her on Saturday; make sure she kept the time free for him.

"Mr. Bentham, I am in rather a hurry."

He looked up from the file that he had not been seeing, to the client whose presence he had forgotten.

"Sorry," he said, with a smile.

On the whole, things weren't too bad at all, he decided.

*   *   *

Saturday, and Jeff was off to a garden center, this time. Odd how his frequent visits to nurseries and garden centers seemed to be having no impact whatever on the neglected grounds. Susan had said as much; he had pointed out that there was nothing to be done until April.

She had arranged a Saturday meeting with Marty, because now that the bedroom itself was finished, they had unpacked everything from the various stowing-away places, including the little safe in which Jeff kept important papers. She had found what she needed. She was right; she thought she had remembered the terms, which had seemed to her less than reasonable at the time. Now, they seemed perfect.

Marty Rogers was greedy; that much was obvious. He was keen to expand, and hoped to persuade her to lend him the money to do so. His principles weren't exactly rigid; she had proved that to her own satisfaction. She had a lot of money, and Marty, she was sure, had a price.

"You want me to do what?" He looked horrified. "I can't do something like that, Susan! And why? I don't see the point."

"You don't have to," she said.

He shook his head.

"Didn't you tell me that Bramcote would be a gold-mine?"

He laughed. "It would," he said. "So?"

"So open an office there."

He looked at her. "How much are we talking about?" he asked.

"As much as it takes."

He had taken the hook, she could tell by his eyes. All she had to do was to reel him in. But it might not be that easy—he was wriggling like mad.

"No." He shook his head again. "It's not right."

"You provided for it."

"That was to protect me against some shyster—not someone like Jeff." There was a slight movement of his eyes as he spoke; a slightly shifty looking away, which was at odds with his boyish innocence. "Though his work has been suffering a little . . ." he said, thoughtfully.

Susan was interested. "Oh? How?" she asked.

"Oh—nothing much," he said, obviously wishing he hadn't spoken the thought aloud. "He's a bit absent-minded—I expect it's the new house. I understand you are rather camping out at the moment."

"Mm." Susan smiled. "Well, there you are," she said.

"No! It's not enough to—no," he repeated, decidedly. "I don't know what you're up to, but I'm not doing a thing like that just because the man isn't quite on the ball. He's probably finding it very difficult to relax at weekends—things will get better when the house is finished, I'm sure."

"Possibly," said Susan, though she felt fairly certain that if Jeff wasn't exactly relaxing at weekends, he would certainly be enjoying himself. "But I don't care what reason you give him." She picked up the copy agreement. "According to this, you don't have to give any specific—"

"No!" he almost shouted. "Why? Why, Susan?"

"None of your business."

"No—no, sorry. I'd like the loan and all that, but the bank's probably right. Three years is a very optimistic view—I wouldn't be able to afford it."

"The bank might want it paid back in three years," she said. "I don't." She got up. "I'll leave it with you," she said.

She had almost got to the door before he spoke again. She smiled to herself.

"How. . . how long would you be prepared to give me?"

"As long as you need," she said, turning.

His mouth fell open.

"Give me a call," she said, "if you decide to accept."

*   *   *

The last Friday in March. Susan was off somewhere frightfully important before going to her health farm, and the kitchen was being done, so someone had to wait in for the carpenter, who had declared his intention of being there mid-morning. Jeff had taken the morning off work.

He hated being at home without Susan; Mrs. Reeves and he seemed to have very little in common, and their faltering attempts at conversation had long ago been given up. Now, as she tried to combat the brick dust and plaster left by the demolished walls, all she did was complain.

But he discovered that he rather enjoyed the carpenter's cheerful company, and had kept him talking for rather longer than he wanted. When the man finally indicated that he really did have to start work, Jeff strolled out into what he now thought of as the garden, though all that had been done was that the high grass had been chopped down, and various parts had been mechanically dug. He hadn't thought much of any of the experts' plans for the garden; he might have a go at it himself. He walked towards the tree.

From the kitchen, he could hear the strains of "The Old Rugged Cross" being sung by the carpenter as he began unpacking the enormous number of packages which these days comprised kitchens. They had had the passage knocked down, and at least it improved the light in the room a little. Susan was having a huge fluorescent overhead light put in above the central work station anyway; Jeff turned, and could see why.

It was only half past eleven, and already the sun failed to reach the kitchen at all. From the oak tree, he could see nothing, not even the carpenter, whose "Nearer My God to Thee" indicated that he was indeed in there.

Not much more they could do about that, he thought, bar knocking the whole place down and starting again. Thankfully, Susan hadn't thought of that.

His visit to Fiona had been good and bad; good, because it was always fun, and they had taken a run out of London in the Rolls for the first time; he had been able to show off both his sleek, expensive girlfriends at once. Bad, because she wasn't going to be free for the two weeks of Susan's health kick. She was even on holiday from work, but her parents, of all things, were coming to visit. Girls like Fiona weren't supposed to have parents who popped up at inconvenient times.

The builders arrived then, to begin knocking holes in the

sitting-room wall for the patio window that Susan wanted. More brick dust and plaster to contend with. They had no sooner stripped off their shirts—it was then that Jeff realized that spring was almost upon them—than "Nearer My God to Thee," which Jeff had been rather enjoying, was drowned by the high-pitched whine of the carpenter's drill.

Drills made Jeff's teeth ache, and he fled to the car, going he knew not where.

*   *   *

Susan had picked up her new car. Cars didn't excite her like they did Jeff, but she was really looking forward to the effect that this one was going to have. She had chosen it, not so much because she liked it—one car was really very like another as far as she was concerned—but because she was certain that it was what Mrs. Kent would drive. A red Mercedes convertible. That sounded like Mrs. Kent's idea of a car.

Marty still wasn't too enthusiastic about her idea, but she would win him over in the end. She had phoned him at work, in order that he shouldn't forget what was at stake. Prestige—clients with more money to burn than even she had. But his side of the bargain continued to stick in his throat.

"Besides," he had said. "The interest on that sort of loan would be crippling."

"Interest free," she had said, to a stupefied silence at the other end. Anything, anything at all, Marty, she had thought. You can have the money as a present, for all I care. Just do it.

It couldn't just happen, he had said. He had to have a reason. So wait for a reason, she had said. He'll give you one, sooner or later. Everyone does.

The builders had finished the garage, and were starting on the patio window this morning. It was really quite exhausting trying to keep track of what everyone was doing, but there hadn't been too many hitches. Some shortage of bricks or something had held up the garage for a week or two; some of the kitchen stuff hadn't arrived, and the bathroom suite that she wanted was currently out of stock. She had tried every outlet in the country, which wasn't as enormous a job as it had sounded, there being only four places exclusive enough to do the suites she had been looking at. They were all out of stock. But, they assured her, this didn't mean that the line had ceased; they merely rotated their styles, and this one was due again in April, they had said. It was April on Monday. She must remember to chase that up before she left for the health farm.

She drove along the now cleared lane to the house, which could be seen from the road as a result of the clearance, but that was all right. She parked the car in the newly completed garage, and smiled at it.

It was lunchtime; no one drilled or hammered or played pop music at full volume. There were no cars or vans. They were all in the tiny car park of the Stag. Here, there was just birdsong and peace. She strolled from the garage to the back door, enjoying the sunshine and the light breeze that had sprung up.

Suddenly, without warning, rapid shots, one after the other, rang out. Instinctively, she dropped to the ground, and there were more as she lay there, her eyes tight shut, her whole body taut with fear.

"I'll get you next time, you bitch!"

She stayed on the ground, her heart beating painfully, her mind and body numb with fright, for long, long minutes before she could move. Her legs wouldn't work; she forced herself to get up, and half ran, half crawled, crouched down below the fence, into the safety of the unit-strewn kitchen.

*   *   *

Jeff listened to the smooth patter as the salesman told him why no home should be without the sleek hi-fi that he was going to buy anyway. Its pencil-slim lines were barely broken by the rectangles which slid back silently to take the cassettes, and the square which did the same for the compact discs. Like the Rolls, it was a slice of sheer elegance, the simple lines of the design masking its complexity.

The turntable was separate, but just as unobtrusively, expensively, slim. The speakers were wafer-thin too, but waist-high, and for a second or two the salesman let him hear just what they were capable of producing.

"I'll take it," he said.

The salesman smiled broadly, and went off to get the inevitable paperwork.

Jeff looked at the other things, and bought what took his fancy. A tiny TV, a complex calculator with umpteen functions, a camera that did everything by itself, binoculars . . . He stopped after he'd bought the binoculars, because he couldn't think of a single thing he wanted to look at through them.

"Just load them into the car," he said, paying with his charge card. His own charge card. Jeffrey Bentham, it said. As long as he wasn't having them delivered, he didn't have to be Mr. Kent.

He drove home, looking forward to unpacking everything that evening, to setting up the hi-fi, and then realized that he couldn't, not until the builders had stopped making the place knee-deep in dust. Still, he had the other things. He could take photographs of the house the way it was, and chart its progress. He could look out of the front window with the binoculars and try to spot real life moving on the horizon, as it bypassed the village up the road.

He drove into the garage, frowning at the brand new Mercedes. He walked around it before leaving the garage, as though walking around it might explain what it was doing there, but it didn't.

He pushed the back door, but it seemed to be locked. Or,

rather, it seemed to lock itself just as he tried to open it. Perhaps Susan had got some sophisticated security system installed while she was at it. He peered through the frosted glass on the new door, and frowned. It must be a trick of the light, he thought, looking again at what seemed to be someone crouched on the floor behind the tall housing for the double oven. Suddenly the figure rose, and the door opened. Susan grabbed his arm, yanking him in before slamming the door and locking it again.

"What the—?"

"That maniac shot at me!" she sobbed.

"What maniac? What do you mean, shot at you? What's happened, for God's sake?"

She looked deathly pale; she was shaking, catching her breath in sobs of relief that someone had come to her rescue. Something had certainly frightened her, but it couldn't have been anyone shooting at her, for God's sake. He put his arms around her, and she held him tightly. She was still crying; the words were incoherent. It was puzzling, but it had been a long time since he had felt that she needed him at all, and he couldn't help being really rather pleased.

"Take it easy," he said, patting her on the back. "Take it easy. Tell me again. Slowly."

"That man next door! He shot at me! Over and over again. I don't know how many times." She looked up at him. "He said he'd get me next time—he called me a bitch."

He smiled. "You must be wrong," he said. "It couldn't have been shots. It must have been a car backfiring or something."

"It wasn't a car!" she said fiercely.

"But why would John shoot at you?"

"John?" she said accusingly. "Do you *know* him?"

"I've met him," said Jeff.

"You're on first name terms with him," she said, clearly holding this to be an offense.

"Well—not really. I mean, John isn't his name."

She pulled away, and looked at him, exasperated. "Then why do you call him that?" she asked.

"He just came out of the—" He stopped. "Never mind," he said. "I'll go and talk to him, see what's going on."

She looked really alarmed. "No, Jeff! You can't. He's gone mad or something. Go and get the police!"

The police would have been here already if they had had the phone connected; Jeff found that he was glad that they hadn't. He liked John the Baptist. And Susan was rather given to being nervous. That couldn't have been what happened. She had just let her imagination run away with her.

"I'll talk to him first," he said.

"You *can't!* You read about them, Jeff. People who suddenly start shooting everyone in sight! Go and get the police, please. *Please!*"

You did read about them. But Jeff put his faith in his own judgment, and went to talk to his next-door neighbor.

*   *   *

Susan put on the kettle, still shaking, looking at Jeff's retreating figure.

She had cursed the new back door, with its pane of glass, when she had been crouched, terrified, in the kitchen. Her heart had all but stopped when she saw the figure block the light at the back door, and the handle move; she hadn't locked it. She had reached out and turned the key just in time, and had fallen back and hidden behind something that hadn't been there when she left that morning. Then she had watched in horror as the figure pressed against the glass, his features distorted. It had been a nightmare. She hadn't even been able to recognize the kitchen, now that it was covered with chipboard and cardboard and woodshavings and smelled of sawdust.

Then she had realized that it was Jeff, and the nightmare

had vanished, only to return. Why was he there? Why hadn't she heard the car? The stab of fear was identical to the one she had had when she had checked the coupon with the football results, but a hundred times worse. It had gone as soon as it had come; she had let Jeff in, holding him close to atone for her momentary suspicion.

But he wouldn't get the police, and that bothered her too. Surely the police should be called when someone shoots at you? Why didn't he want them? Why was he so keen to go and talk to someone who might gun him down before he got there?

She was being silly again. She still felt shaky as she poured herself a reviving cup of tea, and told herself sternly that Mrs. Kent wouldn't let a little thing like being shot at upset her.

She felt better now that Jeff was back, but she wished he hadn't just gone around there without taking any sort of precautions. He had laughed when she had said that; said that he had left his bullet-proof vest at work. *He* hadn't been shot at, of course, or he wouldn't be taking it all so calmly.

If that *was* why he was taking it so calmly. Stop it, she told herself. Stop it. It isn't fair. Whatever he's done, he has never caused you any physical harm, and even letting the thought cross your mind is wicked.

The builders came back then, announcing themselves by removing the hardboard barricade and grinning at her through the hole in the wall. Her hand flew to her mouth in fear, and then she acknowledged them with a half-hearted smile. It was just the shock, she told herself. You weren't rational when you'd been frightened like that.

The whole place began once again to ring with the jokes and laughter of the workmen, the apparently obligatory pop music channel, and electric tools of every sort. She felt silly; with the noise and bustle, her equilibrium had returned, and she laughed at herself.

* * *

"John?"

Jeff walked around the end of the old fence, taking care not to stand on the beds that he had seen John sow. He kept to the grass paths, telling himself that Susan had to have been mistaken. The man he had met just wasn't the type. Eccentric, maybe, but not mad. But at the back of his mind were the newspaper stories. He just had to hope that he was right, and Susan had heard something else.

"John? Are you there?"

A figure appeared in the doorway. "Ben Kent!" he roared. "What do you want? Your rent?"

"No," said Jeff, jumping a bed to the next grass path, and walking up to him. His stride was rather more purposeful, more confident, than he was. John didn't seem to be in a good mood.

He still wore the white raincoat, despite the considerable and unseasonable change in the temperature in the intervening weeks. It was streaked here and there with grass stains and mud. "Because I'm not paying to live next door to that confounded noise!" he declared. "Music, banging, drilling."

Jeff smiled. Humor him, he thought, just in case Susan was right. Maybe he tried to kill people who made a noise. "It's terrible, isn't it?" he said. "But it won't be for too long now."

"I should think not. Want a cup of tea?"

Crazed gunmen did not offer you cups of tea. At least, none of the ones he'd read about had offered anyone cups of tea. He felt it was safe to refuse, and did.

"I can't pay the rent, truth be told," John said. "Never had to, before. I don't mind the noise."

"Good," said Jeff. He didn't care about the rent, and it hadn't yet crossed Susan's mind. It might now.

"I've been hearing very strange stories about you, John," he said.

"Oh? What would that be?"

"My wife says you shot at her, and told her you'd get her next time. She says you called her names."

The man looked totally bemused, then his brow cleared. "Not her!" he said scornfully. "I wasn't shooting at her!"

Jeff shook his head. "So who were you shooting at?"

"Not who—what. That bloody blackbird. Hen bird it is. Don't mind the cock—he comes in the evening. Well, you can live with that. But she's there all the time, at my seeds. So I chase her away with this." He reached back in to the house, and brought out a revolver.

Jeff's eyes widened. "Where the hell did you get that?" he asked.

He slapped the barrel into the palm of his hand. "World War Two," he said. "Belonged to some poor bugger of an Italian. Brought it and ammo for it—it's not run out yet, either. Amazing the things you could get away with then."

"Why did you bring it?"

He shrugged. "Trophy. Protection. A lot of funny people about just after the war. I was just a kid. Never used it till last year. It works."

There were a lot of funny people about now, thought Jeff, who had taken several steps back as the revolver had been slapped. "You can't go around shooting things with that!" he said.

"I don't shoot things! I was in a war, Ben Kent, which is more than you've ever been. I don't believe in killing things. I fire into the air."

"But you can't do that either! You don't have a license for it—don't try to kid me that you have."

John shrugged. "I don't kid, Ben Kent. No license. So what?"

Jeff was open-mouthed. "So *what?*" he repeated. "It's dangerous! It's fifty years old! Anything could happen—it could go off now, so please stop waving it about!"

John stuck it into his belt, cowboy style, and looked up,

smiling. "Emptied the bugger when the blackbird was here," he said.

Jeff looked at it as though it might discharge all the same. But presumably it was empty. You would have to be very devil-may-care to have it pointing at your vital parts if it wasn't. "You have to stop using it," he said, more calmly. "There could be a ricochet—anything. You can't use that to scare your blackbird. Get a scarecrow."

"Bloody crows are even worse."

"You can't use that."

He narrowed his eyes again. "All right, Ben Kent," he said. "I'll go back to what I did before. But the old man's relatives asked me not to. That's why I thought of this."

"I don't *care* what they asked you to do or not to do! You scared my wife half to death!"

John nodded. "I'm not promising," he said.

Jeff sighed. "Try," he said.

"All right," he said. "But I'm not promising." He patted it. "This works better," he said. "But I don't want bad feeling with my landlord. Not when I can't pay the rent." He pulled it out of his waistband, and spun it around his index finger, like a gun-slinger.

Jeff backed off, and left to the sound of John the Baptist laughing again. It was no laughing matter. My God, Susan could have been killed.

Why didn't that bother him as much as it should?

April

You did say April," she said sternly.

"Yes, Mrs. Kent, I know we did, but you see, the problem is that the particular bathroom suite you require is being promoted at our Leeds branch, and we don't actually have one at the moment."

"But Leeds does?"

There was a silence. "Yes," he said.

"Then I don't see the problem," she said. Mrs. Bentham could never have done this.

She was sitting in her room at the health farm, feeling like a new woman after just one week.

The food was wonderful. The whole place was wonderful. She loved the foggy steamroom, and the relaxing Jacuzzis. She loved to walk in the grounds; she even loved the pummeling and massaging, because it was so good when it stopped. The exercises were hard at first, making her muscles ache the next day. But it was a comforting, almost pleasant ache, and now it had almost disappeared. She resolved to continue exercising when she got home.

She went for long walks in the late afternoon, to where there were little holiday cottages. She and Jeff should come here some time, she thought.

"The problem is that *we* don't have one, I'm afraid, Mrs. Kent." There was a distinct note of triumph in his voice. "We should have one—"

"There are roads from Leeds," she said. "Shall I ring there, and order it from them instead?"

The sound of commission going down the drain was almost audible.

"Well, I suppose I could telephone the warehouse..."

"You do that," she said. "And ring me back with a delivery date."

She had even gained access to the kitchen, and persuaded Mario to let her have some recipes. Mario produced steaks, baked potatoes, wonderful salads and sweets, and the fat content was minimal, the calorie count encouraging. She had eaten as well as she had ever eaten, and she had lost four pounds in a week.

She had been going to the beautician, learning how to use make-up. The girl was currently trying to persuade her to change her hair color, and she had finally decided on a dark blonde.

She was running and doing aerobics, being baked in the sauna and beaten up by the masseuse. She was also having her pores cleansed, being encased in warm mud, and having the persistent whiskers that she had been tweezing out of her chin for years removed by electrolysis. She was swimming, and playing tennis.

She ought to be exhausted, but she wasn't. She had more energy than she'd ever had. Mrs. Kent had a lot going for her.

He rang her back with a delivery date. Saturday, damn him, and she was supposed to be here until Sunday. They didn't normally deliver on a Saturday, but it was coming from the warehouse on the Friday, and since she was so anxious to get it . . .

Even Mrs. Kent hadn't had the nerve to tell him that that wasn't convenient. Reluctantly, she had agreed, then had phoned Jeff to tell him that she would be back on Friday night. She didn't trust him to make the necessary abusive phone calls if it didn't arrive, so she would just have to go home early.

*   *   *

The Mercedes had turned out to be Susan's; not only that, but she had driven off in it to the health farm. She had somehow taken lessons and passed her driving test in less than two months; he was impressed. It cleared up the mystery of where she had been all those afternoons when he had come home to an empty house.

Which he was doing every night now, and had been for ten days; he was growing weary of the silence. It was a cold, sharp Thursday morning; Susan was due back at the end of the week, and he was looking forward to her return. He hadn't really been listening when she had rung to say when she would be back, full of how wonderful the health farm was; he should have been having a wonderful time too, and he had been having a rotten time.

The carpenter had been joined by a whole team of people who had somehow stepped over one another with enough efficiency to have assembled a kitchen that looked exactly like the three-dimensional drawing which had been pro-duced for them by the firm's computer. Jeff had stood in the gleaming, futuristic room, looking around at built-in double-ovens, hobs, grills and microwaves, and had poured corn-flakes into a bowl, eating it at the breakfast bar. The wall between the kitchen and the dining room had been partially removed; it was load-bearing, and the load was now supported by a reinforced archway through to the "informal dining area" much favored by the magazines Susan had read on the subject.

Mrs. Reeves, grumbling as usual, had the afternoon before cleaned every inch of work surface in the kitchen, wiped down every piece of equipment. He didn't know what or where half of them were. Some of the cupboards that he tentatively opened turned out to be just that; others proved to be washing machines or dishwashers or tumble dryers or fridges and freezers. Mrs. Reeves had spent a happy hour or so moaning about it not being her job to empty the old fridge and freezer, temporarily housed in the garage, and fill the new ones; no one had said that it was, so he assumed that she was enjoying it.

He supposed that he could get something out of the freezer and microwave it, but he wasn't convinced about that. The new microwave controls looked more like the instrument panel of a Formula One racing car.

The builders had put in the patio window; Mrs. Reeves had made it sparkle. Susan ought to be pleased when she got back, he thought. The place was really beginning to look very good indeed. He finished his cornflakes, and got ready for work. He ought, he realized, to be doing something about the garden.

It was almost lunchtime when a knock on the door of his office was followed by a familiar grin surrounded by designer stubble which could just about pass for a very short beard. The whole was surmounted by an incongruous baseball cap.

"Rob!" Jeff jumped up, hand outstretched. "It's years— how long is it?"

Rob grasped his hand warmly, and pulled up a chair, sitting astride it, his arms along the back. "Nearly ten," he said. "I meant to keep in touch, but you know how it is."

"Are you on leave, or have you gone AWOL?"

Rob smiled. "Retired," he said. "And divorced."

Jeff's smile went for a moment. Retired. My God, that

made him feel old. He sat down. "I'm sorry it didn't work out," he said. "How long have you been divorced?"

"Eighteen months or so. I decided it was time to get out when it was made final. Silly, really. That's what she wanted me to do." He smiled. "So here I am, ex-army sergeant—no job. Need someone like that, do you?"

Jeff shook his head, smiling again. "Not so as you'd notice," he said. "It's good to see you."

"I've been hearing some very interesting things about you," said Rob. "I went to your house, but it's all closed up and empty."

Jeff nodded. "I know," he said.

"Hoped you did." He grinned, producing dents in the dark whiskers. "I thought maybe Susan had rumbled you at last."

"We had to move. It got difficult after some bloody fool published our address."

"So it's true? The pools thing? Lucky bastard."

"I was going to drop you a line, but I wasn't sure where you'd been posted to. It's not all beer and skittles, believe me."

"Ah," said Rob, wiping away an imaginary tear. "My heart bleeds for you. So where are you now?"

"We've got an old farmhouse up on—"

Absolutely no one must know. He could hear Susan's voice, and he checked himself.

"What's wrong?" asked Rob.

"I . . . I think I'd better check with HQ first," said Jeff, in a feeble attempt at humor. "Somewhere in England. I'm afraid the address is still classified."

Rob frowned. "You're joking," he said.

"No. No—I said. It got a bit difficult. We got all sorts of lunatics writing, ringing up—turning up, even. It rattled Susan. She doesn't want anyone knowing where we live."

Rob leaned forward over the back of the chair. "But I'm your oldest friend," he said.

"I know," said Jeff. "It's just that . . . she—she doesn't want anyone knowing. Not even the people here know. So I can't . . ."

Rob sat back, his face a study in sheer amazement. "So you can't tell me, of all people, where you live?" He shook his head. "You're scared to tell me where you live," he said, in the sing-song fashion he had used as a child when daring Jeff to do something.

"Of course I'm not *scared*," said Jeff. "I promised Susan that I'd tell no one, and she's—"

"Well, well. I never thought I'd see the day when Jeff Bentham wasn't master in his own house," said Rob.

Jeff felt himself color slightly, and Rob, who had known him since they were five years old, correctly interpreted the reaction.

"Oh," he said, standing, swinging the chair back to where he had found it. "It's not your house, is that it? It's Susan's house?"

Jeff stood up too. "Technically, yes," he said. "And I think she's entitled to say who should know that she lives there. And quite frankly, you're the last person she'd want to see."

Rob nodded, a slow grin appearing. He jerked his head back towards the way he had come in. "And that's her Roller, is it?" he asked.

"No," said Jeff quickly. "It was a present. It's mine."

"I wish I'd known it was yours. I wouldn't have scraped a coin along it."

For an instant, Jeff thought he really had, then blushed deeper when Rob laughed.

"My God, mate—you need taking in hand. Letting your wife tell you who you can take home? Getting paranoid about a bloody car?"

Jeff smiled, a little weakly.

"Come on—I need somewhere to smoke and drink my duty-frees. And somewhere to stay, come to that. I've just got off the train."

"Right," said Jeff. "Come on." He wasn't sure that he would have been just as brave if Susan hadn't been safely tucked away in her health farm.

"Attaboy, Jeff,'" said Rob.

"And you can stop passing judgment," said Jeff. "That sort of money changes things, believe me." He pretended to cuff him, flipping off the baseball cap as he spoke, and was pleased to discover that Rob the action-man was going bald.

"So," said Rob, once they were on their way. "What's it like, then? Being a millionaire?"

"It has its ups and downs like everything else," said Jeff.

"I'll bet. Like a private jet and a basement games room."

He had to put up with being teased all over again, but he was glad Rob had turned up; he filled the big shiny kitchen, cutting it down to size. He took a cigarette when Rob offered him one, as he had when he was thirteen, and his first drag made him dizzy.

At least he knew better than to keep up with Rob drinkswise, he thought, as the afternoon wore into evening. "You should eat," he said, getting up from the table. "What do you want?"

Rob took another swig of duty-free and looked at him quizzically. "You cook?" he said.

Jeff smiled. "No," he answered, looking up the almost incomprehensible book that had come with the microwave. "But Susan's left things in the freezer."

Half an hour later, they were finishing off the result of Jeff's endeavors.

"Not bad, not bad," said Rob. "I won't mind being billeted here for a while."

"You can stay here for a couple of nights," said Jeff. "But Susan will be back on Sunday night."

Rob lit a cigarette and shook his head, sucking in the smoke noisily. "Oh dear, oh dear," he said.

"Oh come on, Rob! I'm not supposed to have told anyone

where we live—and you know how she feels about you at the best of times."

Rob smiled. "That's never bothered you before," he said. "She just had to put up with me before."

"Things change."

Rob nodded. "They do," he said.

Jeff's eyes widened. Of *course.* "I've got better than a spare room to offer you," he said. "I can let you have a whole house."

Rob pushed his chair away from the table and flopped into the easy chair. "You serious?"

"Of course," said Jeff.

"You don't have to ask the missus?"

"It's *my* house!" Jeff jumped up, suddenly on the defensive. He knocked his chair over, and felt foolish again. Damn the man. He'd been able to get him going since they were kids.

Rob smiled lazily. "Don't get out of your pram," he said. "And don't think I'm ungrateful, mate, but I can't afford to buy your house. What would I want with a semi anyway?"

"Don't buy it," said Jeff.

"What would you want in rent?"

Jeff sat down. "Why the hell would I want rent?"

Rob crushed out his cigarette. "You mean I just go and live in it?"

Jeff shrugged. "No one else is," he said. "She gave away the furniture when she kitted out this place, but we can pick up some more. I'll see you're all right for money."

"No!" said Rob. "The house is enough charity for one day."

"It's not charity! It's sitting there, doing nothing, and you need somewhere to live."

Rob thought about that. "All right," he said. "Thanks. But I'll buy my own bits and pieces. I've got some money. And I'll pay you rent when I've got a job."

"Good. I'll take you over there tomorrow."

Jeff showed Rob around upstairs, which wasn't yet the way

Susan wanted it. "There'll be another bathroom in there," he said, pointing to the anteroom off the master bedroom. "And a dressing room."

Rob raised his eyes to heaven and went off to the less pretentious spare room.

*   *   *

It was Friday morning, and she booked up another week in August, the week before she started at college. She could get herself in trim to face up to all those fresh young faces.

"Certainly, Mrs. Kent. I take it you enjoyed your stay?"

"It was wonderful," she said.

"You look even more lovely than when you came," he said.

She modestly laughed off his compliment, but she felt very smug every time she caught a glimpse of herself in a mirror. That woman wasn't her. She was Mrs. Kent, to the life.

Shopping, now. Lots and lots of shopping, before she went home to give Jeff another surprise.

*   *   *

Jeff took Rob to the golf club. He wanted to introduce him to Neil Holder. Neil was also retired, also at a ridiculously early age, though at least he was a few years older than Rob. He had been a policeman, and was finding himself at a loose end these days. Jeff thought that he and Rob would get on together. They found him, filling his pipe, wearing a cardigan that his wife had knitted for him and his usual benign expression. Anything less like an ex-policeman would be hard to imagine, in Jeff's opinion. His appearance had fooled a lot of crooks, to their cost.

He helped Rob find some stuff for the house; not much, but he had said it was all he needed. He got a bit prickly when Jeff tried to give him the old fridge and freezer; he bought what he needed secondhand if he could, and new if he had to. But there was no housewarming; in the evening they went back to the farmhouse with its multitude of creature comforts.

"If you're staying here tonight, I can get drunk with you," said Jeff. Not that he ever got drunk; he couldn't see the point.

"Great," said Rob. "Make the most of it—it's the last cheap booze I'll have for a while. And your ball and chain will be back on Sunday."

He had made the most of it, and had lost track of the time as the duty-free booze ran out, and Rob had started on the stash in the drinks' cabinet. He was halfway through a very rude, very unfunny joke that Jeff had heard him tell a hundred times before when they heard a car pull up, heard the garage door close, heard Susan's key turn in the back door.

Christ, thought Jeff, his heart sinking.

He could hardly see her through the blue-gray fug; at first, he thought it was someone else altogether.

She was blonde. Well, not blonde exactly, but her brown hair had turned honey-colored; it suited her. She was never all that much overweight, and she had lost what extra pounds she had had. She seemed taller; he frowned, looking down from her perfectly framed face to the elegantly high heels. In between was someone who had walked from the pages of *Vogue*; not Susan.

"Susan!" said Rob, trying to get to his feet while knocking ash into a beer can. The result was not to Susan's liking, and she lifted an ashtray from the sideboard and held it out silently.

He tapped his now ashless cigarette over it. "Susan—you look wonderful," he said. He looked at Jeff. "You didn't tell me she looked like this these days," he said. "I always fancied her, but now. . ."

Jeff dropped the cigarette that he hadn't really been

smoking into the beer can, still speechless, still waiting for the blow to fall.

His eyes left his wife to look at the devastation which had greeted her. Bags, boxes, suitcases, everywhere there was a space. Empty bottles and cans, beer glasses with dregs still in them, overflowing ashtrays. Two days' worth of dirty dishes and cutlery piled into one of the sinks; the discarded freezer wrappings and leftovers in the other, because he hadn't looked for the pedal bin yet.

With a stab of sheer horror, he saw a long, finger-shaped burn on the worktop, remnants of cigarette paper still sticking to it. Underneath, on the tiles, lay a column of white ash, broken in three.

"It's been a long time," she said, with a truly commendable attempt at small talk, given that Jeff knew she wanted to kill both of them.

"Almost ten years. I'm out of the army now, you know. Back home."

"Where are you living?" she asked.

Jeff's heart took a nosedive to the soles of his feet.

"Your old house," he said, swaying very slightly as he stood.

There was a tiny silence, but no visible reaction. "How are you going to get there?" she asked.

He shrugged. The ash which had now reformed with the startling rapidity of foreign cigarettes, fell to the floor with the movement.

"I'll take you," she said briskly.

"Well, that's handsome of you, Susan," he said, rubbing the ash into the tiles with his foot as though she might not have noticed.

"I just think you've done enough damage here," she said. "Come on."

Rob followed her like a lamb, and Jeff watched from the kitchen door as she backed out the Mercedes. The passenger door opened, and Rob got in with a wave of his hand to Jeff.

He looked around. It looked even worse now that some of the smoke was leaving by the open door. He sighed. Perhaps if he got the place cleared up before she got back, it might not be so bad.

*   *   *

She took the key from him and unlocked the door; it would have taken Rob a year. He stumbled in, and offered her a drink from the bottle that he pulled from his jacket as soon as they were across the threshold.

"No, thank you, Rob," she said, as he subsided in the only armchair.

"I've got glasses," he said, encouragingly.

The house was unwelcoming, by anyone's standards. It was clean, but bare. A table, an upright chair, the armchair Rob was in, a portable television. A threadbare rug. Either Rob's taste or his wallet didn't run to lampshades, and the lightbulb created harsh, stark shadows.

"You're cross," he said.

"How long have you been at the farmhouse?"

He frowned as he thought about that. "Just the one night," he said, when he finally got to grips with the question.

She wouldn't have had a house left if he'd been there any longer, obviously. She took a deep breath, and tried to calm down a little. There were far too many emotions struggling for supremacy; she had no intention of letting any of them win.

It was hard to remember that she had lived there for over ten years. It wasn't like her house at all. It smelled different. Unused. Without waiting for permission, she went into the kitchen, which had no lightbulb at all. The light from the living room lit it to some extent, and she could see all there was to be seen. A secondhand cooker, a new fridge. A little picnic table, with assorted plates and bowls and mugs on it.

She looked in the fridge. Enough food to last him for a day or so. She heard him get up, felt his shadow block the doorway.

"You don't have much in the way of furnishing," she said, turning to face him, her heart beating fast.

He leaned in the doorway. "You look good," he said. "I like the way the light from the fridge is catching your face."

She didn't speak; she closed the fridge. Now they were in the half-light.

"No," he said, answering her. "Not much. No built-in appliances. No extractor fan. No central... what is it? Work station?"

"Is that why you vandalized mine?" she asked, standing up.

"Ah... sorry. Sorry." He held up the hand that wasn't propping him up in the doorway. "I'll pay for any damage to be put right. We... we had a drop too much." He pulled a packet of cigarettes out of his jacket pocket, and lit one. He leaned in the doorway, barring her exit; he looked down at his feet, not at her. "It'll have to wait until I've got a job, though," he added.

She had known him as long as she had known Jeff; she had always been afraid of him, of his total masculinity. Of how he made her feel.

"Come and see me when you're sober," she said. "I might be able to help you out with a job. It won't be much, but it'll be better than nothing."

His head shot up, and he was startled into temporary sobriety. "Really?" he asked, startled.

"Really."

He took a draw of the cigarette, letting the smoke drift out of his mouth. "Fancy that," he said, and smiled at her, his eyes glazing back into semi-consciousness. "I'll be able to pay Jeff some rent after all."

The almost exotic smell of the tobacco that had drifted out

through the kitchen window, alerting her to Rob's presence in the farmhouse, hit her again. She breathed it in.

"And—Rob. Anyone who knows our new address knows us as Kent, not Bentham. No one knows where the Benthams have gone."

The bleariness left his eyes. "Kent," he repeated. "He didn't tell me that bit." Then he grinned his slow grin, and his frank gaze slowly took her in from head to toe. He shook his head when he had finished. "Boy," he said. "Did the money do that for you?"

"Yes," she said candidly.

His cigarette dangled between the forefinger and thumb of his free hand. He drew on it deeply, then dropped it on the floor, standing on it, and in what seemed like slow motion, he pushed himself from the doorway, exhaling smoke.

She swallowed.

"Jeff's had himself made over too," he said.

A nod; that was all she could manage, as he came up to her. She could smell the smoke, and the alcohol; she wanted to run. She couldn't breathe in here, with him. It had always been the same. She didn't exactly run, but she took advantage of the unbarred exit, and walked briskly out of the kitchen, through the sitting room, to the front door.

"When do you want me?" he called after her. He emerged slowly from the kitchen, still smiling. "To see you about the job," he said.

"Monday morning," she said, quickly. "Nine o'clock." She turned, letting herself out, almost breaking into a run as she went to the car.

It was a while before she could drive away; his unsettling presence had started a physical reaction that she knew wouldn't let her go. But before, when it had happened, he had only been on leave; she had never spent more than a few hours in his company, and had hardly ever been alone with him at any time. He would go back to his unit, and she could get over it. Then he had married, and stayed away.

Over the years, she had barely thought of him. On the odd occasion when Jeff had mentioned him, it had been like some other life, like some faint memory of childhood foolishness. She had grown out of it.

But he was back.

*　　*　　*

Jeff had found a black refuse bag into which he had at least put all the rubbish; he had removed all the empties from the surfaces, and wiped them, even making an attempt to make the cigarette burn less noticeable, but without much success.

On her return, which was sooner than he had thought it would be, he had abandoned his task; she would be better at it, and anyway he felt that he had done enough for one evening.

"He had nowhere else to go," he said, when she had inevitably demanded to know what Rob was doing in their old house. He reached for the packet of cigarettes, but it was empty. He realized with a smile that Rob had left an unopened packet on the table. He sat down and took one out.

"You're not smoking those things in here," she said sharply.

He looked at the packet. They were a bit smelly, he supposed.

"Why on earth did you start smoking again after all this time?" she demanded.

"I felt like it," he said, getting up. "I'll pop down to the pub, I think."

She didn't argue; he had thought she would.

He made half a pint last almost an hour, and smoked two cigarettes. It was usually quiet, but tonight someone was playing the jukebox, someone else was playing the fruit machine, and someone was playing a trivia machine that played incessant tunes every time a question was answered, right or wrong. People crowded up to the bar, pushing into him as he sat there. Eventually, they had all left but him.

"You were busy tonight," he remarked to the landlord.

"Always busy, Fridays," he replied. "I've seen you in once or twice lately, haven't I?"

"Yes."

"Is it your wife that's brought us in the extra business at lunchtimes?"

Jeff frowned.

"Builders and such. Working up at the old farmhouse. For a Mrs. Kent, they said. You Mr. Kent?"

Jeff nodded. Yes. He was Mr. Kent.

He walked back up to the house, thinking how best to approach Susan, who hadn't been as furious as he had expected. Perhaps he should make it clear that he was glad to have her back; if he hadn't been so horrified, he would have been more than pleased to see her. And he ought to say something about how she looked. He smiled. She looked wonderful. He'd had a bit more to drink than he should have done, he supposed. But she wouldn't mind that.

He let himself into the kitchen, and went out into the hall, catching sight of himself in the mirror. Oh God. He looked as though he'd been on a two-day binge, when all he'd done was watch someone else on a two-day binge. But he'd better make an effort.

He went into the cold bathroom, and ran the water. After half an hour, he emerged bathed and shaved and smelling sweet.

He would apologize. She would understand—he hadn't seen Rob for ten years, after all.

She was asleep. Ah, well. Jeff crept in beside her, and dropped off almost as soon as he lay down.

*   *   *

She wasn't asleep.

She had come home to find that the devastation was mainly surface-deep and that Jeff had done some clearing away. The place looked not unlike the way it was supposed to look.

"Sorry," he had said, as soon as she walked in.

She had had to say something, and she hadn't known what. She had asked why Rob was living at the house, not because she cared, but because it was what he would expect her to say.

He had made to light one of the cigarettes; she had stopped him quickly. It was bad enough having the smell hanging around; she didn't want him adding to it, reminding her. The smell was inextricably bound up with her reaction to Rob, and it would only confuse her if Jeff started smoking the damn things. *"Rob's on leave—I've brought him back for some dinner."* That was what that smell meant. He had always smoked those cigarettes; he said it was because he could get them wherever they posted him to.

Jeff had taken exception to the ban and gone to the pub; she had been glad to get rid of him. She had tidied up, allowing Mrs. Bentham back into her life. She had opened the windows to get rid of the smell of spirits and tobacco; the house had got very cold, but the smell had obstinately remained, and she had given up once things looked more or less normal. She had washed all the dishes; she hadn't introduced herself to the intricacies of the dishwasher, and besides, she had wanted something to do.

She wasn't sure what could be done about the burn on the worktop. Perhaps she would have to replace the whole section. But she couldn't get angry about it.

She had gone to bed, and had heard Jeff come in at eleven-thirty. He had stayed downstairs a long time; she had heard the bathwater run away, heard the hum of his electric shaver. That was why she had pretended to be asleep when he came to bed, and why she was lying stiffly beside him until he began to snore softly.

She couldn't sleep. There was too much on her mind to sleep. The patio window was in, at least. The light in the sitting room had been left on, and had spilled out onto the rough ground when she had walked from the garage. She had to get the sitting room papered and painted, she had to get curtains and carpets, and sofas. That would be better than a three-piece suite, she told herself. Two, perhaps even three two-seater sofas. It was a big enough room. And a couple of armchairs. A coffee table—there was a beautiful Japanese coffee table in that oriental shop. Big, low, square. A lacquered top, just right for Rob to leave a cigarette on.

Next door in the little anteroom the component parts of the *en suite* bathroom lay in their packaging for the plumber to get busy on Monday. The bathroom suite for downstairs was being delivered tomorrow. She had to get it all organized; Jeff had done nothing. Too busy entertaining Rob.

She gave up trying to think of other things. The house might be what was on Mrs. Kent's mind, but it was Mrs. Bentham who was having problems, and it was to that particular problem that her mind kept returning.

It had been a shock, coming home to find Rob Sheridan there. He made passes at every woman who crossed his path, and had been routinely chatting her up ever since she had met him. She had always been nervous of being alone with him, afraid of the strong physical attraction she felt for him. But it had been years. *Years.* She had almost forgotten that he existed.

It had still been there, despite the state he was in; she had found it difficult to talk to him, and had used abruptness to cover her confusion. Even drunk, he had not been fooled by that.

One of her newfound charitable friends needed a van driver; Rob could drive anything from a three-wheeler to a removal van. She could get him a job. That put her on a different footing with him from how it used to be, she told herself. She was Mrs. Kent now. Confident, moneyed Mrs.

Kent, who could get people jobs and make people deliver bathroom suites, and didn't have to be afraid of anyone.

She wasn't afraid. She had always called it that, to herself. Blamed fear for the racing pulse and the rush of adrenaline. Fear of what? He had never done more than smile and look. That was all he had to do to get her hot and bothered, even smashed out of his mind. He still made her feel the way he always had; he still made it difficult for her to sleep after she had merely been in the same room as him, never mind alone with him.

It was Mrs. Kent who had volunteered to drive him home, who had deliberately ensured that she would be alone with him; but it was Mrs. Bentham who lay awake all night with the ache.

*   *   *

There seemed to Jeff to have been no time between closing his eyes and being aware, as one is, that he was being observed. He came to, wide awake after his almost unconscious sleep, to find that it was dawn, and Susan was propped up on one arm, looking down at him.

He moved in the luxury of the kingsize bed, and looked at her; she looked even better in the soft morning light than she had last night.

"How long have you been awake?" he asked.

"A while," she said.

"You aren't worrying about John, are you?" he asked. "He hasn't used the revolver once, honestly."

She looked for a moment as though she had forgotten who John was, then her brow cleared. "Not really," she said.

"Because there's no need. He's harmless. He doesn't shoot anything, never mind people."

"Good," she said.

"And don't worry about Rob," he went on. "He won't breathe a word about where we live, I promise. He knows you want it kept secret—he won't say." Encouraged by the fact that she didn't seem about to have a row with him, he carried on. "I'm sorry about last night," he said. "I wasn't expecting you back until tomorrow. I'm sorry about the smoke and the mess—I wanted it to look nice for you when you got back, and I go and... I am sorry, honestly. We can get a new worktop, can't we? I didn't mean to let him get drunk, but you know what he's like."

She didn't speak; he wasn't sure whether that was good or bad.

"He's out of the army," he continued. "He's just a bit lost. I'm sorry you had to take him home. I know what he's like, and I know how you feel about him—did he bother you? He'd had too much to drink—don't take it personally."

She got out of bed.

"Where are you going?" he asked.

"I have things to do."

"Come back," he said, catching her hand. "It's not seven o'clock yet, and you look gorgeous."

*   *   *

She tried to pull her hand from his. His smooth lawyer's hand.

"Come on," he said, sitting up. "It's Saturday morning. We can have a lie-in." He pulled her back down, kneeling behind her, his arms around her waist. "You've been away for two weeks," he said, leaning his chin on her shoulder, his voice wistful.

Rob's chin would be rough. She tried to imagine it.

"Susie," he said, wheedling now. His lips touched her ear. "I've only had that hairy ex-sergeant for company—"

She turned her face to his. "Stop talking about him," she whispered, a little desperately, then kissed him with rather more passion than was her norm.

He smiled, rolling her onto her back, pushing her nightdress up, needing no second invitation. She didn't want him any more than she had last night, but she needed to relieve the tension in her body somehow, and for once she had as little time for foreplay as he had. She closed her eyes, and pretended it was Rob. It helped, a little.

But even so, the bang that echoed through the early morning air, scattering the birds, and rattling the old sash windows, was none of Jeff's doing.

It hadn't helped that much.

*   *   *

"It's a gas-gun," Jeff said, as he came back from his second visit to his explosive next-door neighbor.

The smell of bacon and eggs was allowed to hang in the air until Susan remembered about the cooker hood, and Jeff's eyebrows rose as one of the overhead cupboards turned out to be some sort of noisy fan that stopped your breakfast smelling. He *liked* his breakfast smelling.

"What the hell's a gas-gun?" she asked, briskly arranging his plate.

"A bird-scarer," he said. "He needs it to protect his crop, he tells me."

Susan had jumped every time it had banged; Jeff felt that she really was making a bit of a meal of it.

"But it's gone off every twenty minutes since dawn!" she said. "How long are we supposed to put up with it?"

"Well...until the end of the summer, I suppose."

She stood, his breakfast in her hand, staring at him. He rescued the plate, and sat down at the breakfast bar, presuming that to be where one sat to eat breakfast. But there were no knives and forks and he didn't know where he was likely to find them. She had been up ever since it had happened, sorting out the kitchen, and he didn't know where she had put things.

She was producing some sort of homemade muesli with

oats and things. Jeff wrinkled his nose a little as he watched, then got up and began opening drawers, ever hopeful of not having to eat bacon and egg with his fingers.

"You *must* be able to do something!"

Jeff sighed, as he found the cutlery. "I can't. He's entitled to use a gas-gun to scare the birds—it's in his lease."

"It's what?"

He presumed you used a spoon for her concoction. He took one out.

"It's in his lease. He showed me it. We can check with our copy, but he'll be right. He only stopped using it as a favor to the old man's relatives, who were trying to sell the house, but I told him not to use the revolver, so—"

"It's a menace!"

Jeff sat down again, and started on his breakfast at last. It was a bit on the cool side now. "It isn't dangerous," he said. "Just noisy."

It blasted again as they spoke, and she jumped, spilling some oats onto the floor.

Every twenty minutes, dawn to dusk, day in, day out, all spring and summer. That's what they had to look forward to. But he was out all day, and it was only at breakfast time that it really mattered to him. In the evening, the windows tended to be closed, and the double-glazing would help. The television was usually on, and it was only operational until dusk. June might be a bit of a bind, but he could live with that.

"The old man was as deaf as a post," he explained. "He didn't give a damn what he used—revolvers, gas-guns—it made no odds to him. So there it is, in black and white in the lease. It's described as 'use of automatic audible crop protection systems,' but it's the right to use a gas-gun, make no mistake. No one can do anything." He looked up as she sat down with her muesli. "I hate to say I told you so," he said. "But I told you so."

"I was waiting for that," she said.

"It was far too cheap, Susan—there had to be a catch. If you'd let me look at the title deeds, I would have found it. I don't know who was acting for you, but I'd have a strong word or two to say if I were you."

She ate in silence, munching at her awful breakfast. He could only thank God her health kick hadn't extended to him.

"It's not that bad," he said, his tone conciliatory now that he had got the smug bit out of the way. "We can get upstairs double-glazed too—we'll hardly hear it."

*   *   *

The gas-gun continued to bang, every twenty minutes, all day. Every time it did, it made Susan jump. Every time it did, she remembered what her imagination had been doing the first time. Every time it did, she felt like a confused fourteen-year-old.

If only Rob hadn't happened, she would have enjoyed finding out that the house had a major drawback. As it was, she couldn't survive until autumn—she doubted if she could survive until lunchtime.

Jeff was getting ready to go to some mythical place of interest; it wasn't fair. He was getting away from the instrument of torture next door, and leaving her with it. It was April, she pointed out. The garden could presumably now have something done to it. And she made her feelings clear about his bringing Rob to the house, and letting him live in the other one rent-free.

"He hasn't got a job," he said.

She didn't tell Jeff about the job. She wished she had never said it. But she had phoned up about it that morning, and had arranged for Rob to have an interview on Monday.

She was dreading Monday, and waiting for it to come all at the same time. Damn Rob Sheridan. Damn him.

The bathroom suite arrived, as promised; she needn't have come home at all.

*   *   *

Jeff had to listen to a great deal more of what Susan thought of their next-door neighbor before he could get away, and on to the motorway. Fiona's parents should have left that morning, and he could see her again at last.

Still the magic worked. Cocooned in the luxury of the car, he could forget irritations like the gas-gun and Susan's overreaction to it. All right, it had startled him too when it had gone off, given the rather frustrating moment it had chosen, apart from anything else. But it was just a loud crack every now and then. Hardly a sonic boom.

He drifted along in his silver beauty, smiling at the world. It was cold, but sunny; the morning light strobed through the trees, lying in strips along the road ahead.

There was just a little dent in his good humor by the time he left Fiona that evening. They had had lunch, then had strolled about London pretending to be tourists before going back to her flat and playing their tantalizing game until they could stand it no longer, and they had made love. Nothing there to worry him. The worrying part came as he was leaving, and it stayed with him all the way back along the motorway.

Three words. That was all, as she kissed him goodbye. Just three words that nibbled away at his peace of mind. He had known, at the beginning, that it was a mistake. Love them and leave them—it had always been the safest way in the past. And all weekend, he was aware of something other than Susan nagging at him, though, my God, he had never known that she had such persistence in her.

She knew there was nothing to be done about the gas-gun, so she nagged him about everything else. The garden. The cigarette burn, which he had mistakenly thought she had decided to let pass. The fact that he had failed to call the plumber when the upstairs bathroom suite arrived. Letting Rob come to the house in the first place. Letting him stay there in the second. Letting him have the old house in the third, and letting him have it rent-free in the fourth.

"It's the best way," he had said, able at last to counter one of her accusations. "Rent books are trouble."

But worse trouble than that awaited, as he thankfully escaped Susan's wrath on the Monday morning, and went back to work.

* * *

"Sober," Rob said, standing at the back door.

Susan could feel the electricity, and he was just standing on her doorstep at nine o'clock in the morning. "Is that deliberate, then?" she asked, indicating her own chin.

There was a little rasping sound as he ran his hand over the stubble, and smiled. "Don't you like it?" he asked. "I know it's a bit old hat, but I couldn't do it when it was all the rage."

"You'd . . . you'd better come in," she said.

"So," he said, plonking himself down at the breakfast bar, somehow making it seem too small, "what's the job?"

"It's a delivery firm—they need a van driver. I don't know what the conditions are or anything—you'd have to find that out at the interview."

He pulled out his cigarettes, and tapped one out of the packet. "Sounds great," he said.

He was still wearing the baseball cap. He had been wearing it on Friday night. She found herself wondering if he slept in it, and wishing she hadn't wondered. She could feel herself blushing, for God's sake.

The gas-gun went off.

"Jesus Christ, what was that?" Rob was on his feet.

She had jumped again. Perhaps it was because of the

business with the revolver shots rather than its more recent connotations, she tried to tell herself. But she knew why it made her jump, it having blasted its way into her life just when it did.

"The bird-scarer," she said.

"You need a bird-scarer?"

She explained about John, and his smallholding. She didn't mention the episode with the revolver; she felt silly enough already about that. "We'd better be going," she said briskly. "I said you'd be there at nine-thirty."

He smiled again, reaching across to knock his ash into the ashtray. "You trusted me, then," he said.

She didn't answer; she opened the back door.

"This job's mine, is it?" he asked.

"As good as. Maybe you should take off that hat when you go in."

He smiled, and threw his cigarette out of the open door. "I will," he said.

*   *   *

Jeff called a cheerful good morning to the girls in reception, and poked his head around Marty's secretary's door. "Is he in?" he asked.

"Yes—he said he wanted to see you as soon as you came in," she said.

"Oh, right." Marty was about to read the riot act, which was always quite difficult for him, looking as he did, like a bright sixth-former, despite being well into his fifties. Jeff smiled at the girl, knocked on Marty's door and went in.

"I can explain," he said.

"I know an old friend of yours turned up," said Marty. "Jenny told me."

"Yes," said Jeff.

"But that really isn't an excuse to go swanning off and leave everyone in the lurch for two days," said Marty.

113

Jeff hung his head in melodramatic shame. "I know," he said. But he knew he couldn't keep up the comedy act. Marty had known him a long time. He'd understand if he told him the truth. "I'll tell you, Marty—on Thursday, I was thirteen again. Thirteen and having to prove to him that I was as big and tough as he was—which I never was, of course." He smiled. "Thirteen, and smoking behind the bike sheds. Accepting dares that scared the shit out of me because I didn't want him to think I was—"

"Jeff," interrupted Marty.

Jeff realized he had been going on. "Sorry," he said. "But that's what happened, Marty, I swear. Do you know, I even think that I—" He broke off. "I think I even play around just to impress him," he muttered. "And I don't do that as often as he thinks, either." He looked up again. "I'd have lost face if I'd had to come and ask if I could leave, don't you see?"

"No one expects you to *ask*," said Marty, looking acutely uncomfortable. "What you are expected to do is make alternative arrangements. Get someone to cover you. But you don't. And . . ." He took a deep breath. "And quite honestly, it's just another example of how difficult this situation has got."

Jeff frowned. "What situation?" he asked, genuinely puzzled.

Marty sighed. "Jeff, there are other people working in this practice. Other junior partners. Who have felt for some time that you are treating work like some sort of hobby ever since . . . well, you know."

"It's not rude, Marty," said Jeff, irritated by his own folly in thinking that Marty would understand. "Ever since Susan won the pools."

"Right," said Marty, his face growing pink. "You come to work in a Rolls Royce, you won't even tell anyone where you're living—this isn't the first time you've not been here when you should have been. They are here because they have to earn money. And, quite frankly, they feel that you have an unfair advantage. Your work isn't as important to you as it should be. And now, you just walk off and leave everything—" He swallowed. "If they can handle your clients in your temporary absence, then they could do so permanently, and make themselves more money. Money that they need, and you don't."

Jeff stared at him, panic beginning to bubble up. There was a hard look in Marty's pale eyes that he had never seen before.

"I want to buy you out, Jeff," he said. "I no longer want you to be a partner in this firm."

Jeff jumped to his feet. "But you can't *do* that!" he cried.

"I can," said Marty. "I am doing it. Look at your partnership agreement if you don't believe me."

"I don't understand," he said. "I don't understand. Who— who's complained about me?"

"It's just a general feeling," said Marty. "But if you look at the agreement you'll see that I don't need to have a complaint about you. I can buy you out whenever I want to, Jeff. And that's what I'm doing."

*　　*　　*

"I start next week," Rob said, getting into the car beside her.

She should have felt in charge of the situation. Her influence had just got the man a job. He was a passenger in her car—wasn't that what the driving lessons were all about? He ought to be the one who felt awkward, out of place.

He was the one who was wearing jeans and a T-shirt, a baseball cap on his head, sporting what looked like a three-day growth, whatever he thought it was.

She was driving her own Mercedes, wearing an outfit that had cost the earth—a sum accounted for, apparently, by its artful simplicity. Which meant that she could have picked up an outfit for a tenth of the price which would have looked just as simple. But she hadn't, even though she did feel in her heart of hearts that the designer's customers were a great deal more simple than his designs.

And so did Rob. He admired her new look, but he wasn't fooled by it. She was just who she was; Mrs. Kent vanished in his presence, and Mrs. Bentham, married at seventeen, came right back. And Rob knew her better than he had a right to, better than Jeff ever had; Rob had shared an intensely personal experience with her, and he played on that knowledge, though he had never mentioned it since.

She couldn't play games with Rob, and she didn't want to. There was only one thing she wanted to do with him, and the longer she was in his company, the more obvious that became, to both of them.

She didn't understand it. She had never felt like that about Jeff, and she hadn't even felt it about Richard Price; that had been a clinical experiment which had proved to her that the whole thing was at best a bit of a bore, even with someone who had women falling at his feet.

She deposited Rob at the house, stopping barely long enough to let the man get out. She didn't wave, or hoot. She just drove off, her mind and body at uncomfortable odds with one another.

*　　*　　*

Jeff had driven straight home; even the car couldn't help, not this time. Anyway, his partnership agreement was at home. Rogers couldn't do that to him, not after twelve years of working with him. He squealed to a halt outside the garage, and walked quickly to the back door, fumbling for his key, tears pricking his eyelids. The last time he'd cried, Susan had just lost the baby.

He walked through the kitchen to the hall. Marty couldn't buy him out just like that. He couldn't . . . he was halfway to the door when he noticed the smell. Rob's unmistakable cigarettes.

He sniffed again. Rob must have been here. What the hell would he be doing here at this time on a Monday morning? Susan would be furious.

Oh, well. Who cared? He carried on, and half ran upstairs to the bedroom, to the safe where he kept all the important stuff. He unlocked it, and looked in. Used to keep all the important stuff, he thought. She had all that sort of thing now.

The partnership agreement was at the top of a small pile of documents—the deeds to his own house, his birth certificate, receipts for income tax purposes and his will, all the documents held together with a rubber band. She had made her own will now, of course. She had got Marty to do it. It was in Jeff's favor, but no one else's. Oh, there were a few small bequests to people she knew, though she never saw them now. But if he went first, then all Susan's money was going to charity. He supposed it made sense, when he thought about it. She really didn't know anyone else all that well. Just him.

The *will* should be on top, he thought, as he picked up the agreement, and unfolded it. But the thought was chased out of his head by what he was reading.

* * *

Jeff's car was there when she got back. It wasn't parked in the garage; he always put it in the garage. It was pulled carelessly up to the parking spaces outside, overlapping the one it was in. It was almost as though someone else must have been driving it; Jeff was so careful about everything like that. But no one but Jeff had ever driven the Rolls. Something must be wrong.

"Jeff?" she called, when she got in.

There was no reply. She went to the foot of the stairs and called again. Puzzled, she went up, to find him in the bedroom, sitting on the bed.

"Jeff—what's wrong? Are you ill?"

He looked up at her, his face streaked with tears; it shocked her.

"Jeff—what's happened?" She went to him, sitting beside him on the bed.

"Marty," he said. "He's . . . he's terminated my partnership."

Well, well. So Marty had come through. She had almost given up on him; she had thought that he didn't have it in him. But the greed had won out over his better self.

Jeff's distress startled her a little, but it didn't move her. She had cried too many tears to worry about his.

"But why?" she asked. She wanted to know; Marty had said that he had to have a reason.

Jeff shook his head. "I don't know," he said. "I think he's jealous—the money. I don't know. He says it's because I took a couple of days off when Rob came back."

She frowned. "Why shouldn't you take a couple of days off?" she asked.

"Well . . . I . . . I didn't tell him. Rob turned up at the office, and I just—well. I just left with him."

"Why didn't you say what you were doing?"

He sighed, a long, shuddering sigh. "I don't know," he said, miserably. "But that bloody partnership agreement gives him the right to get rid of me anyway. Even if I hadn't done anything." He blew his nose. "He called me in this morning, and just told me."

He must have left the office almost immediately; she was glad she and Rob had been gone by the time he got home.

"It's worse than you know," he said, opening the safe, and taking out the copy agreement. "Read it. Read it."

She took it from him, but she had no need to read it. She had read it very carefully already. Marty, sharp operator that he was, had sewn his junior partners up with piano wire when he had drafted the agreement. And they, greedy for status and a share of the profits, had allowed their training to desert them. Jeff would never have let a client of his sign an agreement like that. But good old Marty wasn't the type to do the dirty on a chap.

Which had been true, she supposed. Good old Marty had never called on the clause before, and he had paid his junior partners well enough, making it unlikely that they would choose to break the agreement without careful thought to their future. But then, he hadn't been offered quite the financial incentive that she had offered in return for his turning nasty.

The partnership agreement meant that Jeff couldn't set up on his own within a thirty-mile radius of any office belonging to Rogers and Partners. He couldn't work for any other firm of solicitors within a thirty-mile radius of Rogers and Partners. He could be employed as a solicitor in any organization which did not entail his seeing clients, but not as a Crown prosecutor in any district in which Rogers and Partners had an office, and not for any firm which had previously used Rogers and Partners for its legal work.

The partnership agreement meant, in effect, that he couldn't work without moving away from the town, and she had no intention of doing that. So, he either had to move without her—and by extension without her money—or he just had to stay put. She didn't know whether the full impact of it had hit him or not yet, but it would.

Poor Jeff.

*   *   *

It was an overcast April day. It hadn't rained, but the air was damp and cool, as though it had. A light wind stirred the branches of the trees as Jeff and ex-Superintendent Neil Holder walked onto the green at the ninth. Rob was caddying for them both, because, like them, he had nothing better to do. Well, Rob had work of a sort to go to, but he wasn't exactly a career van driver, and he was on afternoons, so he had said he would caddy. He and Neil had hit it off; Jeff had known that they would.

"I'll give you that," said Neil, knocking away the ball. Jeff picked it up, and tried to tell himself he was having fun. But golf was supposed to be a relaxation, not something you did instead of working. Neil was in his mid-fifties, and had believed that he was looking forward to retirement. Counting the days, he'd said. But now that it had happened, he had the same wistful expression as Rob had had when he had turned up in the office, and as Jeff knew that he wore almost permanently.

Neil holed out, picked up his smoldering pipe from the edge of the green, and they went to the next tee. Jeff sighed aloud.

"What I don't understand," said the ever-direct Rob, correctly interpreting the sigh, "is why you ever signed an agreement like that in the first place."

Jeff waited until Neil had driven off. "Because," he said slowly, "I was being offered a hell of a lot more than I would have got as Marty's—or anyone else's—employee. We had to move—and I couldn't have afforded it otherwise."

"I suppose," said Rob. He held the brand-new golf bag while Jeff decided what to take off the tee. "God—do you remember that flat?"

Jeff chose his club, and teed up. "Remember it?" he said. "I'm still trying to forget it."

"What was wrong with it?" asked Neil, just as Jeff addressed the ball.

Jeff's shot went way to the right, the ball disappearing into the bushes that lined the fairway. He didn't know why he played with Neil Holder. The man was still settling all the old scores from the magistrates' court. He was also a keen amateur golfer who had at one time considered turning professional. Jeff was supposed to be being given hints and tips. All he got was lessons in gamesmanship.

"Nothing was wrong with the flat," he said, as they set off.

120

"Well, Susan didn't like being that high up, but I didn't mind. It was all right. No—it was the company we found ourselves keeping that was the problem."

"You lived in the Brompton Road highrise?" said Neil incredulously.

It was the only place in the town that could be described as "that high up." They had got off lightly, Jeff supposed. Other towns had dozens of the things. "We did," he said. "Ten years before the mast. By the time we left, someone had tried to set one of the flats on fire."

"Can't say I blame him," said Neil. "Bloody eyesore."

Jeff looked a little hopelessly into the depths of the bushes. "Yes," he said. "That wasn't what made our minds up though—it was when someone was raped in the lobby. It frightened Susan—it frightened me, too. We had to move."

"Is that it?" said Rob, pointing to a smudge of white that Jeff had taken to be a piece of litter.

He peered at it. Sure enough, that was it, under some twigs. "Can I move that stuff?" he asked Neil.

"Feel free. I don't suppose you regarded *him* as more victim than villain, did you?" Neil asked, with heavy sarcasm.

Jeff's professional attitude to crime had been strained rather to its limit, he remembered. "I didn't then," he said, moving away the twigs, accidentally pushing the ball into a better position. He glanced up, but Neil hadn't noticed. "And I don't now. I agree with you. Lock them all up."

He regarded his selection of clubs without the faintest idea which one was likely to help. He actually found the game a bit boring; he very rarely went to the lessons that he'd paid for. He'd been a member for a couple of years; he had made good contacts, and he liked the clubhouse. He just didn't like playing golf.

"Have you been there lately?" asked Rob.

"The flats? No," said Jeff, pulling out his apparent choice of club. "I make my clients come and see me. Used to," he amended. He closed his eyes and hit; he opened them to see it land, pitch, and roll onto the edge of the green. He smiled broadly. Perhaps there was something to this game after all.

"How the hell did you do that?" asked Neil, walking across to his own ball.

"It's worse than ever," said Rob. "I went there to see a flat—I tell you, *I* didn't feel safe, and I've been under fire in Northern Ireland. God knows how women must feel."

"Second generation thugs," said Jeff, trying to time his remark to coincide with Neil's swing, but it didn't work. The ball flew onto the green, over the pin, checked, and spun back towards the hole. "They'll be even better at scaring people than their fathers were."

"Shall I tell you something, Jeff?" said Neil, as Rob loaded both bags onto the trolley and they walked down to the green. "I didn't always disagree with you about victims and villains." He looked just a touch embarrassed, as if he were about to confess some slightly shocking secret. "I've . . . I've been having a bit to do with the council's youth schemes, as it happens. Gives me something to do. I've just come back from a course—all a bit airy-fairy for me, but they had some good ideas. These kids are bored," he said. "I think that's half the problem."

"I'm bored," said Jeff. "You're bored. Rob's bored. We don't get our kicks raping women."

Neil marked his ball. "No," he said. "We play golf. For as much a month as they get to live on, if they're lucky."

Jeff looked at his putt. He crouched down like they do on television and looked at his putt. He walked to the other side of the hole and looked at his putt. People went on about borrows and slopes from left to right, but he was damned if he could ever see what they were talking about.

Rob handed him the putter. Jeff looked at the hole, and the ball. Then the ball and the hole. He made a few practice putts behind the ball, then squared up to it, pulling back the putter.

"Very few of them rape women," said Neil. "To be fair to them."

The ball went twenty feet past the hole, traveling to its right. Jeff sighed.

"Oh, bad luck," said Neil, placing his ball on his marker, and tapping it towards the hole. "You'll give me that," he said, sweeping it up as he spoke.

Jeff walked to his ball. Neil was giving him two strokes a hole, and they were on the tenth. So far, he had won one. All he had to do was get down in two to win another, and keep the match going. The thing was, did he *want* to keep the match going? He hit at the ball without any preparation, and it rolled past the hole again, leaving him a five-footer coming back. Good. He was bound to miss it.

Neil smiled. "This to stay alive," he said, in the whispered tones of the golf commentator.

It landed in the hole with a satisfying thunk. Sod's law.

"Dormy eight," said Neil. "Good putt."

"They might not all be raping women," Rob said. "But they're sniffing glue, vandalizing buildings, breaking and entering—and eventually, they'll move up to real drugs. Then they'll rape women. And mug old-age pensioners, and hold up petrol stations."

Jeff picked a wood. Neil sucked in his breath. Jeff ignored him. He drove, sliced the ball out of bounds, and drove again. He sliced the ball out of bounds again. He paid up, and the match was over.

He couldn't tell Neil he'd done it deliberately; for one thing, it would hurt his feelings, and for another he wouldn't believe him. But he had, and he felt inordinately proud of that.

"Yes," said Neil, as they walked to the clubhouse. "I know what they're like. That's why I'm hoping to get some sort of youth project going in the town. Try and get to them before they get to that stage."

"Ping-Pong and soft drinks?" said Rob, his voice sarcastic.

"No," said Neil, stopping in his tracks. "It would just be a headquarters—we'd organize things for the kids to do. You would be just the man to help, as it happens."

"Me?" Rob looked astonished.

"You. You're strong, tough—you've just said. You've been in Northern Ireland; you know about guns and bombs and staying alive. That'll impress them a bit more than a retired policeman would."

"You want me to teach them how to make bombs?"

Neil smiled, shaking his head. "It was just that I got an idea when I was at a Lodge meeting the other night."

Jeff laughed. "Now I've heard it all," he said. "You're going to make them join the Freemasons."

"No, no—hear me out. I mean that we create something for boys from, say, thirteen to seventeen that's *hard* to join. That you can't talk about to nonmembers. Not like a youth club. We don't throw open our doors and say come and join us—that way you get three kids who are swotting for their exams. We say you can't join unless you're tough enough."

Jeff saw the flicker of interest in Rob's eyes before he shook his head, dismissing the idea.

*   *   *

Susan peeled potatoes for the evening meal, thinking about Jeff. He had moped around for a few days, but then he had begun going to the golf club more often. He was even taking golf lessons; if he was at all good, he would become instantly and irrevocably absorbed, that much she knew. But he didn't really know the first thing about playing golf; he watched it on television, that was all. So it didn't seem destined to fill his days.

Serve him right, she thought. She glanced out of the window as the car arrived, and her heart somehow contrived to sink and leap at one and the same time as she saw Rob emerge from the Rolls.

"Brought Rob for some lunch," said Jeff, walking through the kitchen and out into the hall to hang up his jacket.

Rob wasn't wearing a jacket; he was in jeans and a T-shirt, as usual.

"I'll go, if it isn't convenient," he said.

"No," she said. "It's just cold meat and salad—there's plenty."

"It must be summer," said Jeff, coming back into the kitchen.

"The salad stuff's from John," said Susan. "Freshly picked. It looks lovely."

"See?" said Jeff, taking cans of beer from the fridge, and sitting down at the table. "The gas-gun has its uses."

It was due to go off any second. Susan would find herself waiting for it; it made her jump all the more that way. "Could we evict him?" she asked.

Rob joined Jeff at the table. He opened a can of beer and drank some, his eyes on her, while Jeff was pouring his carefully into a glass. She didn't think she could stand much more of this.

"Evict him?" Jeff was saying. "The man brings you food, and you want to evict him."

She spooned mixed salad onto the plates with much less care than usual. Some fell onto the worktop as the gas-gun boomed.

"Anyway, he's entitled to use it, and that's that," added Jeff.

She banged the salads down. "His rent's three months overdue," she said.

Jeff picked up his knife and fork. "You can't just evict him," he said. "You have to ask him to pay it first."

"I have," she said. "He said he had no money—he said that the old man never wanted his rent."

Jeff's knife paused for just a second in the act of cutting his roast pork. "Did you give him some sort of deadline?" he asked.

"I told him I wanted four months' rent by the end of this month," she said.

"Right." Jeff loaded a forkful of salad. "We'll have to wait and see if he pays it," he said.

Rob was still watching her as he ate, his eyes amused. The gas-gun banged, and he seemed to *know* its connotations. She shot a look at Jeff. He might have told Rob the circumstances, she thought. But he couldn't possibly know the rest. That had been locked firmly in her imagination, and that was where it would stay.

Rob reached over for the salt, his knee pressing against hers. It wasn't the first time; he'd done it the other night when Jeff had brought him home for supper. He had smiled, apologized with "Sorry—was that your knee?" and Jeff had made some remark about leaving his wife's knees alone.

This time he didn't apologize, and he didn't smile, and his eyes had stopped being amused.

"What's the matter?" said Jeff.

Susan stared at him. This was hell. This was sheer hell.

"You've gone pink—you're not choking, are you?" he asked, alarmed.

She shook her head. "I ... er ... I feel a bit ... I think I'll leave mine."

Jeff frowned. "Are you sickening for something?" he asked.

Yes. Oh God. Yes.

"Just—you know," she said, getting up and leaving the kitchen.

Jeff came after her, of course.

"I'm all right!" she snapped. "I might have a bit of a temperature—maybe it's flu, or something. Go and talk to Rob."

"If you're sure."

She was sure. She was *sure.*

She couldn't take this. He played on it deliberately; he always had. She had to stop him coming here.

*   *   *

Jeff drove home from Fiona's, the Spirit of Ecstasy slowly but surely working her magic on him. He was seeing a lot of Fiona with all this newfound freedom, despite her telling him she loved him. She hadn't said it again, anyway, and he didn't have the energy to go looking for someone else. He didn't think he could go through all the awkwardness of a new relationship. He could deal with Fiona if she got heavy. She hadn't yet—perhaps it had just been an automatic endearment, after all.

And it was becoming quite difficult at home, though things should change in September, when Susan started at college. That might help. Perhaps she was just bored, like Neil's tearaways. He would come home from wherever he had taken the Spirit of Ecstasy—garden centers, bookshops, Fiona—and she would be there, calling to him, wanting to know why he hadn't done this or had done that.

College would help. Or maybe she should get rid of Mrs. Reeves—perhaps she simply didn't have enough to do. But college really ought to help. When she was out all day, the gas-gun wouldn't make her so irritable. She might stop nagging him at last. But five months was a long time with a nagging wife.

The garden was top of the list. John's rent was next. And Rob. She didn't want him coming around, she'd said. She had always been the same about him; some sort of jealousy, he supposed. Women being envious of male bonding, or some such nonsense. Perhaps she thought he neglected her when Rob was around. She had had the nerve to give Rob a rent book; Jeff hadn't wanted to take his money, but Rob felt obliged to pay, now, and did.

Rob worked shifts; when he was on mornings, he and Jeff would go off for the afternoon to the races. It was only natural to ask the man in for a bite of supper, but he'd had to stop doing that—it was all too evident that Susan didn't want him there, and it had begun to make even Rob feel uncomfortable.

Jeff had taken to going into the pub on his way home from wherever he had decided to take the Spirit of Ecstasy; he would have half a pint of beer, and go home at seven. It annoyed Susan; it was the only reason he did it.

Rogers and Partners had just opened another office, in Bramcote of all places. God knew where Marty had got that kind of money, but he had, and that extended the thirty-mile radius within which he was virtually prohibited from working to an effective hundred miles, so getting another job was totally out of the question, unless they moved right out of the area.

Fiona had suggested that he get a job in London, which was far enough away under the agreement. But the idea was that he stayed with her during the week, and he wasn't prepared to risk his marriage, or the money that went with it, for Fiona. He liked the good life; he'd discovered that very quickly. He liked Susan too, when she wasn't nagging him to death. In some ways, he liked her more than he had; the money had given her a bit more confidence in herself, and he couldn't remember the last time he had felt that twinge of annoyance at her apparent stupidity. If only the gas-gun didn't get on her nerves so much, they'd be fine.

Maybe he should give Fiona up, he thought. If Susan got wind of it, he'd be finished, and perhaps she was getting just a bit too serious. And yet, he didn't want to give her up; having somewhere else to go might just be keeping him sane. He'd just have to carry on being careful.

But that night, as he pored over his bank statements and the neat list he had made of his outgoings, he realized that he could afford Fiona or the Rolls, but not both.

It was no contest.

May

At least Rob had stayed away for the last couple of weeks, and she was beginning to feel a little more relaxed. It had always been the same; it was his physical presence that caused the problem. Once he had been out of sight for a week or two, she could hardly believe that it had ever happened. Except that this time things were different.

But she told herself that it would be true this time as well, if it wasn't for the gas-gun. The house was finished, and Jeff had begun working on the garden, but she didn't think she could stand a sharp reminder every twenty minutes of Rob's effect on her.

She had thought she might be able to evict her tenant, but the four months' back rent had appeared, together with the next month's, though God knew where he got his money from.

But perhaps what was irritating her most of all was that Jeff was adjusting; he filled his days with leisure pursuits, and was simply getting on with his life again. She should have known; he had always been like that.

129

She couldn't stand it anymore, and another move was indicated. Which was why Elsa was here again.

"It won't be easy," warned Elsa. "In fact, you should really wait until winter. Then let the new people find out about the gas-gun."

"I can't," said Susan. It wasn't morality which was holding her back; she just knew she couldn't survive until winter. "It's not even June yet, and it's driving me up the wall," she said.

"Well. . ." Elsa picked up her cup of coffee and walked to the patio window. "The old man died three years ago the March just gone," she said. "The house went on the market that May. It simply couldn't be sold. And one spring and summer was enough for the garden to revert to wilderness—it hadn't been that far off it in the first place. So then, even when the man next door was persuaded to stop using the dreadful thing, no one wanted to know, because there was so much work involved. It's too far out of town for most people, and not far enough out to be regarded as countryside. Its views are hardly picturesque."

Susan had never taken much notice of its views; she supposed that that was because it didn't really have any. Just scrubby grass and the paraphernalia of living, like water towers and pylons. "But look at all I've done to it!" she protested.

"It's beautiful," Elsa agreed. "Inside." She looked out at the garden, which looked worse, if anything, now that Jeff was digging bits of it.

"Jeff says the land needs to be properly drained, or it'll flood when the brook's in full flow. That's why we can't do much with it. Not until that's been done. He's planted some seeds in the beds—they'll be up in June and July, he says."

Elsa nodded. "It does flood," she admitted, without even a suspicion of shame. "But you simply make sure prospective buyers aren't here when the brook's in full flow, in that case." She turned from the window. "The garden needs cosmetic surgery," she said. "Make it look good. Quickly. Then, maybe, someone will at least come inside to see what you've done to the place."

Susan wondered how easy it would be to get Jeff to ignore the basics and bung down some turf. He had said the other day that he would be glad of John's bird-scarer once he'd sown the lawn. And, naturally, you did that at whatever time of year you did it. Which wouldn't be now.

Elsa finished her coffee. "Believe me, Susan—if you want out of here, there has to be something to greet prospective purchasers other than that. And you can't just abandon another house. Even pools winners can't afford to do that."

No. She had spent a great deal of the money now that she had given Marty his loan. She would just have to convince Jeff, that was all. It might not be impossible; during the month, things had got back to something like normal. Jeff was rather subdued, and he no longer disappeared on Saturdays, but he did go out for drives in the Rolls; perhaps he had found someone a little closer to home. He certainly wasn't interested in her.

But apart from that, it was all rather like it had been before; he worked in the garden, she in the kitchen, and neither of them involved the other very much at all.

⁜   ⁂   ⁑

Jeff had set up his hi-fi at last, and as May grew older, and the evenings longer and appreciably warmer, he would sometimes turn the speakers toward the patio window and put on a CD, listening while he was working. Usually something light from the classics, punctuated by a crack like a gunshot every twenty minutes. Sometimes, if he timed it right, the bang came between movements.

He was working in the garden. It might stop her going on about it for a while, at least, and anyway, she was right. They had to move; if getting the garden in order would hurry that up, then it was worth it. But in the meantime, he had to live with her, and she was getting impossible. She definitely needed something to do, in his opinion.

She wanted turf down. She wanted John out. She wanted this, she wanted that. He kicked the spade savagely into the clay, and entertained a vision—the very briefest of visions—of burying her in it. But less stern measures could be taken; he was contemplating black market tickets for Wimbledon. Maybe Susan would like to come—tennis was one of the few sports in which she took an interest.

He hadn't been to see Fiona again, and it was when he realized that he had to give her up that the old desire to do some gardening had taken hold; he was releasing some nervous energy and keeping Susan happy at one and the same time. He had no real desire to keep her happy any other way, not the way she was at the moment.

The landscape gardeners had all been crossed off his list; all too fussy and frilly. He could do it better himself, he had said, and then he had done nothing except keep the grass down. Susan had reminded him of that throughout April. Well, he was making up for it now.

John's rent had made quite a significant hole in his finances; he had thought he had said goodbye to all the penny-pinching, but his bank reserves weren't limitless, and being "bought out" by Marty had barely amounted to a gold-plated handshake. And having bought all the gardening equipment, he had almost cleaned out his account.

He had had to pay his golf subscription, which had doubled from last year and was almost into four figures. The Rolls drank petrol, especially with his habit of driving all over the countryside in it, something he was doing even more. He could pay off his credit card purchases monthly, but not forever. So even the economy he had made where Fiona was concerned wasn't making much difference. He had been reduced to asking Susan for money.

"Whatever you want," she had said, looking a little startled.

"Yes," he had said. "I know. But, well, I have to ask you, you have to write a check..."

"I'll get extra credit cards for you." She had smiled. "Like you did for me. That'll be better, won't it?"

"Yes," he had said.

It had made him feel uncomfortable. But she was doing all she could. She wasn't to know how it made him feel.

He straightened up, feeling his back, and looked at the huge amount of land. He had to decide whether he wanted to get professionals to cultivate the bulk of it, or leave it virtually wild except for the garden area. There was something attractive about just letting nature look after it. Not that that mattered now, really, since they were both determined to sell. The new owners would do what they wanted with it. He looked back at the area he'd marked out for the lawn.

Turf. Whoever heard of such a thing. When Jeff Bentham embraced something—whether or not he actually enjoyed it—he did it properly. The land really should be drained, but he had been prepared to concede that that was possibly not vital. Apparently Elsa had said that previous flooding had been confined to the area of the brook, and he could work around that. But he would be laying a top quality lawn—he'd been thinking about marking some of it off for a tennis court, but that was obviously not worth doing now. But even so, a lawn meant hoeing and raking from now until August, before he even began to prepare the seed-bed. And he still had to work out exactly how much of it was to be lawn.

Turf!

He had told Susan that he was just as keen to move as she was. Privately, he thought that he was even more desperate to get away from the gas-gun. He could ignore it, but she couldn't, and its effect on her was driving him mad. But even if they were selling it, he didn't want to put down turf. He wasn't having someone think that he ran over the ground with a mechanical digger, flattened it, and stuck turf down.

The row about the turf was just about par for the course now; they were rowing a great deal lately.

He was working on the border by the old fence, trenching the heavy clay two spits deep, working compost into the piles of earth as he filled up the trenches. It was hard, sweaty, dirty work on this unusually hot and oppressive afternoon, but hard work helped, sometimes.

"Excuse me?"

He straightened up to see Elsa. He had almost forgotten what she looked like. She looked good, on this fine spring day; she wore a cotton dress and bare legs. He smiled. Why hadn't he thought of her before? She would be much less expensive than Fiona. Oh, yes, he could fancy Elsa.

"Is Mrs. Kent in, do you know?" she asked, hovering by the gap in the now shorn hedge.

"Yes," he said, a little surprised at the formality. Elsa had become a fixture while they were looking for a house; she and Susan had long since been on first-name terms. "Just go through."

She hesitated. "Do you think I should?" she said.

Jeff frowned. "Yes," he said. "Of course. Go through."

"I'm glad she's taken my advice," she said, as she came in. "And got a gardener—" She stopped in her tracks, and blushed furiously.

It was a nice sight. He smiled at her, enjoying her confusion.

"Oh, I'm so sorry," she said, her normal poise totally shattered. "I'm terribly shortsighted. Do forgive me, Mr. Kent."

Jeff's smile vanished.

*   *   *

"Oh, Jeff won't mind," Susan laughed. "I think he'd be quite flattered—gardening is his first love."

Elsa looked embarrassed. "I think he was a bit cross," she

said. "I normally wear contact lenses, you see. But I've lost one. And I only use my glasses to drive. So—when I saw this man..."

Susan shook her head. Jeff wouldn't care at all—Elsa must have imagined his crossness. "Forget it," she said. "And while we're on the subject of the garden, I've only managed to talk him out of putting in a drainage system. He says he won't be sowing the lawn until September, and that it can't be used until this time next year."

Elsa sighed. "But how soon will it look like a lawn?" she asked.

"October," Jeff said appearing at the door. "More or less. Like a very new lawn. Bits of nasty earth will show through." He went to the sink and started cleaning himself up.

It wasn't like him to be snide, but Elsa hadn't seemed to notice. "He'll have stopped using the bird-scarer by then, won't he?" she said.

Jeff shrugged. "About then," he said.

Elsa turned to Susan. "If you can just hang on until November," she said, "I think we'd have a good chance of selling."

The gas-gun went off in the silence that followed, this time making them all jump.

Susan didn't believe she would survive until November, but she nodded. "I'll try," she said.

Jeff went upstairs, and came back after a few minutes, changed. "See you later," he said, shrugging on his jacket.

"Where are you going?" Susan asked.

"Out," he said, as he opened the door.

"I can expect you back at seven, can I?"

"You can if you want," he said, and the door banged.

Elsa tried not to look uncomfortable, but she failed miserably.

Susan laughed it off with a little shrug of her shoulders. It couldn't have been because of Elsa's mistake. Jeff wasn't like that. *She* was; she would hate to have been mistaken for the gardener. But not Jeff.

*   *   *

He sat at the bar, alone. He hadn't drunk much; he had driven for miles, trying to find the peace of mind that had started to desert him with Fiona's whispered "I love you" and which seemed to be receding faster than he could call it back.

He had always been able to look on the bright side, eventually. Of anything. He thought of the setbacks that he had weathered; the flat, he had concluded, was better than living with his mother. Before that, living with his mother had been adjudged better than being homeless. And before that . . .

Before that, it had been a tearful Susan admitting, in response to his persistent questioning about what was wrong, that she was pregnant. Within hours, the initial shock had turned to pride. He had fathered a child. He had created another being. Then the dreams of fatherhood, the wonderful permanence of knowing that someone would carry on your genes, and your name. Because it was going to be a boy; he had made his mind up about that.

But the dreams had been shattered by a miscarriage, and he had had to learn to accept that, and look on the bright side. They had been too young to be tied down. They couldn't have afforded a child. It had probably been for the best.

So—no one to carry on the name. He sighed. What name? Even he didn't have it now, as Elsa had so innocently reminded him.

He checked his watch, raised his eyebrows, and drained his glass. "Five to seven," he said, aloud, to no one in particular. "Goodnight, all."

Arthur, pulling a pint at the other end of the bar, nodded to him over the heads of the other customers, whose goodnights—courteous, not unfriendly—followed Jeff to the door. If no one spoke behind his back, it was only because it had all been said.

Outside in the overcast spring evening, Jeff knew that heads were shaking sadly, though he had, of course, never witnessed them. The communal giving up of a lost cause was almost tangible, and the little pub itself seemed to shrug its shoulders as he walked around to the tiny car park.

Mr. Susan Kent, that's who he was, and everyone knew it. No job, no money of his own. He'd had to cheat money around in order to pay John's rent without Susan tumbling to what he had done. Poor John. He'd better find the money for his rent from somewhere; Jeff couldn't keep paying it, even with the assistance of the money he was getting from Rob, and if it didn't get paid, John would be out of his pathetic little smallholding before he knew what had hit him.

He allowed himself a little fantasy of John the Baptist barricaded into his cottage, loosing off all six rounds in his revolver at the invading Susan, who fell lifeless and uncomplaining to the ground.

He smiled at the Rolls, silver-gray as the sky; it was too large, too imposing for its setting, but it was the only thing left that made life worth living. The improbable heat of the day had not abated, and Jeff touched the button that caused the windows to slide smoothly down as he drove towards the house which sat at the top of the hill, looking down its nose at the town.

The garage door lifted majestically at his approach; he drove in alongside Susan's car, and slid to a stop, the car's nose one centimeter from the back wall. He never misjudged it.

He sat for a long time with the silent engine running, and turned his head slowly, thoughtfully, towards the open garage door. He could, at the touch of another button, close it again. No one would hear this masterpiece of engineering as it pumped out its deadly gas.

He could see the garage filling up with wisps of fumes, growing hazy as it curled round the walls, billowing around Susan's Mercedes, blotting it out, enveloping the Spirit of Ecstasy, wafting through the window to be breathed in with the smell of varnished wood and polished leather until there was no more breathing.

*   *   *

Susan was in the middle of making the dinner when the phone rang. She answered it to the vicar, who wanted to know if she had been asked to present the minibus.

"Yes," she said. "Your wife gave me the message—it's in my diary. I'm delighted—I didn't think you would get it this quickly."

"I think they pulled out all the stops so that the children would have it for the summer," said the vicar.

"That's wonderful. And of course I'll present it—you have told the local press, haven't you? The more publicity you get the better." She had a diary by the phone; her charitable works were keeping her busy. She had actually forgotten, what with one thing and another, but there it was, in her diary for the next day. *Saturday, 1st June 2:15 P.M. M/B.*

The vicar had been in London presenting a petition to the appropriate government minister protesting at the closing down of so many places like the one he was now trying to provide from charitable contributions. With the best will in the world, even Susan's personal contributions couldn't make much of a dent in the total required, and he needed press attention.

"Oh, yes. My wife told the local paper, and they said they would notify the television people—and national newspapers, they said, though I don't suppose that's very likely."

"No," said Susan. Her personal news value was nil now, thank goodness. Though it would have helped highlight the point that the vicar was trying to make. She liked him; he had set himself a totally impossible goal, purely to draw attention to the problem. His committee now included representatives of the social services, the medical profession, councillors, and even—when the business of the House allowed, which as far as Susan could see was never—their local MP.

"I'll see you tomorrow," she said.

She put down the phone, and looked at the clock. Dinner was at half past eight, and she had no idea where Jeff was. He was usually back by seven. It was half past seven now, and there was still no sign of him.

She flicked through her diary, which was pleasingly full, and went back to the kitchen to see how the casserole was doing. She was on quite a number of committees now, and involved in fund-raising for all sorts of things. She had surprised herself, as she had when learning to drive. She did have a contribution to make, other than cash, which as Jeff said, wouldn't go far no matter what she did. She had ideas. Ideas that other people listened to, and sometimes even implemented. Lots of people knew who she really was; the vicar obviously did, and there were others. She didn't mind. She had never minded.

But poor Jeff didn't seem even to have wondered about that; his male chauvinism was so deep-seated that she would swear that he still hadn't realized what she had done. It was almost no fun if he didn't even know why he felt so miserable. She had known; for twenty-five years to the day she had known.

She just hadn't realized *how* miserable she had felt. Not until the money had released her from it. But he hadn't worked it out, not yet. Perhaps not ever. It was galling to know that he thought that all this had just happened to him; to know that he had no inkling of the preparation, and the thought and the care and control that had gone into it. The sheer self-control entailed in refusing to be Mrs. Bentham anymore, after spending all her adult life being her.

139

But the gas-gun chipped away at that self-control, every time it went off. Every day. All day. Turning her back into Mrs. Bentham every twenty minutes, scared to have Rob in the house. Her answer to these irritations, totally unplanned, unpremeditated, and uncontrollable, was to nag Jeff. She would find herself doing it; she didn't mean to, or want to, particularly. But she nagged him, nonetheless.

Thunder murmured in the distance; perhaps a thunderstorm would cool things down a little. Sunless heat had taken over from sunless cold. The bird-scarer cracked.

"You could move back into your old house," Elsa had said. But she didn't know about Rob.

*   *   *

He didn't know how much time had passed before he snapped out of his fantasy, and watched the exhaust fumes drift harmlessly out into the open air. A long time.

Switching off the engine, he contemplated upturned wrists, shuddered, and left the car. He walked around to the front door, as he always did. He had objected to that unused front door. It was like some sort of dead end. So he used it. As his key turned in the lock, Susan's voice reached him. She always seemed to call just a fraction too soon, before she could possibly have had time to hear and react, like an actress jumping her cue.

"Jeff? Is that you?"

"Yes, dear," he said, sniffing the appetizing aroma drifting out from the kitchen.

She came out of the sitting room into the hall, looking immaculate, as she always did, nowadays. She was rich now—richer than most doctors and lawyers, who were so much higher up in the social ladder than she was, so she had to look her best. And Susan's best, whether it was sixties' fashion or nineties' elegance, was very good indeed.

"Where have you been?" she demanded. She never asked lately, if she could demand. "Do you know what time it is?"

"I went for a drink. It's about twenty to eight, I think." He walked past her into the sitting room. Picking up the paper, he sat down with a sigh.

"Not there, please, Jeff. I'm reading."

He looked up from the paper. "I thought you liked the window-seat when you were reading," he said.

"It's pitch dark," she said, though this seemed to Jeff to be something of an exaggeration. "There's going to be a storm."

"Mm." Jeff got up. "The brook's running high as it is," he said, with some satisfaction. "We might have a flood." He switched the television on, just as the gas-gun went off.

"Oh, not in here, Jeff, please!" She was closing the patio door as she spoke. "Use the portable if you want to watch that thing!"

"Sorry, dear," said Jeff. "I'll tell you what. I'll go out again. I'm sure we'll both be much happier."

"Stop calling me dear—and you can't go out, I've—"

He pushed open the patio door again and strode off across the garden, down through the bushes and the trees, far away from the house, down to where he'd found John the Baptist, where his hens came to lay. Down to the edge of the brook, and the tangle of bushes which were being edged aside by the rushing water.

It *was* high, running fast, with the intermittent rain they had had for days. He liked the brook; he liked to hear the water run, see it flow over and around stones and roots and branches, smell the dampness of the earth and feel the coming of summer.

But this evening, it reminded him of nothing so much as a newly dug grave.

*   *   *

At eight-thirty, she served one portion of casserole, and put the shallow dish back in the oven. She helped herself to some buttered noodles, and left the rest to cool on the worktop. He could heat them up in the microwave when he came in. If he came in.

He had been behaving oddly before their row, really. The business with Elsa had been odd. And calling her "dear" —which he had done throughout their brief conversation, had been odd. Perhaps he *hadn't* forgotten what day it was; perhaps he was having trouble dealing with it. That would at least be something.

She enjoyed her meal; it was the first she had allowed herself that had not had its origins in Mario's kitchen at the health farm. She skipped the starter and the dessert; it seemed a bit over the top. She ate at the breakfast bar, preferring not to sit in solitary splendor at the laid table in the dining alcove.

She consigned her plate to the dishwasher as the gas-gun blasted, and the front doorbell rang. She jumped, and went to the door, trying to make herself relax. She would be all right if it wasn't for the gas-gun. She simply had to try to sell the house. Someone might not mind the dreadful thing; God knew, Jeff didn't seem to. He might not be unique. Maybe they would find someone just as stone deaf as the previous owner. Maybe, she thought grimly, that was how the previous owner became stone deaf.

Any relaxation she had managed to achieve on her way to the front door vanished when she opened it.

"Can Jeff come out to play?" he asked, removing a cigarette from the corner of his mouth.

She felt her hand tighten on the doorknob. "He's out," she said.

"Oh. I saw him the other day—I thought he could do with cheering up."

She looked around outside; no sign of a taxi pulling away. "How did you get here?" she asked.

"I walked."

It was nearly four miles. She raised her eyebrows. "You were keen," she said.

He smiled. "I needed the exercise—it's not too far if you cross the fields."

She could hardly send him away again. "Come in," she said.

"There's a storm brewing, though," he said, as he came in, bringing with him the smell of sweet, heavy tobacco smoke. He looked around for an ashtray, and she handed him one. Even that was like an electric shock; touching something that was touching him. He ground out the cigarette. "Will he be long?" he asked.

"I've no idea." She walked back out into the hall, back to the kitchen, just to get away. But she had known he would follow her; she had meant him to.

"Something smells great," he said.

She looked at the oven, and back at him, and made up her mind. "Sit down," she said, replacing the lid on the noodles and putting them in the microwave.

She got a glass, a placemat, and a knife and fork from the table, and set them down on the breakfast bar. She took the open bottle of claret from the sideboard, and put it down beside the glass.

She could feel him watch her all the time, as she opened the oven and took out the casserole and the empty plate. She arranged the meat on the plate, spooned the vegetables around it, and put the plate back in the oven. She would make him the sauce that she hadn't bothered with herself. The casserole dish sat on the hob, the sauce bubbling and thickening, steam rising. He smiled as she pulled open the cooker hood. She set the microwave; after a couple of minutes it pinged, and she removed the noodles, adding an extra knob of butter for luck. She removed the plate, poured over some of the sauce, put the rest in a sauceboat, and presented him with the result.

143

He looked at the little parcels of meat. "What is it?" he asked, his voice slightly suspicious.

"Beef," she said.

He cut into a parcel and sniffed, closing his eyes as the aroma of chopped bacon, garlic and thyme, with overtones of brandy, rose from his plate. "Nice," he said, helping himself to noodles, then looked up at her. "I take it you've already eaten?"

She nodded.

He started eating, and smiled broadly. "What would I have got if you'd been expecting me?" he asked.

She poured the wine, and he looked up. "You're joining me in a glass of wine, surely?" he said.

She hesitated, then nodded. "OK," she said, reaching over for the other glass. She sat down, and poured more wine. He touched his glass with hers, and she felt it again.

He tucked into the beef for a few moments, then put down his knife and fork. "My powers of observation are not all that keen," he said, reaching for the sauceboat and the remainder of the noodles. "But I'd guess you and Jeff have had words."

She nodded, sipping the wine.

He carried on eating for a few moments. "And you've used them all up, have you?" he said.

She frowned.

"Words," he said. "I think you've said about two since I got here."

She smiled. "Sorry," she said.

"Oh, well, that's three. What's Jeff going to eat?"

"I don't care. There's pickled salmon in the fridge, if he's hungry."

He smiled, mopping up the sauce with the noodles. "That was the starter, right?" he asked.

"Right. There's almond soufflé in the fridge, too, if you're interested."

He finished his meal, and sighed with satisfaction. "No," he said. "I'll pass on the pudding."

He patted his firm stomach, and she was glad of the health farm; no need to feel inferior. Her figure wasn't quite how it had been at seventeen, but it wasn't bad.

He picked up the bottle. "Drink up," he said.

"No." She covered the glass with her hand.

He filled his glass. "Was this special?" he asked. "Or does he eat like this every night?"

"It was special."

"What's the occasion?"

"Silver wedding," she said.

Rob pushed his stool a little way away from the breakfast bar, and stretched his legs out, pulling his cigarette packet from his pocket. "Is that right?" he asked, the unlit cigarette between his lips, his face amused. He searched for matches, and lit up before he spoke again. "He's forgotten, has he?" he asked.

She shrugged.

"It's like that, is it?" He looked at his empty plate. "So why all this?"

She shrugged again. "An excuse to cook something a bit different," she said.

He nodded slowly, and sat back, looking at her.

"What?" she said, when she couldn't stand it anymore.

"You still do the cooking," he said, with a slightly puzzled expression.

"Yes. I love cooking." He knew; he understood. Jeff didn't.

He drank some wine. He made her want to cry, and she didn't know why. Smoke drifted across the table; she didn't fan it away.

"Come on," he said, picking up the bottle. "Where's the harm in another glass?"

"No, really," she said. "You'll want a lift back, I expect."

He sipped the wine, not speaking. Just looking at her

thoughtfully. Then he finished it off, and stood up. "I'm ready when you are."

He'd been there an hour. Dusk was beginning to creep around the edges of the evening, and she hadn't noticed the gas-gun at all.

She didn't really know much about leaving the house, getting into the car, driving it to the old address; she wondered if there was some sort of law about driving while under the influence of your passenger. She knew the way from the farmhouse to their old house with her eyes closed anyway, which was a good thing, because they might just as well have been.

She pulled up at the house, still automatically going through the driving-lesson moves in her mind. Lights. Brake. Handbrake. Neutral.

He leaned over and switched off the engine. Still, neither of them spoke. Her thoughts were racing, and her heart seemed to stop altogether when he touched her. But it hadn't, or where was the throbbing coming from?

"Is there any point in us prolonging the agony?" he asked.

He was in agony too. That hadn't occurred to her. She barely shook her head.

*   *   *

The sky grew dark before its time, the pylons merging into the blue-black of the dying light. The final patch of silver sky, painfully bright by comparison, closed up, and smoky clouds puffed up behind the high ground, descending like a slate roof, keeping in the heat, not allowing it to escape.

At Jeff's feet the stream bubbled and danced as if in excited anticipation of the storm, and rain began to fall from the stone-colored blanket of cloud. Killing himself was a fantasy. But he could leave. He could get into the Rolls, which was, after all, legally his, and drive the hundred miles required by the agreement.

He gave a huge, shuddering sigh. No, he couldn't. He couldn't set up on his own; he didn't have anything like enough money to do that. Besides, he didn't want to leave; he had liked things the way they were, and he didn't understand what had gone wrong. Anyway, if he left, he wouldn't have the money at all.

His problem was legal, more than anything else. It was her money. She had won it, fair and square, on her own. Nothing to do with him. And women paying men was new enough to the British courts; they were very strong on men paying women, but not so hot when it was the other way around. He couldn't claim to have offered her moral support while she clawed her way to riches—they had just landed in her lap. It was the degree of financial dependence that determined things, and until the win, for almost twenty-five years, she had been totally financially dependent on him, not the other way around. The wrong judge, and he'd get nothing.

Susan would point out that she had denied him nothing when he had become dependent on her. She had paid off the mortgage on his house; she had bought him a Rolls Royce, and sundry other expensive goodies. He had lost his job because of his own folly; she had done everything she could to cushion that blow, and had done nothing at all to jeopardize the marriage. He would simply have walked out on it.

He wouldn't get a halfpenny.

It wasn't fair, he thought, to blame Susan. He'd got himself into this mess, having to show Rob how grown-up he was. And Susan couldn't be happy with things as they were, though the money did seem to have been rather luckier for her than it had for him. She hadn't really seen what was happening to them, hadn't noticed that in amongst the fun part of spending the money their marriage had all but disintegrated.

*   *   *

Rain pattered onto the windowsill and dampened the curtains which just failed to cover the wide open windows. An early moth, fooled by the unnatural heat, attracted by the light, fluttered around the bare bulb, banging against it over and over again, until it spun in dizzy circles to the floor.

Susan knew how it felt.

Her body glistened as she held onto Rob, unwilling to lose physical contact with him. He smelled of soap and smoke and freshly generated perspiration; he tasted of wine and tobacco, and his stubbled chin was rough against her face as they kissed. She drew her lips away from his, and smiled; he smiled back, and laid his head on her shoulder, his lips at her breast.

Her fingers were still entwined in the thick hair at the nape of his neck; on top of his head it was thin and wispy and tousled. She stroked it down, kissing the bald patch.

"Nice way to spend your silver wedding," he said, his voice indistinct, his lips brushing her skin as he spoke. He pushed himself away, but she still kept in contact with him.

It was a criticism. She didn't care, and she didn't reply. She was like the stunned moth; out of it now.

He rolled over onto his back. "The payoff," he said. "Going to bed with his best mate. Is that what this is about?"

This time she shook her head.

"No," he agreed. "Sorry. I know it's not."

He seemed to be at as much of a loss as she was for reasons. It had been there for over twenty-five years, whatever it was. Just another thing Jeff hadn't noticed.

"Why did you and Liz get divorced?" she asked.

"She didn't care for army life," he said.

"Were you unfaithful to her?"

He shook his head.

It was hard to believe, given his reputation. "Is that like Jeff isn't unfaithful to me? One-night stands don't count?"

"No," he said.

"I had a one-night stand. Well, a one-hour stand, actually. In a hotel bedroom."

He grinned, and she could see the dimples through the bristles.

"That sounds nice and sleazy," he said.

"It was."

"Who was the lucky man?"

She smiled. "You wouldn't believe me if I told you."

"So what happens now?" he asked.

"I'd better go," she said. But she didn't move.

"What's the rush? Is there some part of Jeff's anatomy you've forgotten to cut off?"

She lay back, her fingers still loosely entwined with his. "He doesn't even realize," she said, her voice a touch bitter.

"That just makes it more cruel."

She thought about that. Perhaps it did; perhaps it wasn't as unsatisfactory as she had thought. She smiled.

He sat up on one elbow and looked down at her. "I thought you had to go," he said.

She nodded. She did have to go. She had to break the contact, make space between them. She had to be able to think. With an enormous effort of will, she pulled away, and got out of bed. Her clothes were scattered on the bed, on the floor. That was all there was in the room; a new bed, their clothes, the make-do curtains, and the moth which danced around the light again.

That and the heat, the sound of the rain, and the still crackling charge between them. She had thought the realization of her gas-gun-interrupted fantasy might break the spell, but it hadn't, because the reality was better than she could ever have imagined. She wanted to get straight back into bed with him; he knew that, he wanted it too, and he disapproved. He would hurt her if he could; she knew that.

But just like the moth, she would retire somewhere to recover, then come winging back up towards the heat and the light and the danger. She knew that too.

"Don't forget to wish Jeff a happy anniversary from me," he said as she left.

*   *   *

Time had passed without his noticing again; the gas-gun had stopped long ago. Darkness had gathered, and the rain had begun in earnest. Jeff turned and walked back to the house. The garage was open; her car had gone.

The patio door had been left ajar, and he would be blamed, no doubt, for the rain that had stained the carpet. He closed it behind him, and stood in the darkness of the sitting room, looking out at the distant headlights of the cars on the bypass. He had been there some time when he heard her car, heard the garage door close. She came in the front door, unusually, going straight upstairs; that wasn't like her either. Jeff sighed, and waited until she had closed the bedroom door before he went out into the hall, and through to the kitchen.

His dinner had been disposed of; one empty plate lay on the breakfast bar, along with a half-full wine bottle and two glasses. He frowned, as he reached into the cupboard for another glass, and poured himself some claret. The table was set.

That was when he realized. The meal, the wine—almost twenty-five years, he had thought earlier. He was so used to saying that, thinking it. Almost twenty-five years, as though it never got to be more than that. But it did, and they had moved into their twenty-sixth year of marriage this very day.

*   *   *

She looked at herself in the bathroom mirror. My God. She had stubble-burn. She showered and washed her hair, going into the little dressing room to dry it. She had heard Jeff moving about in the bedroom after she had come out of the shower; she didn't know what to expect when she came out of the bathroom, and with all her being she just wanted to stay in there.

Sometimes after they had had a row, he would be loving and conciliatory; that was the last thing in the world that she wanted. She put on a nightie that covered her from head to toe—he called it her passion-killer, and that was just what she wanted it to be.

He might still be angry, of course. That wouldn't be so bad. Either way, she had to come out; she couldn't spend the night in there.

*   *   *

Jeff had listened to the shower, falling at a slightly different tempo from the rain, like some sort of counterpoint to it. He had listened to the hairdryer, to her teeth being brushed. She was in the bathroom for a long time; when she emerged, her face was pink, as though she had been scrubbing it. Probably one of those grainy facial scrub things that she had bought at the health farm, he thought.

"I'm sorry," he said. "I forgot."

"It doesn't matter," she said.

Thunder growled in the distance, coming their way, as Susan got onto the bed; it was too hot to get under the duvet, he supposed, since she was wearing a nightdress which came down to her ankles and buttoned up to the neck; too warm for the weather, but it signaled her non-availability. Hardly necessary, these days, but perhaps she thought he would be foolish enough to try tonight.

"I can't say any more than I'm sorry," he said.

"I've told you. It really doesn't matter."

She arranged her pillows for reading, and picked up a thriller. He put out his lamp, but Susan kept hers on, reading as though her life depended on it.

It mattered, all right. No wonder she had been cross when

he came in late. And then he had walked out on her anniversary dinner. He really didn't think that there was any way to make it up to her; everything he thought of would, quite rightly, be thrown back in his face.

Another flash, this time darkening the bedside lamp for an instant; another roll of thunder. Susan put the bookmark back in the book, rearranged her pillows, switched off the light and lay down.

But she didn't intend sleeping, and she didn't intend that he should sleep. He didn't blame her.

"I think I'll go mad if we have to stay here until winter," she said. "That thing banging away all day, and now this."

He smiled. "Not much anyone can do about a thunderstorm," he pointed out. As he spoke, the rain stopped, as though someone had switched it off. "Except me, of course," he added, in a feeble joke.

She sighed. "I'm going to ring Elsa," she said. "And get her to put this place on the market now. And I want you to speak to your friend John and ask him to shut that thing off while we're showing people around."

"Good idea," he said.

"And Jeff—I want you to put down turf," she said. "I don't care if it's the wrong time of year, I don't care if it all dies in a month. You want to move as much as I do, and this is the easiest way."

"Yes," he said. "You're right."

*   *   *

It was all very odd, not to say a little alarming. If it hadn't all started when Elsa was there, and before she had seen Rob, she would even have wondered if he knew. But he couldn't know.

Her game wasn't working out. Revenge was fun, but it wasn't everything. She had never intended spending the rest of her life torturing Jeff, but she had thought she might get more mileage out of it than she had. It was beginning to pall already, and it was less than satisfactory, since the irony of the situation seemed to be entirely lost on him. That might be more cruel in Rob's philosophy, but it was frustrating.

And it was frightening to think how easy it would be to reverse it all; however bewildered and miserable he had become, it would all be forgotten if she just eased up. Jeff would put her behavior of the last few months down to a hiccup caused by the head-turning win, and resume operations as before. They would move to wherever he wanted to set up a practice, she would keep house, and they would live happily ever after.

But that wasn't going to happen. Rob had asked her what happened now, and the truth was that she didn't know. She had never thought beyond this point. Jeff was supposed to have had a soul-shattering revelation by now; she had set him on the road to Damascus, and nothing was happening.

She had set out to alter her marriage, not destroy it; she had expected some sort of catharsis, something concrete on which they could build the rest of their lives together. For they would be together; she had never meant to lose him. But she was at a loss to know how to bring about his conversion.

She had imagined a row, she supposed. Not the sort of niggling arguments they had been having for weeks now, caused by Rob's sudden reappearance. Rob was irrelevant. She was operating on some primitively instinctive level with him; she would beat against the light until she got burned or it went out; it couldn't last long, in either event.

Jeff was the one that mattered. And he had been acting strangely; perhaps it was the first stirrings of his conversion. A little gentle probing might bring it out into the open, and phase two, whatever it was, could begin at last.

*   *   *

She was pretending to sleep to start with. He knew the difference, after all these years. But eventually her breathing altered, and she really was asleep. He lay awake, wondering why his old, comfortable life lay in shreds.

The rain came on again, as suddenly as it had stopped. Instant, pounding rain, and the rhythm sent him to sleep eventually; he awoke as dawn lit the corners of the room. He was perspiring; Susan looked coolly beautiful in the half-light, and his morbid fantasies of suicide were forgotten. Leaving her wasn't such a hot idea either, he thought. He was lucky. He *was*. He didn't ever have to worry about money again; he had a wife who looked like a film star, who was prepared to forgive his overlooking their silver wedding anniversary. He had the car. If they did move, got away from John and his bird-scarer, Susan would stop being so nervous all the time, and life would be tranquil again.

But he knew it wasn't as simple as that. Moving was essential, certainly, but he had to try to make her understand what had happened.

The thunder came back with the dawn, suddenly and deafeningly. Susan, startled, opened her eyes and looked as bewildered as she had the day she thought that John was shooting at her.

"It's only thunder," he reassured her.

"Did it wake you too?" she asked.

"No," he said. "I was awake."

Light filtered into the room; a soft, watery light which gave Susan an almost ethereal air. The thunder crashed again, directly overhead, as the rain battered against the house.

"Where did you go last night, anyway?" she asked. "I had to throw your dinner away. Where were you? What were you doing?"

"Thinking," he said.

"What about?"

He smiled. "Suicide," he replied, and got out of bed, pulling on his dressing gown. "Shall I make us a cup of tea?"

*   *   *

Suicide.

Susan didn't believe him. Suicide? She shivered, suddenly aware of the drop in the temperature that had come with the storm, and got under the quilt. Last night's rumbling had been a preview; this, whirling about the unprotected house, was the real thing.

Suicide? She was pushing the thought away.

He was back, bearing a tray with two cups of tea. He put it down at her side of the bed, and walked slowly around to his own.

"In the last four months," he said, sitting on the bed, not looking at her but at a tiny flaw in the duvet, "because of this money, I . . . I seem to have got lost somehow."

He'd noticed.

He looked at her then. "I don't want to spoil things for you," he said. "But I'm a casualty of this pools win. I've had to change my name, move my home, give up my job and become dependent on you—I want to try to make you understand how that feels."

She stared at him, trying to check the surge of anger that had risen at his words. There had been resentment, bitterness, a desire for some kind of revenge, but there hadn't been anger. She had always been in control.

But she wasn't anymore. "Yes!" she shouted. "You've had to change your name and move and become dependent on me! And believe me, Jeff, *believe* me—if I could have worked out how to make you pregnant into the bargain, I would have!"

It was Jeff's turn to stare, as thunder crashed.

"You want me to understand?" she yelled. "*You* want *me* to

155

understand? What it's like to be told where you're going to live? To have to ask for everything you need or want?"

He pulled away a little from the ferocity of her attack, shaking his head as she spoke.

"And why? Why? Because of a few minutes in the back of a borrowed car? Because I let you go all the way—that's what we called it, remember? All the way," she repeated bitterly, her voice quiet, then she launched into the attack again. "I wasn't going to tell you about the baby, and I wish to God I hadn't!"

Jeff swallowed, his head still shaking, his eyes still bewildered.

"Before I'd had time to *think*, I was married and living with your mother!" She leaned forward, a quarter of a century's pent-up rage suffusing her face. "I didn't know whether I was coming or going, but I was sure about one thing. I was not going to turn into an earth mother at seventeen!"

Lightning bathed the room, and Jeff's puzzled eyes widened with realization, and his mouth opened. He dropped his gaze to the vicinity of her womb, then looked back at her again, his eyes empty.

She knew what she had told him. She didn't take her eyes off his; she was breathing hard, the fear of him that had touched her in moments of stress hardening into real dread as he stared at her like a dead man.

Slowly, he got off the bed. She backed off, but he didn't pursue her; he left the room.

She heard him go downstairs, heard the front door open. Frowning, she got up and looked out at the driving rain. Lightning tore through the dark skies as she saw him walk around the house, across the short, wet grass, down towards the brook.

She struggled with the heavy sash window, pushing it open with a grunt. "Jeff!" she called into the rain-filled morning. "Jeff—what in the world are you *doing?* Come back! Jeff! Jeff!"

*   *   *

He heard her call him from the bedroom window. Her voice sounded thin and flat against the blustery wind, and he hadn't looked around. No point; he couldn't answer her. He didn't know what he was doing. He was going to the brook, that was all.

He smiled as he walked through the rain, his dressing gown growing heavy as it became drenched. He had wondered what the attraction was for John's hens. Now he knew. They went there to think. To sort things out. To hatch things out, come to that. Or so they thought. But they never got the chance, because along would come John the Baptist and take their eggs. He had thought he was going to hatch something out, once. Did they feel like he had, when they found their eggs gone?

An abortion. It was almost funny. He watched the water break over the banks of the little stream and form deep puddles in the earth, into which the rain poured more water. It looked like a miniature Missouri, wide and rolling. If only it was. He could just step into it and disappear.

An abortion. It had never crossed his mind to suggest such a thing, but if it had, he knew what her reaction would have been. Shock, horror, revulsion. It was against the law. It was against nature. And now that he, in common with everyone else, knew a great deal more than he had ever wanted to know about abortion, he knew that it had been late, and dangerous.

An abortion.

"I'm sorry," her voice said from behind him.

He turned to see her, a Burberry pulled around her for protection from the elements.

"Sorry you told me, I take it," he said.

"Yes." She raised her voice against the wind. "I'm not sorry about the abortion. I never have been."

Rain drove into his face as he looked at her. It whipped her honey-blonde hair forward from the back of her head, as she stood, her hand on the slippery wet bark of the oak tree, trying to keep her balance on the muddy ground.

"Where did you get the money?" Odd thing to want to know, he thought, as he asked the question. But they hadn't had a halfpenny—he had been on the subsistence allowance of an articled clerk, and she hadn't had a job.

"The money my mother left me," she said.

Her mother's Post Office savings. He nodded, then frowned again. "But... how did you know where to go?"

"I asked someone."

"Who?"

"It doesn't matter."

No. Slowly, like the first drops of rain had fallen into the stream, it all began to fall into place. The move, only brought about by the publication of their old address—why would any newspaper do that, unless they had been told they might? The change of name, unnecessary and unworkable. Overreaction, he had thought, and he had humored her. Marty Rogers' newfound investor, and the partnership agreement, lying on *top* of the other things, when he had had it tied in a bundle, at the bottom, for years and years. She had found it. She had read it. And she had engineered it all.

This was what she had intended doing with her money. What she was doing. She had *told* him. "I'm already doing it," she had said. Why? Why had she wanted to do a thing like that? They had been happy—they had had a good marriage. Why had she rubbed out his whole life? He felt tears in his eyes again as he looked at her. Twice before. Twice before in his married life he had cried. Once when they lost the baby. Once when he lost his job.

But neither of them had been lost; she had aborted them both.

June

She had finally got Jeff into the house, and into a hot bath. He had stayed up in the bedroom; he hadn't eaten. He hadn't spoken to her. She had gone up, eventually, ostensibly to get ready for the presentation, but more to see if she felt happy about leaving him there on his own.

And now she was here, at the church hall, waiting to present the minibus. There was a great deal of standing around at charitable functions, Susan had discovered. Standing around, and waiting. Waiting for all the right people to turn up, waiting for various speeches to be given, waiting for the sweet sherry that inevitably made its appearance, then standing around drinking it. All before you got to the reason everyone was there.

She had spoken to Jeff, as she had got ready. She had told him that she was sorry. She had told him that she couldn't put things back the way they had been, but that even if she could have done, she wouldn't have, because they had never been right. She wasn't going to lie to him; he had to know where they stood.

ELIZABETH CHAPLIN

"I just wanted you to understand," she had said.

He had nodded; he hadn't said much, but he wasn't alarming her anymore. He said he would be going out for a drive, and she believed him. She didn't think that suicide had ever really been on the agenda.

The minibus sat out on the courtyard, which steamed now as the sun beamed down from a sky cleared of the low, menacing cloud which had hung around for so long. Summer seemed to have arrived, but everyone knew that this might be all there was to it; it might be twenty-four hours long. They were out in summer dresses and sleeveless tops already.

Except for the people stuck in the church hall, that was. Someone had tried to make it look welcoming by putting flower arrangements here and there. All she (for it was the vicar's wife, Susan was sure) had achieved was to make people ask if there was a flower show on later.

It had happened; the catharsis, the blinding light on the road to Damascus. But now that it had, she had no idea what would result, or even what she had hoped would result. She didn't know what he intended doing; they had been together a long time, and perhaps there was something to be salvaged from the rubble. His dawn histrionics weren't going to weaken her resolve; if he wanted to leave her, that was fine. If he wanted to stay, that was equally all right with her. But she was never going back to the way it had been, and he had to know that.

The table at the end of the hall had held the pre-poured glasses of sherry, and still offered some plates of tired-looking sandwiches, dried-up sausages on sticks and some suspiciously undercooked chicken legs. Trifle sat in a large bowl. No one had yet availed themselves of the food.

She found herself assessing the cost, and tutting silently. She knew how much a head they had paid for this so-called buffet—not much, to be sure, but if she couldn't produce something more appetizing for that price, she would be ashamed of herself.

What about Rob? a voice in her head asked quietly. What about him? What had happened with Rob was simply a moment's madness; it wouldn't happen again. It mustn't. She wasn't a moth; she had a will of her own. Rob didn't enter into the equation. The issue was her marriage; Rob had no business there.

But he is there, said the voice.

Yes. And she had been right last night. They had to move. Not just out of that house—they had to move away. Whatever it was that she and Rob found when they were together, it couldn't have any sort of future. If she and Jeff moved, Rob would just get on with his life, and Jeff could start up on his own. But things would be different. She'd be at college—she was still determined to shape her own destiny. Then perhaps even university.

Her legs were aching, as she smiled and listened to whoever was talking to her as though she were actually interested in what he had to say. People were eating now, all talking about the thunderstorm, of course, and how they had been startled from sleep at dawn, but she doubted if any of them had had quite the night she had had.

One step at a time. She would get on to Elsa, tell her she wanted to get rid of the house. That much she knew she wanted to do, at least. For now, she was doing all she could do; she was getting on with her life.

"And the whole thing was, of course, a complete and utter shambles!"

She was supposed to be commiserating. Laughing? She didn't know, and searched her companion for clues. He didn't seem to find it very funny. "Oh, dear," she said.

"Served them right!" he said.

"Well . . . yes." She looked around desperately for the vicar. If he could just hurry things along a bit, she might get out of here before she actually dropped.

*   *   *

Jeff heard the doorbell, but he didn't move. He had followed Susan into the house when she had asked him, there not being much else he could do in his rain-soaked nightwear; he had had a bath and dressed, and he had stayed in the bedroom until she came up to change to go somewhere.

And now he was sitting in the kitchen, looking out at the garden. Even with the passageway gone, the sunlight only lit the kitchen until about ten o'clock; outside the sun shone down, and the kitchen was still gloomy, which suited his mood. He had opened the back door, and was looking out at the patch of garden which he was taming. The area marked out for lawn, the neat border which would be in bloom soon, the tree surrounded by fine gravel, ready for a summer-seat; perhaps a summerhouse. That would be nice. At least, nice in theory. He was never convinced that he knew what summerhouses were used for, other than to provide a locus for the body in murder mysteries.

The gas-gun boomed, and the doorbell rang again, twice. He got up slowly, hoping it was Rob.

Fiona. He blinked a little.

"Hello, Jeff."

"What are you doing here?" he asked.

She gave a short sigh. "The minibus, ostensibly," she said.

The—minibus—ostensibly. Jeff examined each word in turn, but they didn't make any sense. "Sorry?" he said.

"The minibus. Your local paper belongs to our group." She shrugged. "They thought we might be interested because it was Susan."

"I'm—" He cleared his throat. "I'm sorry. I don't know what you're talking about."

"Your wife is presenting a specially adapted minibus to some disabled group today. So I said I'd cover it."

He frowned. Just another thing that Susan hadn't bothered mentioning, presumably, like the driving lessons and the abortion. "She's not here," he said. "She left about an hour ago—shouldn't you be wherever the presentation is?"

Fiona raised her eyes to heaven. "I'm not covering the bloody presentation!" she shouted, startling him. "I'll get that from the local man—I wanted to see you when I knew she wouldn't be here."

Oh. He took refuge in silence, as he had with Susan, when she had been saying she was sorry, checking him out for suicidal tendencies before she went off to wherever it was she was going. Still, look on the bright side, he told himself. No one will blame you for walking out on the marriage now. Look what she's done to you.

"Can I come in?"

He shook himself back to some sort of normality. "Yes—yes, of course." He showed her into the sitting room. "Can I get you something? Tea, coffee—a drink, perhaps? There's a nice dry white in—"

"Why haven't you been to see me?"

"No money," he said, sitting down. She remained standing.

"No money?" she repeated, incredulously.

"You knew I'd lost my job."

She sat down opposite him. "Yes, but—well, I didn't suppose it would affect you all that badly financially, not with things as they are. Are you saying Susan's spent it all already?"

"No, of course not. But that's her money, not mine."

Fiona nodded. "But does that mean you can't even get down to London?"

He sighed. "I could get there," he said testily. "But I can hardly expect Susan to foot the bill for wining and dining and buying you presents, can I?"

She stared at him, her mouth slightly open, reminding him of when he had originally propositioned her. It made him feel a little uncomfortable, as it had then.

"Do you think that's what it was all about?" she asked.

He didn't answer. Of course it was, he thought. He bought

her goodies, and she showed her gratitude. That was all he had ever asked of her, and he had clearly done the right thing in giving her up, albeit from necessity.

"Do you think I wanted you because you brought me *presents?*" She sat back and looked at him, shaking her head. "You have to leave her, Jeff," she said.

So that was what it was all about. Saying she loved him, suggesting he find a job in London. She was tired of presents. She wanted more than that. At least he understood her, unlike Susan. "You're backing a loser," he said. "I don't have any money anymore."

She frowned, her eyes disbelieving.

Jeff sighed. "It's the truth," he said. "I'm not just giving you the elbow. I'm broke."

"My God," she said.

It had finally sunk in that he hadn't been worth her trip from London.

There was a long moment when she just looked at him, shaking her head very slightly. Finally, she spoke. "I don't *want* your money," she said, slowly, carefully, leaving spaces between the words. "I don't want presents. God alone knows why, but I want *you.* Do you understand?"

He had never thought of that. Women. There was no accounting for them. And they weren't worth it—if she thought he was going to jump through some sort of hoop for her, she could forget it. He really didn't care if he never saw another woman as long as he lived. She was a nice diversion, but he didn't need this kind of hassle on top of everything else.

"You had no right to come here," he said. "I don't want this boat rocked, do *you* understand?"

"Money? That's what it's all about?"

"It is now," he said.

She sat forward again, and her voice was low and urgent. "For two pins," she said, "I'd tell her about us."

He stiffened. "Blackmail? I've told you. I'm not worth anything. You tell her, and I kiss goodbye to the money."

She shook her head. "I'm not talking about money," she said. "I'm talking about survival, Jeff. Don't you understand what she's *doing* to you? How much of your life still *exists?*"

He stared at her. "How do you know about that?" he asked, alarmed in case she had already been speaking to Susan.

She closed her eyes briefly, then looked at him, her gaze steadily holding his. "Because I listened to you, week after week. Not because you took me out to dinner—not because you bought me presents—because I wanted to listen. And you *told* me, week after week, what she was doing to you!"

He frowned.

"You have to *leave* her, Jeff. Or there'll be nothing of you left!" She looked away from him, at the floor. "And I will tell her," she said quietly. "If it's the only way to rescue you."

This was all he needed, he thought, fighting the rising panic. Whatever happened, he had to stop her telling Susan. "I have to sort things out," he said. "I need time to think."

She looked up again. "Don't take too long, Jeff," she said. "And don't think you can come and jump into my bed now that you know it's for free. And don't think that I'm blackmailing you, because I'm not. I don't care where you go when you leave her—that's up to you. But I care about you, and I won't let her destroy you."

She got up, and went to the door.

"Leave her, Jeff," she warned. "Or I swear I'll tell her." Speech over, she was gone, with a slam of the front door.

He heard her car start up, and walked to the window, watching it wheel around to the main road. He went to the back window, in time to see it signal the turn for the town, and he sat down with a bump.

He had a great deal of thinking to do, and he automatically went out to the garage, got into the car, and drove off, feeling better almost as soon as the engine purred into life.

*   *   *

Phil was making his way down the hall towards Susan, ushering her out into the sunlit courtyard. He made a speech, thanking her, making a pitch for more contributions from the onlookers.

Then someone uncorked champagne, and Susan jumped; everyone laughed.

Phil took the bottle, bubbles streaming down the glass, and handed it to her. "Shake it up," he said. "Spray it over the bus. The photographer's ready."

"I can't," said Susan. "I don't know how."

Phil smiled. "I think once you've shaken it up it sort of does it whether you want it to or not," he said.

There were some acts of flamboyance that weren't even in Mrs. Kent's make-up. "I can't," she said. "I'll do it wrong."

"I can't do it," said the vicar. "It wouldn't be right if I did it. You're giving it to me."

"I'll do it," said a voice, and Susan looked up to see Rob, shirtsleeved and smiling. He took the bottle from her.

Somehow her voice said the right things. "This is a friend of my husband's," it said. "Rob Sheridan." She glared at Rob. "Philip Houseman," she said.

"Pleased to meet you," said Rob. "Right. Let's do this right." He shook it up like a veteran of a dozen grand prix wins, and moved his finger slightly. The sparkling liquid shot out into the air, and champagne showered the bus, Susan, and everyone else within ten feet. The photographer was delighted, and everyone clapped. It was over; eventually, the small crowd left.

"It's a lovely little bus," Rob said, and Susan watched, bemused, as he and the vicar walked around it, talking, discussing the various features. Rob got a demonstration of the hydraulic lift for the wheelchairs, the clamps, the seating that could be rearranged or removed altogether if desired.

He was offering to drive it, if ever the vicar was stuck for someone.

She felt as if she were in a dream. Rob didn't belong to this part of her life; he had no business being here. And how in God's name had he known where to find her? Even Jeff didn't know where she was. And her diary gave no clue.

They came back towards her, the vicar chatting to Rob. He beamed at her. "I really can't express my gratitude," he said.

Rob smiled, and there was an awkward little silence.

"Well. . . perhaps you would both like to come in for some afternoon tea? Nothing special, I'm afraid, but my wife would make you more than—"

"Er—it's . . . it's very kind of you," said Rob. "But Susan has offered me a lift to an appointment, and we really ought to be going."

He smiled. "Of course, of course—you are both very busy people. Thank you again, Susan," he said, shaking her warmly by the hand. "This will make such a difference."

They got into the car; already, she could feel apprehension building. "How did you know where I was?" she demanded.

He smiled. "Some woman came to the door," he said. "Said she was covering the presentation of the minibus, and she told me all about it." He smiled. "She wanted to know your new address."

"So you gave her it." She started the car.

"No, no—not just like that. I said I thought you wanted it kept quiet, but she knew all about it. Even knew you'd changed your name."

Susan frowned. "Was she from one of the free papers?"

"No," he said. "A Sunday paper. . . which one did she say, now?" he shrugged. "I was half asleep—she got me up." He laughed. "She even knew about the space-age kitchen, so I assumed I could tell her where the house was, and I did. What's wrong with that?" he asked.

"Did you get her name?"

"Yes, but it's gone too."

"Fiona Maxwell?" she asked.

"Yeah—that's right—you do know her, then?"

"I know her," said Susan.

So Fiona knew all about everything, did she? Jeff hadn't been to see her for a month; that was why she had broken cover, presumably.

"You know why she was here, don't you?" she asked, as she put the car in gear.

"To cover the presentation," he said, puzzled.

"Did you see her at the presentation?"

He frowned. "No," he said. "Now you come to mention it."

"Quite. I'll tell you why she was here, Rob. She was checking up on her investment."

"What? Who is she?" asked Rob.

"Jeff's mistress."

"Oh."

Forget Fiona. She drove off. "What's this appointment I'm supposed to be taking you to?"

"I think you know."

The diversion caused by Fiona had merely served to delay the moment; she drove without speaking to her old house. Her marriage was falling to pieces around her, and she was going to forget all that because she had to try to beat her way through burning glass to the white-hot glow inside. You couldn't sustain a relationship at this level. It had to calm down or explode in your face.

She had thought that there might be a lessening of the tension, but if anything it was worse, as she pulled into the little driveway. "Can you open the garage door?" she asked.

"Just leave it here," he said, undoing his seat belt, and getting out.

"I don't want people seeing the car," she said.

"Why not?"

"Because I don't know what this would do to Jeff if he found out."

He grinned his slow, lazy grin. "Concern?" he said.

"I hurt him this morning. I didn't mean to—" She stopped. "I don't think I meant to," she said.

"So you want to put the car in the garage?" His voice was amused, but his eyes were hard. He got out of the car and leaned back in. "Such a thoughtful little wife," he said. "Jeff's a lucky man."

She watched as he lifted the garage door, then leaned across, slammed the passenger door, and reversed out and away.

*   *   *

The Spirit of Ecstasy led the way through leafy lanes, dappled with sunlight as Jeff drove. The windscreen sparkled; the leather had a soft sheen; the wood faintly reflected his hand as he touched the cassette player. It should have been perfect.

But he was in trouble. If he thought he'd get nothing if he walked out on the marriage, what chance did he have if he was divorced for adultery? With the journalist who had covered the pools win? None. Anything Susan had done since would positively be applauded.

So he was walking nowhere, and Fiona was telling no one anything. It was as simple as that.

Oh, why the hell hadn't he stuck to his golden rule? Why had he ever gone back after the first time? Why had he gone back after she had told him she loved him? He had to hang on to her too. If he didn't, she might carry out her threat. Hell hath no fury, and all that.

There was one way out of it. A fantasy way; he didn't really take it seriously.

He had to keep Fiona sweet. Make her believe that he was going to leave Susan for her—damn it, this was the position he swore he would never find himself in. But he was in it, and that was the only way. Just keep the danger level to a minimum, that's all, he told himself.

His life was in disarray; a damage control operation was the only possible course. He headed the car homewards, feeling at least that he had a goal.

He and his wife had some serious reconciling to do.

* * *

The Rolls had gone. Susan pulled into the shade of the garage, and sat for a moment, gathering her thoughts. Reason had nothing to do with her sudden departure; she had not exercised her freedom of choice. She had got scared, and she wasn't even sure what she was scared of. Scared of having started something she couldn't stop, scared of emotions that she couldn't control. All she had known was that she was scared, and like the moth, she had flown away from the danger that had momentarily eclipsed the light.

Rob arrived by taxi minutes after she got into the house.

"Why did you do that?" he demanded.

"I was afraid," she said.

He sat down at the breakfast bar. "Afraid of what?"

She sat down too. "Rob, I can't keep going back to the house! The neighbors know me. It would get back to Jeff in no time!"

"Does that matter?"

"Yes! This—you—it has nothing to do with anything! I'm not going to let it break up my marriage!"

Rob ran a hand over his thinning hair. "For Christ's sake, Susan! What marriage?"

"I still have a marriage!" she shouted back, defensively.

He sighed. "Where is he?" he asked.

"I don't know. His car's gone. He's probably gone to her place."

He jabbed a forefinger down on the table with each item as he spoke. "He's got a woman chasing up here after him all the way from London," he said. "You told me yourself you hadn't had anything to do with him for weeks. He's been practically suicidal for days, and now he's gone. And you say you've still got a marriage." He stood up. "Right. I believe you. Tell Jeff thanks for the loan of his house and his wife. I might see him around." He opened the back door.

She felt as though her life was seeping away as he spoke. She had just found it, and it was running away from her; she wanted to cry. "Don't leave," she said.

He closed the door, and she breathed again. "Fiona Maxwell came chasing up here after the money," she said. "That's what she wants. Not him."

"So what if she does?"

"It's *my* money."

His eyes widened. "Money isn't important, Susan," he said.

It was her turn to look astonished. "Oh, yes it is," she said. "It's what makes me independent of Jeff—and you— and anyone else who thinks he can tell me what to do! It's important, of *course* it's important!"

Rob sank down again, elbow on the breakfast bar, his hand over his eyes, massaging his brow. "What do you want from me?" he asked, eventually.

"I don't know."

He sighed. "What did you mean, you hurt Jeff? More than you'd done already?"

She nodded.

"What did you do?"

She looked at him. "I told him about the abortion," she said.

"You *what?*" He looked horrified.

"I didn't tell him you'd helped me."

He relaxed a little, and lit a cigarette. He had smoked it all before either of them spoke again.

"I'll take you back," she said.

*   *   *

Jeff drove back to the farmhouse, back to Susan. He was rehearsing the conversation in his mind; she was saying everything he wanted her to say, and it was all going his way. But he was a lawyer; he knew it didn't work like that. People didn't come like that. Even the ones you had coached said the wrong things in the witness box. Impromptu conversations went their own way entirely, and he had some hard work ahead of him.

The Mercedes wasn't in the garage; she must still be at this presentation, whatever it was. He stopped the Spirit of Ecstasy one centimeter from the wall, and got out, stiff and aching from his dawn soaking. The gas-gun went off, and he walked towards the back door, too weary to walk around to the front, not caring anymore.

He stopped on his way through the kitchen, sniffing the air. Rob's cigarettes. Of course. Fiona knew Rob was living in their old house; she must have got their address from him, and Rob had probably come to see if he'd done the right thing. Susan must have run him back; Jeff wondered if he'd get an ear-bashing about Rob releasing sensitive information to the press. Probably. But perhaps not; she seemed to want to make amends.

In the sitting room, he turned on the television. Might as well, while he had the chance to watch it without being nagged. Golf. Bloody golf. He'd gone right off it since Neil Holder had started giving him instruction.

Sitting there, unable to put his plans for reconciliation into action, he had time to think, and he realized that his plans were very short-term. Keeping Fiona at bay and hanging on to Susan—that was just a holding operation. He couldn't do it for the rest of his life; it would be no life at all.

He picked up the remote control, changing the channel, and the garish colors of a sixties western filled the screen as the hero slowly drew his gun. The screen filled with a close-up as his finger squeezed the trigger; the barrel clicked around in slow motion, and the gas-gun went off. The timing made Jeff smile, and then it made him think.

This was a moment that he would be able to pinpoint afterwards. Oh, the seed had been there for some time, planted somewhere along the line by a fleeting thought, an idle fantasy. But if the actual moment of conception was lost among many possible moments, this was the moment when he knew, beyond all doubt, that he had conceived.

He knew the solution to his problems.

*   *   *

Susan dropped Rob off; when she got back, Jeff was in the sitting room.

"I've been thinking," he said as she came in.

She nodded, and walked to the open back window, looking out at the garden, dug and hoed and weeded, ready for the turf. The irregular lines of the lawn had been marked out with infinite care and patience. It would look haphazard, but it had been planned with his usual meticulous attention to detail.

"I understand," he said.

That was it? Was that what St. Paul had said, when he saw the light? I understand?

"Do you?" She doubted very much if he did. He understood that he had lost his identity, but he would have to become submerged in hers for twenty-five years before he understood how she felt.

She felt his arms come around her as he stood behind her, and she closed her eyes. Conciliation, then. All right. If that was what he wanted. She didn't care how it was going to end.

It had worked; all her hard work had paid off. Mrs. Kent had won through. She ought to feel triumphant, but she didn't. Perhaps she *was* just Mrs. Bentham. Perhaps Susan Kent had been a seventeen-year aberration, after all. She was born to cook and clean and tidy up for Mr. Bentham, and now that she had changed all that she didn't like it.

But she was *winning*; why didn't she feel as if she was? He had even said that he understood. And surely that was all she had wanted from him.

"I never meant to hurt you," he said.

No, she didn't suppose that he had. She couldn't even say with any degree of truth that he had hurt her. He had simply taken her over.

"But I did, obviously. And you hit back. I can understand that."

There he went again, understanding. That was what she had said, of course. That she had just wanted him to understand. But that hadn't been the right word. Understanding wasn't enough. He would have to have been her, and she couldn't achieve that with all the money in the world. All she had done was hurt him.

"You didn't do it deliberately," she said in her first acknowledgment of her cruelty.

"No," he said. "Thoughtlessly. Perhaps that's worse."

Hardly.

"It hurts. I'm not pretending it doesn't. But if you feel you can do it—please give me another chance."

Was this what she had wanted? Jeff begging for another chance? She didn't think so. She allowed herself to be turned around, and looked into his eyes. The emptiness was back, and it scared her.

"I'm not talking about behaving as though nothing's happened," he said. "I don't want to go back to how it was before. But we can start from here, can't we?"

She didn't answer.

"Will you try?"

Why not? She didn't know what she wanted; they might as well do what he wanted.

"We can't throw away twenty-five years just like that."

No. That was what she had tried to do. She had tried to throw away more than half of her life, and it couldn't be done. She shouldn't have done what she had; he shouldn't be having to plead with her.

She was nodding, looking into his expressionless eyes. "But—" she said, then didn't know if she could make demands. But they had to move house, to have any chance at all. She had to get away from Rob.

"What?" he asked gently.

"Not in this house." They had to leave, now.

"We'll leave as soon as we've sold it," he said, the slight puzzlement on his face failing to reach his eyes.

"Can't we leave before that?"

"As Elsa pointed out," he said. "We can't leave a string of empty houses behind us."

Yes, they could. To hell with how much it would all cost. To hell with everything. "Jeff, I want to leave!" she urged. "I want to go away—somewhere you can set up on your own."

"Yes," he said. "Of course we'll move." He kissed her then, slightly self-consciously, and they went upstairs.

She didn't want the next phase of the conciliation process, but she let it happen. Not from a sense of duty, as it had always been before; not as a substitute, as it had been on the morning of the gas-gun's entry into her life. This time, she was afraid not to. Afraid that he would guess that the light was there, burning brightly through an open window, and that she would flutter helplessly towards it if she was given half a chance. If the light was extinguished, the moth would forget about it; she didn't want to see that solution dawn in those lifeless eyes.

*   *   *

It was one thing to plan a murder; it was quite another executing that plan.

Jeff had always been a reader; whodunits had figured

175

largely in his formative years. Of course, the whole point of a whodunit was that the murderer—however clever—was unmasked, and justice was done, so all that the fictitious murderer could offer him was imperfect murder. But it hadn't got to be perfect, so he would draw on-at resource, together with his own knowledge of police and forensic procedures.

The perfect murder, he supposed, was one where no one knew that anything at all had happened, and life went on without the victim's demise ever being brought to light. He smiled. That wouldn't do. That wouldn't do at all.

But if all one required of a perfect murder was that its true perpetrator was never discovered, then perhaps it was fair to call this the perfect murder.

But he needed rather more than niceties of language if he was going to carry his plan full term. He had, in the first place, to decide what would appear to have happened.

An accident, misadventure? Sudden death is sudden death, and an inquest follows. Pathologists, forensic scientists, the coroner himself, would all have to be fooled. Doubts raised at the inquest could be enough to get the police interested. Sudden death is sudden death.

Jeff worked hard, preparing the ground for the turf which he had ordered. He stopped for a moment and leaned on the fork. He knew the gas-gun was important, but he wasn't sure why it was. It was as if the plan was there, in his head, but he had to find his way to it. The gas-gun had been the key; now all he had to do was uncover the rest.

He set to again. All right. He needed a shotgun. There should, he was certain, be nothing underhanded about that; he should quite openly buy a shotgun, get the necessary license, learn how to handle the thing.

Why? He had to have a reason. Rats, he thought, with a smile. He'd seen them now and then, skittering about through the undergrowth. Rats. He had never mentioned them to Susan, because he knew the idea would alarm her; she was jittery enough these days without worrying about rats. He stopped work again as he thought about that. It was a pity he hadn't mentioned them before now, he thought. But he could remedy that. Before long she would be buying a gun herself.

Shades of Victorian murderers rose up before him. Rats were an old, old excuse, they said. An excuse that had very rarely worked then, and certainly wouldn't work now. In their day, it was arsenic, but the principle remained the same, whatever the means.

If you buy something, they said, whether rat poison or a gun, with the intention of killing, then that intention is severely examined if a human death results from the purchase.

If he told Susan that he had seen rats, she would move house before he could blink, and that was the last thing he wanted.

But the more he thought about it, the more he knew that a shotgun was essential. It was *important*, though as yet he didn't quite know why, that no one should hear the fatal shot. He had to have a gun, and he had to have a reason for wanting one.

A hobby—what could be more natural? He would buy a sporting gun.

No. He smiled. He couldn't buy anything. He had no money. Susan would have to pay for it. In fact Susan would suggest the hobby, too.

Nonetheless, said the Victorian murderers, Susan would not be buying the gun for her own use. You would be the user of the gun. And sporting gun or not—isn't that buying something with the intention of killing with it?

Yes. And he didn't want to shoot birds—he liked birds. Even John the Baptist didn't shoot birds—he would never speak to him again if he took up shooting. But, he said to the Victorian murderers, as he turned the soil, you can shoot without killing.

Clay pigeon shooting. There must be somewhere that you

could join, somewhere you could learn. Not that he gave a damn whether he could ever shoot clay pigeons. He wouldn't need to be a sure shot to do what he had in mind. But they would teach him one end of a shotgun from the other, and that was all he needed to know.

He would take his plan one step at a time. He whistled cheerfully as he got on with the gardening.

*   *   *

Susan once again found herself wondering at her own foolishness. Jeff worked hard to get the garden right for the prospective purchasers, and behaved as he always had, except that he possibly included her a little more in his life. He was restless, but that was only to be expected. He wanted to move as much as she did, but Elsa was having no luck.

There were times, now and then, when the life seemed to go out of his eyes, but she was beginning to think that that was her imagination. It was usually in bed, where she found it impossible to push Rob to the back of her mind. She couldn't rid herself of the feeling that Jeff knew. But he was probably no different from how he had always been. It was her problem, not his.

He still wasn't disappearing to mythical garden centers on Saturdays, despite Fiona's visit, so he was trying to change things. She tried too; she made him his favorite meals, she watched what he wanted to watch on television. They didn't go out much.

"You know," he said one night, "I think I should take up some sort of a hobby."

"A hobby?"

"Yes," said Jeff. "I just think I should do something—I don't honestly like golf. And besides, I really don't think I can spend any more time with Neil than I already do."

She smiled. "I thought you were going to help him get this youth club off the ground," she said.

He shook his head. "He wants me to," he said. "But it isn't my sort of thing. He's found some premises. He seems quite keen."

"What sort of a hobby?"

Jeff shrugged. "What do the idle rich do?" he asked.

She felt guilty. He wouldn't go back to Marty even if she could arrange it; anyway, she had interfered enough with his life. He was adjusting, as he always did, and she should help him to adjust.

"You used to say you were going to write a book one day," she said.

He smiled. "Trouble is," he said, "I never knew what about."

"The garden should keep you busy for a while," she suggested.

"Mm. I don't really count that," he said. "Not if we're selling."

They were selling. She had begged Elsa to give the house the hard sell to anyone who looked remotely possible.

"If I'm joining the green welly brigade, I'm going to do it properly," said Jeff.

"A farm?" she asked, startled. She couldn't really see him getting up at dawn to milk cows.

He laughed. "No," he said. "Not what they do for a living—what they do for fun. What do they do?"

"I'm not sure," she said. "Ride, I suppose. Do you fancy learning to ride?"

He shook his head. "I'm a bit scared of anything bigger than me," he said, and smiled. "Besides, they'd expect me to hunt. And I rather like foxes."

"Fishing," she said.

"Too cold and damp."

"Well, unless you want to shoot defenseless birds, that's their three main pastimes ruled out."

"No thanks," he said. "I don't want to ride anything bigger than I am or kill anything smaller than I am."

She laughed. "You are a hopeless member of the green welly brigade," she said. "You don't even want a Range Rover."

But he was right, of course. He should do something. She had had years of experience when it came to filling in her time. But they were female pursuits. Afternoon television was soap operas and recipes. Voluntary work was female-dominated. Even the charity committees on which she found herself these days were almost exclusively made up of women.

"The Citizens Advice Bureau!" she said, triumphantly. "They'd love to have a solicitor for free."

And Marty couldn't do anything about it, she thought. Jeff could sit there dispensing free advice to people who would have paid through the nose for it. Why hadn't she thought of that before? Bramcote Citizens Advice Bureau would be perfect, but she didn't suggest that.

"That's a good idea," Jeff said. "I might just give them a ring in the morning." He smiled a little ruefully. "Though they won't want me all day every day," he said. "If they want me at all. They might just want to avail themselves of my advice from time to time."

Susan sighed. He was giving her a hard time, and she didn't blame him, not really. It wasn't going to be easy to get back on an even keel, of course. Not even if Rob disappeared and Jeff got a wonderful job tomorrow.

"What sort of thing takes your fancy?" she asked.

He thought for a moment. "Well—since you mentioned it—I do quite like the idea of learning to shoot. Not birds, though—clay pigeon shooting. I've always thought that could be fun."

She smiled. "Then do it," she said. "If you don't like it, you'll think of something else." She reached over and squeezed his hand. "Once we've moved away from here, you can get a proper job, or start your own practice," she said. "It's not for long."

Oh, if only she didn't know that the light was there, shining enticingly through the curtains that she was desperately trying to hold shut.

* * *

You couldn't shoot and play golf, he discovered. At least, he couldn't. The bruise on his right shoulder was permanent; his golf swing—never the best feature of his game—was reduced to a kind of baseball bat level.

"Giving up golf?" Neil looked astounded.

"Well, I'm bloody awful at it anyway," said Jeff.

"And you're a crack shot, are you?" he asked with some sarcasm.

"I'm not bad. We had clay pigeon pie the other night."

Neil laughed.

"I've got some equipment set up at home," Jeff went on. "You can come and have a go, if you like."

"No thanks—I don't want a dicky shoulder."

Jeff picked up his pint, and winced as his shoulder complained. "They say you get used to it," he said.

"What—not having the use of your right arm?"

"I wouldn't mind having a go now and then," said Rob. "My shoulder got used to a worse kick than that well over twenty years ago. I'd like to keep my eye in."

"You?" Jeff didn't know how Susan would feel about that, and he didn't want to do anything at all to upset her.

Rob shrugged. "Why not me?" he asked.

Yes. Why not Rob? She was supposed to be making amends, and he was supposed to be behaving naturally. So despite the fact that the last thing he wanted was Rob coming around the house any time he felt like it, he smiled. "Yes," he said. "Yes—of course you can. Any time you like."

He had things to do. However it was to be done, he had to

get the timing right, for one thing. But Rob wouldn't be there all the time, and banning him even from the grounds would look a bit odd.

And he could make a start even if he wasn't alone; he was in the garden most of the time anyway.

*   *   *

Susan had listened as Jeff had told her that he had tried to get three tickets for Wimbledon, but he had only been able to find two; he had promised Neil, he had explained, so he would have to take him.

Susan had been pleased to hear it; she had tried to look disappointed, but a Saturday off seemed like heaven. It was sheer hard work, this attempted reconciliation. And she did feel rather under an obligation to do what he wanted; if he had been able to get three tickets, she would have found herself on a rain-soaked seat at a tennis match she had no desire to see.

She dropped him at the station, and drove off, back to the farmhouse and the gas-gun. Once, that would have been far from her idea of heaven, but today she would have it to herself.

She thought it might be Elsa, when there was a knock at the back door. She opened it.

Oh, my God. Susan felt as though the breath had been knocked from her body.

"Jeff said I could come and play with his new toy," said Rob, smiling lazily at her.

It wasn't fair. Light bulbs didn't seek out moths to destroy. "Then play with it," she said.

"I can't."

He walked in past her; she stood at the open door, her heart pounding.

"I need someone to send the things up," he said.

She swallowed. "I don't know how to do it," she said. "I expect he meant you to come when he was here."

He smiled. "Isn't he here?" he asked. "I thought he was. His car's here."

She closed the door, and turned slowly towards him. "I imagine that you know as well as I do that he has just got on a train," she said.

He sat down and took out his cigarettes, lighting one. "Watched you drop him at the station," he said. "Watched him safely onto the train. I even watched the train pull out. Wimbledon, isn't it? Champagne flowing like water, so conscientious Jeff leaves his car at home."

"Why are you here?"

"Why do you think?" He released a stream of smoke. "You won't come to me."

"Of course I won't!"

"Right. So I've come here. With a perfectly good excuse, if your next-door neighbor should mention my visit. But that's as far as I'm prepared to go with this charade."

She hadn't moved from the door; she wished she hadn't closed it. The room seemed smaller with Rob in it. Smaller, with just one focal point. Rob, perched on a stool at the breakfast bar, cigarette drooping from his mouth.

"What charade?" she asked.

"Keeping your so called marriage together," he said. "I don't know why you want to do that, but I'm prepared to believe you."

"I love him," she said stubbornly.

He nodded slowly. "Maybe," he said. "But you want me."

"I don't even like you."

"No." He crushed his cigarette out in the ashtray. "It doesn't seem to make much difference." He smiled slowly. "But I'll tell you this," he said. "If that's your idea of love, I'm glad you don't love me."

"I think you should go."

"I know you do. But this isn't a one-way street, sweetheart."

He held out his hands, and she found herself taking them, being pulled gently down onto his knee.

"You see," he said. "The problem is that I love you."

"No," she said, trying to twist away from him, but he pulled her back, and minutes later they were on their way upstairs, Rob leading the way.

He headed towards the main bedroom, but she pulled him away. "In here," she said, stopping at the spare room.

"Why draw the line at using his bed?" he asked.

Her hand was on the door handle; she paused. "You came here, remember," she said, opening the door.

*　　*　　*

Jeff had been going to ask Susan to come to Wimbledon with him when he had arranged for the tickets, but he had decided against that, because he needed some time off from her and her nerves, which were getting as bad as they'd been in the Brompton Road highrise. He had two tickets for the first Saturday; he had asked Rob, but he couldn't make it.

So Jeff made a surprise visit to Fiona, which is what he should have done in the first place. Keeping her sweet. She didn't make it all that easy for him when he got there, but he did have the tickets, and she had intended watching Wimbledon on television, so he persuaded her to join him.

He made no attempt to get her into bed, making it clear that he respected her decision with regard to that. That impressed her, too. There was no talk of telling Susan anything. He had spent a pleasant afternoon with her, and was on the train home, sitting back with a feeling of considerable satisfaction. He had appeased Fiona, and he had even had a bet on the entire day being a washout, and had won.

As he thought of that, another piece of the plan revealed itself. Who had devised it? Not him. He was taking no active part at all. Just following what it said, often quite mystified as to its purpose.

Betting, it was saying to him. Betting. A wager. A contest. A clay pigeon shooting contest. With whom? Neil? But Neil didn't want to know about that. Rob did, though. A contest between him and Rob? *Shooting?* Someone who had just learned how to load a shotgun and someone who knew how to handle an army rifle? But who said it had to be a fair contest? Rob would win. Macho man Rob would like that. Showing off for Susan.

A contest meant witnesses, and it was, he conceded, difficult to see how there could be witnesses without hampering his plan.

But he watched the scenery passing by, and he knew he was right.

*   *   *

Outside, rain fell once more as Susan and Rob lay in each other's arms.

"If you want the truth," he said, turning away from her, "I like Jeff a lot more than I like you."

The condemnation was as much a part of all this as the sex. The excitement, the tenderness, the joy—all wiped out by the put-down. Was that how it had to be? Was there something perverse inside her that *liked* lying in the arms of someone who despised her? The same sentiments were probably true of her; she didn't feel obliged to voice them as soon as her pulse rate had returned to normal.

"Why are you here, then?" she asked.

He sat up, and looked down at her. "I've told you why."

"Love?" She shook her head.

He looked away in a gesture of exasperation, then turned his head back. "Why do you think I helped you when you wanted to get rid of the baby?"

She frowned. "You knew where I could go," she said.

"I knew—I didn't have to tell you. I didn't have to arrange it," he said. "And I knew how Jeff felt. I knew what it would do to him. But I helped you get rid of it."

"Why did you then?" she asked hotly.

"Because what you wanted was more important to me."

She sat up angrily. "And I'm the only one who wants this? Is that what you're saying?"

"You're the only one who wants it this way. I'd rather be straight with Jeff—and lose him—than do this to him. But you want to have your cake and eat it. Like you've always wanted. And I'm doing what you want, like I've always done."

She gasped. "Like you've *always* done?"

"For years. Every time we saw each other. I never touched you before because you didn't want me to. But this time you did. And I obliged instead of telling you to go to hell."

Her mouth was open. "Are you saying you're doing me some sort of favor?" she asked.

"I'm saying I love you," he said obstinately.

"Rubbish! It's some sort of physical attraction, that's all. Chemistry, whatever."

"I'm damned if you believe that," he said. "This is something our bodies get up to on their own? Forget it, sweetheart. This is what *we* get up to, and we have to take responsibility for it."

"We don't have to call it love!" she shouted, then took a moment to calm down. "You asked what I wanted from you," she said quietly. "This is what I want. I don't want to know what's going on in your head—I don't want to know what you think of me. Our hormones might respond to one another, but it has nothing to do with love!"

He was shaking his head. "But it has. Because I fell for you, and I wanted you," he said, his hands on her shoulders. "From the day I met you. That's what your hormones react to—someone who really wants you. It turns you on."

She pushed him away. "Jeff wants me—I never feel like this with him. I never have."

He made an impatient noise. "Jeff never wanted you!" he shouted. "All he wanted in the first place was a bit of fun, but you got pregnant. And then he wanted the baby. Not you."

She didn't speak.

"And you wanted him and not the baby," he said. "Simple as that."

"I was seventeen," she said. "I didn't know what to do."

"Oh, yes you did," he said, his voice low. "You could have come to me first—but you didn't. You made him marry you. He married you because of the baby, and now he's staying with you because of the money. He still doesn't want you, but you're going to hang onto him all the same."

They were sitting up in bed, eyes locked, faces set. His was angry, hers hurt. And still the electricity hummed between them. It had to fizzle out. People couldn't live at this pitch.

"But I need you," he said. "I've got you now. And I'm not letting you go." He pushed her back down, his mouth on hers.

She closed her eyes, and listened to the steady rain outside the window as she gave herself up to him again, flying furiously towards the light, knowing that the heat would defeat her. It had burned her before, and it would burn her again. There was no reason, not even emotion. Just sheer blind instinct, and she couldn't be held responsible for that.

It was so good, after the home-truths, if that's what they were. She hadn't known then, and she didn't know now. All she knew was that she was being lifted up again onto a different plane by someone who could make her fly, soaring and sweeping through the air until she circled to the ground, exhausted.

They fell asleep; she awoke to dull evening light, and

panic. She shook Rob awake, hurrying him up as she pulled on her clothes and smoothed down the duvet, then looked up to find him *watching* her instead of getting dressed.

"Hurry up!" she said. "Jeff could be back any minute!"

"So?" he said. "Wouldn't that be a nice finishing touch? Jeff finding us together? Why the concern now?"

"Why the instant condemnation?"

She left the room, running downstairs to the sitting room, going to the window, watching for Jeff.

"Because I feel guilty," he said, suddenly behind her.

She turned. He was carrying his shoes; his belt was unbuckled.

"I don't," she said. "But then he's never been unfaithful to you." She didn't feel guilty. She felt scared. She looked over her shoulder, checking for a taxi.

The television suddenly flashed into life, and she frowned, looking at it.

"You never know," said Rob, his voice hard. "We might see him in the stand, and have time for a real row."

The sun shone down brilliantly on the center court as two familiar but non-current players battled it out. Across the top of the screen was a message confirming that play had been abandoned without a ball played, and that this was a recording.

He snapped it off again. "Pity," he said, a muscle working in his cheek as he controlled the anger he still felt. "I need a row." He sat down, lighting a cigarette before he carefully unlaced his shoes, put them on and laced them up again.

Slowly. He did everything slowly, and Jeff could be here any time if there hadn't been any tennis.

She didn't plead with him to hurry; there was no point. He exhaled smoke, and stood up, addressing his belt.

"Don't come here again," she said.

"Where then?"

"Nowhere! I don't want Jeff hurt anymore!"

He paused in the act of buckling his belt. "God, you're a

selfish bitch," he said. Then he did up his belt, picked up his jacket, and left without another word.

She wasn't. She *wasn't*.

She sat on the sofa, her legs curled under her, her arms folded, trying to hold on to what she had when she was with Rob, when he wasn't despising her. But it wasn't real. She and Jeff were real. She had hurt him too much already, and the only answer was to move away. But Rob mustn't know where they'd gone; he would follow. And Jeff would never understand; he would never agree to move without letting Rob know where he was going. Not again.

She didn't know how to get out of this.

* * *

Jeff opened the sitting-room door. Susan was alone on the sofa, her legs curled up beneath her. She looked up quickly as he came in. Jumpy, as usual.

"How did you get on?" she asked.

"I won money on the tennis." He smiled, drawing a wad of notes from his pocket. His money. His own money. He knew why women went to bingo now.

She frowned. "But it was a washout," she said.

He nodded, smiling. "That's how come I won," he said. He sniffed the air. "Either you've taken to cheroots, or you've had a visitor," he said.

"What? Oh—yes. Rob came—he wanted to shoot, but I can't work that thing."

Oh, God, wouldn't you just know? "He knew I was going to Wimbledon," Jeff said, pouring himself a drink. "Would you like something?"

"Yes," she said. "Brandy."

He raised his eyebrows at the unusual request, but he didn't comment. He just poured her a generous measure. "Did he stay long?" he asked.

"He had a cup of coffee," she said.

"Sorry," he said, easing himself into the armchair. "I'll tell him to come when I'm here next time he wants to shoot."

"It's all right," she said.

Tears didn't seem far away. He sipped his drink, unsure of how to proceed with the conversation. Normal. Behave normally. If she's upset, ask her what's the matter. "Is there something wrong?" he asked.

She drank some brandy. "I think you should start looking for where you'd like to set up," she said.

"I will," he said. "As soon as we've got someone interested in this place."

"No!" she said, with sudden ferocity. "Now. I think you should find somewhere. Somewhere you'd like to live."

Somewhere *he* would like to live? On his own? Without his loving wife and the next-door neighbor's gas-gun? The holding operation. It had worked with Fiona, it could work with Susan. No drama. Just keep them both at bay until the birth. Or death.

He smiled. "I think you've got some say in where we live," he said.

"I don't *care* where we live!"

He really believed she meant it. She wanted out of this house desperately. Not yet, Susan. Not yet.

"Don't be silly," he said, his voice gentle. "I know you hate this place, but it won't be forever."

He got up and went to her, sitting on the arm of the sofa. She looked up at him, her eyes glistening.

"I know you don't like John being next door," he said. "And you don't like the gas-gun, and you don't like being so far away from everyone. But we'll be out of here soon."

The tears were falling now. "I want to leave now," she said.

"We will leave. Don't worry. Don't get so worked up over nothing. It's just because you've been here on your own all day—I know how it made me feel when you were away."

He kissed her, but she turned her head so that his lips met her salty cheek.

"It won't be long," he said. "We'll be out of here by the end of next month. You'll see." He patted her. "Just don't let things get you down," he said.

At least she stopped demanding that they leave right now. But for how long? How long could he contain the situation?

*   *   *

The gas-gun woke her at dawn, with a start of fear. Jeff slept on beside her, lying on his back, snoring every now and then, quietly, like a dog.

He knew. He was playing with her last night. All that elaborate sniffing of the air, and the deduction that Rob had been visiting, when he'd told him that he was going to Wimbledon. And then she had to say he'd had coffee—there were no cups; he must have noticed that. She couldn't do this; she wasn't cut out for it. And she didn't *feel* guilty, but perhaps it was a guilty conscience that was making her so afraid.

Whatever it was, she couldn't live like this—they had to move. Now. They couldn't wait for Elsa to produce purchasers— they had to go.

She got up as Jeff shifted in his sleep, in case he woke and wanted to make love, as he sometimes did, on Sunday mornings. She didn't think she could bear that.

*   *   *

Jeff opened his eyes, pleased to find himself alone. It had come to him last night; slowly, the dust had shifted from the plan, and it had all been there. Whoever had drawn it up had been guiding his actions for weeks. The calculator, the hi-fi—everything. Everything was part of the plan. It wasn't his plan. He had conceived it; he was not its begetter. He

191

had been chosen. He had been chosen to execute it, in front of witnesses. Witnesses who would prove that he couldn't possibly have done it.

And the holding operation was more important than ever now that his plan had taken shape. Fiona must be kept sweet, the reconciliation must work, and they must remain living in this house.

This was one baby that Susan wasn't going to abort.

July

His calculator had a stopwatch as one of its many and mostly impenetrable functions. He had never used it, never thought he'd have a use for it. But he was using it now.

Nineteen minutes and seventeen seconds, it told him. The gas-gun went off every nineteen minutes and seventeen seconds. He timed it for an hour in the morning and an hour in the afternoon every day for three days, as he weeded and hoed and watered, making the cosmetic improvements advised by Elsa. It never varied, bless it. Nineteen minutes and seventeen seconds, every time.

He took time off from gardening and the calculations to smile at the birds. At first they had risen in a cloud of panic every time the thing thundered, scattering far and wide, and going, presumably, to plunder someone else's "crop," which was what John the Baptist called his oversized vegetable garden. But now, weeks of explosions had taught them that the noise didn't hurt, and they would flutter up a few feet to rest on the oak tree and on the guttering, then go straight back down again.

The dry weather was making matters worse, as far as John was concerned. A lack of worms, he told Jeff seriously. The birds were coming in greater numbers, and causing more damage as they pecked at the dry earth, disturbing delicate roots even when they weren't actively eating the shoots of his second crop. Jeff lent him his sprinkler.

"Said on the radio they were going to ban them," John said.

"Well, they haven't yet." Jeff grinned. "Anyway, I won't tell on you if you don't tell on me."

"That's not right, Ben Kent."

Jeff shook his head. "It's not right that your crop will die from lack of water," he said. "Or my lawn."

John looked disparagingly at the turf, knitting together now with the help of its nightly watering. "Grass," he said, in the tone of voice that most people reserved for obscenities. "Can't eat grass, unless you're a bloody rabbit."

"She wanted it," said Jeff, with a jerk of his head at the house.

John nodded sympathetically. "I had one of them once," he said, taking the sprinkler, and striding off around the end of the fence with it.

"A sprinkler?"

He looked at him scornfully over the fence. "A woman," he said.

Jeff watched him go, smiling after him as he walked along the grass paths through the neat rows of organic vegetables, which, despite his complaints about lack of rain and predatory birds, grew large and plump and delicious.

What exactly had John *done* with his woman?

*   *   *

Susan glanced out as she went to the phone; Jeff was digging up yet more of the unyielding soil as he continued to plan the garden. All the man was doing was trying to come to terms with life, a life that she had fashioned for him; if his occasional faraway look bothered her, it was her own fault.

Except that it wasn't far away; it was as though she wasn't there at all. And it was, in a way, the mere fact that it did only happen occasionally that bothered her. Sometimes it was in intimate moments, though these had grown infrequent again; other times, there seemed to be no reason at all for his strange withdrawal. But she didn't really believe that she was imagining things.

And now he'd joined a gun club, of all things. If he wasn't in the garden, he was there. Still, she hadn't seen him so cheerful for a long time; she could hear him whistle to himself in the garden.

The phone had called her away from the window.

"Hello?"

"Ah—Susan? Neil Holder here."

"Oh, hello, Neil—Jeff's in the garden. I'll give him a shout."

"Ah well—it's you I want to speak to really."

"Oh—fine. What can I do for you?"

There was a little silence. "Well . . . it's a bit—I was going to talk to Jeff, but I thought that I really should ask you directly."

Susan frowned. "Ask me what?" she asked, mystified.

"Well—it's just that—well, someone told me how you . . . well, I just wondered "

"Neil," she said, "do you think you could just try asking me whatever it is?" She knew the awkward preamble; she had heard it dozens of times since January.

"Well, I don't know if Jeff's mentioned to you that I do a voluntary job with the Council . . . well, it's not a job really, not yet. But I'm trying to see if there's some way we can do something about the level of vandalism—you know—and I'm trying to set up some sort of . . . well, you know, club, or whatever."

195

Susan waited until he had finished. "You need a donation," she said.

"Well . . . it's—I just . . ." Another silence. "I'd like to show
you what I want to do," he said, suddenly grasping the
nettle. "If you could meet me at the old boys' club."

She frowned. "Where's that?" she asked.

"Brompton Road," he said.

Her heart sank. She hadn't been back there, not once,
since they had finally escaped. The number of times it
figured in reports of the magistrates' court in the evening
paper suggested that it had got no better. Jeff had always
said that half his income came from Brompton Road.

"When?" she asked.

"This evening, if possible."

Mrs. Kent wouldn't hesitate, she told herself. Mrs. Kent
wouldn't be afraid of groups of youths on street corners. It
was light until nine o'clock, anyway, if it stayed fine, and it
had been fine all week.

"About seven?" she suggested.

"Oh, yes. That would be great."

"I don't remember a boys' club," she said. "Where is it?"

He told her. "It was built after you left," he said.

She hung up. They had only left twelve years ago, and it
was already known as the "old" boys' club. It had presumably failed before, and would again. Who the hell had got her
into this? Not Jeff—he didn't like it when she gave money
away. The vicar, presumably.

*   *   *

"Brompton Road? Do you want me to come?"

"Neil will be there," she said.

"I hear it's got worse," he said.

"It's all right—you're busy."

That never used to bother her. He wasn't sure he could
take much more of Susan being nice to him. "Neil's gone

soft, if you ask me," he said. "Finding something for them to do isn't going to help. Locking them up would be more effective."

Susan smiled. "You both seem to have changed your tune," she said.

"I'm not paid to defend them anymore," said Jeff.

"And he's not paid to accuse them," said Susan.

Jeff shook his head. "You'll be throwing your money away," he said. "A youth club? Can you see these kids joining a youth club?"

She shrugged. "I can at least see what he's got in mind," she said.

"It's your money," Jeff said, opening the patio doors and turning the speakers towards the garden. He surveyed the tapes, and selected one.

"I won't do it if you don't want me to," she said.

He wasn't looking at her; he hesitated for just an instant as he inserted the tape. "Why not?" he asked, his voice a shade bitter. Too bitter; he had to watch that. They were supposed to be being reconciled. He was supposed to be contrite, not bitter. He turned to look at her, but she had gone.

She was in the hallway, pulling on a jacket.

"How long will you be?" he asked, as the music started.

"Not long."

They both walked into the garden, bathed in evening sunshine.

"Not more than an hour," she said. She pecked him on the cheek, and walked to her car.

He went back to his horticultural activities, she hooted, the gas-gun cracked and Handel wafted through the evening air.

She wouldn't do it if he didn't want her to. He picked up the fork and stabbed it into the ground.

*　　*　　*

They were both being too solicitous of one another's feelings, Susan thought, as she drove away from the house. It
was as though they were newly married. In fact, it wasn't at
all unlike when they were newly married. That had been
awkward and unnatural too.

But they had settled into something that had worked well
enough for twenty-five years; surely it hadn't all just evapo-
rated? She smiled tiredly to herself. Perhaps this was her
punishment. Back to the beginning, and start all over
again. Doing what Jeff told her, not doing anything he didn't
want her to do. And being a little afraid, always, of what he
might do.

Which was still, she told herself sternly, all in her mind,
and nothing to do with Jeff at all.

Finding herself back in the long, wide, neglected thor-
oughfare to which they had moved from Jeff's mother's just
made the whole punishment idea seem more likely. It had
got worse; old houses were being demolished, but the
leveled land was up for sale with no takers. New houses
were growing old before their time.

The tower block—the only one in the town, because it had
been such a disaster—still somehow stood; it looked even
less inviting than it once had. She drove slowly, looking for
the landmarks Neil had given her to locate the old boys'
club. Eventually, she saw what resembled nothing more than
a very large, condemned public lavatory. That must be it.

The building, square and ugly, was surrounded by weeds
of such strength and height as to be almost frightening in the
urban street. The wire fence enclosing them had been
trampled to the ground, the mesh torn from the concrete
uprights.

She brought the car to a halt, looking for some sign that
Neil was there, but there was no other car. A group of
watchful youths—she could see Jeff's point about the likeli-
hood of their joining a youth club—stood around a fish and

chip shop doorway, passing around a bag of chips, eyeing her as she got out.

She closed the car door, and licked nervous lips as they called out, a couple of them sauntering towards her.

"Nice motor," said one, walking up to it, touching the aerial that she had forgotten to retract.

"There's a couple of quid in it for you if it stays that way," she said, startling herself. It was Jeff who had told her that that was how to keep your car intact; years ago now.

"Yeah?"

She nodded.

"All right," he said.

She felt proud of herself, and turned away from him, towards the depressing building. Who in his right mind would want to spend his evenings here? she wondered. Though, she reasoned, if they hung around outside, they might as well hang around inside.

Its windows, set high in the walls so that it was impossible to see in, and presumably out, were broken; some were boarded, some stuffed with paper, but most of them were left gaping, with jagged remnants of grimy glass still clinging to the frames. Towards the rear was one intact, open window. It looked out of place. The prefabricated walls were adorned with spray-painted graffiti, some of it by a rather talented hand.

"You going in there?" asked her minder.

"I think so," she said.

"Some bloke's in there," he said.

She didn't let him hear the sigh of relief. "Good," she said, setting off purposefully through the gap in the concrete posts where once there had been a gate.

She pushed open the door, which had been left slightly ajar, and went into the dim interior, trying to accustom her eyes to the gloom. "Neil?" she said.

"No." Rob emerged from the shadows.

She tried to gather her thoughts. "What is this?" she asked. "Is Neil here?"

"No. I told him I'd meet you."

She stared at him. "You involved Neil?" she said, her heart thumping so painfully she could barely speak.

He smiled. "He's a man of the world," he said.

"But—but *why?*"

"I'm doing a spot of DIY," he said. "I've got a key." He held it between finger and thumb, and walked past her to the door, closing it, locking it.

She didn't turn around. He stood behind her at the door, and all she could hear was the blood pumping in her ears. His hand touched the nape of her neck, and her head went back a little. His lips touched hers.

"Here," she said. It was supposed to have been a question, but it came out as a statement.

"Why not here? It's not all like this. I've been busy— come and look."

She allowed herself to be led through the broken glass which still lay on the floor towards a door at the back. Rob opened it, and immediately the damp, neglected smell was replaced by the smell of fresh paint; the little room had newly emulsioned walls and gloss-painted woodwork. A rough wooden table sat in the middle of the floor, covered with pots of paint and brushes standing in cleaning solvent. She looked up at the window; the glass had been newly replaced, and the smell of drying putty mingled with all the others in a potpourri of DIY. On the floor was an army bedroll, a bottle of wine and two glasses. She turned to him, speechless.

"Mind your jacket," he said. "The gloss is still tacky. Glass of wine?" He pulled a penknife from his pocket, and extracted a corkscrew from its complex system of tools and blades.

She shook her head, her eyes never leaving his.

"I won't bother either, then," he said, folding the corkscrew back in, pocketing the penknife. It was for all the world as if they were in a drawing room, until he took the key from his pocket, and held it out to her.

She could leave; he wasn't going to try to stop her. She took the key from him, but she laid it on the table, and turned back to him; they were kissing and hugging and trying to undress one another, sinking down onto the bedroll which was as hard as if it had been the bare concrete floor, and she didn't care.

*　　*　　*

The walk from the oak tree to the back door was fifty seconds at a reasonably brisk pace, and one minute seven seconds at a more leisurely stroll.

Which should it be? How much time he took beforehand didn't matter; all that mattered was that the timing once he was inside the house was right. So he had to decide right now how long that walk was going to be. And suppose someone called him back? Engaged him in conversation? Perhaps he should leave himself more time than he needed for the walk. It could mean that he was inside the house for longer than he would want, and Susan would, of course, be in there, if everything went according to plan. But he could do something that wouldn't arouse Susan's suspicions.

Jeff smiled. What suspicions? How could she possibly know what he was going to do?

All right. He would leave himself two minutes for the walk to the house. Tomorrow—providing he could get rid of Susan for a while—he could find out how much time he needed inside. The gas-gun cracked, and he took a deep breath.

What he had to do above all else was practice with the gun. And since it would obviously take a great deal of training before he got it right, he had to think of some way of getting rid of Susan for long enough at a time, often enough. He would have to give that some thought. And even if he did, it would be best if he could think of a way of silencing it. It would hardly do for John the Baptist to get nosy.

It wasn't going to be easy. Last night, it had seemed so simple. But quite apart from the timing, which was vital, and which had to be absolutely spot-on, there were the unforeseeable problems. Someone coming in to use the bathroom, someone coming to the door... but don't panic, he told himself. The beauty of the whole thing is that you can call it off, at any time. Right up until the last second. If anything goes wrong, you just don't do it. And no one will ever be any the wiser.

He watched the birds as they flew up at the next utterance of the gas-gun, and settled back down again. He knew that he had a lot of work to do, but he was looking forward to that. It was exciting; he was actually enjoying himself for the first time in weeks.

"Ben Kent!"

Oh, what now? He went over to where John stood, and saw that he was holding a wine bottle and two mugs. He frowned.

"You want some? Elderberry. Best I've made."

Jeff loathed elderberry wine. But he smiled, and said he'd love some.

*　　*　　*

She lay, her legs still entwined in his, waiting for him to push himself free of her, and pass judgment on her.

He reached out and gently brushed a wisp of hair from her face. "Tell him about us," he said.

She shook her head.

"Do you still want me to go away?"

She shook her head again.

He smiled. "Do you still think it's just hormones or chemistry or something?"

She smiled too, and shook her head again. She wanted to cry, and this time she could feel the tears coming.

"So tell him."

"I can't," she said. "I can't—Rob, you're his best *friend!*"

It was Rob's turn to shake his head. "Not anymore," he said. "I don't know who it is, but it stopped being me twenty-five years ago."

She closed her eyes as the tears streamed down her face.

"He's *my* best friend," Rob went on. "There's a difference."

She opened her eyes, wiping the tears with her hand. "I can't tell him," she said. "He wants us to try again—he's not even seeing that woman anymore. He's just getting himself back together again. I can't tell him."

Rob's eyebrows raised a fraction. "Are you so sure he'd mind?" he asked.

"Of course he'd mind! He was practically suicidal without this! He's happier than he's been for ages—I can't hurt him again." She wiped away new tears. "Please, Rob—can't we just carry on the way we are?"

"The way we are? Look at the way we are, for God's sake!"

It seemed sordid again now. It hadn't—it hadn't, when they were making love. She wished they were again, that she could just love him, and not have to think about the situation at all.

"You could move," she said. "You don't have to live in our old house! I could buy somewhere—"

"No!" he shouted.

She covered her face, and took a deep breath. Slowly, she drew her hands away. "All right," she said. "But you still don't have to live there."

"I want to live with you," he said. "Anywhere. Leave him. Leave the money, bring the money—I don't give a damn about the money."

Neither did she, anymore. But she did about Jeff, just like he did. She shook her head.

Now, he pushed her away. "You know what I think?" he

203

said, getting to his feet, pulling on his jeans. "I think that I'm an ex-army sergeant who drives a van for a living and he's a solicitor. You want one for blow and one for show."

It had been a long time coming. She got straightened up as best she could without a mirror, terribly aware that she had to complete her financial transaction with the sharp-eyed youth outside. She picked up the key.

"Susan."

She turned.

"Come away with me for a weekend."

She sighed. "Oh, sure. You and I disappearing for the same weekend. Even Jeff would begin to wonder about that."

"Then tell him you're going to that health farm or somewhere. For a week. But go somewhere I can join you for a couple of days."

She didn't answer. He had been thinking this through, obviously.

"I want to be with you!" he said. "I want to spend *time* with you. It'll do you good—you don't look very well. You need a break, and I need to be with you. Please."

"All right. But if Jeff doesn't want me to go away, I won't."

"Fine," he said, his voice flat.

She looked around the little room. "Was I brought down here entirely on false pretenses?" she asked. "Or are you supposed to be talking about this donation he wants?"

"Oh—yes. The Council's paying for the place to be done up, but he wants to put in a pool table and sound equipment for live bands and discos and things."

"Does he think it'll work?"

Rob opened the door and they walked into the darkened hall, their feet crunching on the broken glass.

"He doesn't know," he said. "He wants to sell alcohol-free lager and make it as much like a pub as possible." He led her through boxes and planks of wood to the door. "It's worth a try," he said.

"Tell him to do whatever he wants to the place," she said. "I'll sign the checks. But no opening ceremonies, all right? An anonymous donor."

"Right." He unlocked the door. "I'll come out with you," he said. "It's getting dark."

The youth materialized as they reached the car, which was indeed intact.

"Sorry," said Susan. "I was longer than I thought." She gave him a fiver.

He smiled. "Any time," he said, and winked knowingly as he strolled off to rejoin the group outside the chip shop.

"Can I give you a lift?" she asked.

"No," said Rob. "I'll walk."

"It's a long way."

"I'll walk."

She watched as he strode away. A weekend would be nice. Time to talk, to go for walks, to get to know one another. Time to take time. He might even leave out the sting in the tail.

* * *

Jeff couldn't believe his luck. Talk about timing. He'd been trying to think how he could get her out for long enough, and here she was asking if he'd mind her going back to the health farm for a week or so. She hadn't asked if he would mind last time. Now, she wanted his blessing? No matter. She would get it.

"If you want to, of course, you should go," he said. "I promise not to let Rob move in."

She smiled a little wanly.

"There's nothing wrong, is there?" he asked solicitously.

"No," she said. "It's just that it made me feel so good last time, and I . . . well, I think I need a tune-up."

"You look fine to me," he said.

She looked up at him. "You're sure you don't mind?" she asked.

He mustn't seem too eager to get rid of her. He sat beside her on the sofa, and put his arm around her. She shifted slightly. "Look," he said. "We've been through a lot—getting back on an even keel isn't going to be easy. We both know that. You *are* too tense—I think it'll do you good. So don't worry about me. I have no desire whatever to be massaged and beaten with twigs or whatever it is they do to you. I'll be fine."

She smiled, and kissed him. "You're too good for me," she said.

No, Susan, he thought, as she went upstairs. We're much of a muchness, you and I. It's just as well we married one another, when you come to think of it.

*   *   *

She waited on the empty platform, sitting on a hard metal vandal-proof bench.

The country station had survived thanks to holiday traffic and weekenders; most of the latter had arrived by the train that he had said he would be on. She had scanned the suddenly busy platform, eagerly waiting to catch a glimpse of him. But the platform had cleared, and he hadn't been there. She could have gone back to the cottage, but all she had done was sink down onto the bench, and she hadn't moved.

Other trains had come and gone; she had taken no interest in them. An hour ago, her heart had lifted as the next train that might be carrying him had appeared in the distance; it had arrived at the platform full of promise, in the strangely quiet way that trains did these days. It had deposited just a handful of people, who had hurried down the steps, under the lines, then emerged at the other side, heading for the exit.

The train had sat there for a moment, waiting for its departure time. While it was there, there was still hope, still a possibility. But the whistle had gone, and it had left, the noise from the engine at the rear growing almost to a scream as it passed her.

The sole representative of British Rail was sweeping up the dust of the hot summer day; he glanced at her now and then. No trains at all now, no other members of the public. Just her, and the shirtsleeved man who brushed the platform.

Two hours to go before the last train, the last hope.

She sat quite motionless, her arms folded tight, hugging herself as if she were cold. The warm July sun hung in the sky, dipping down towards the roof of the ticket office, glinting off the rails which stretched out and curved into the hazy distance, empty and silent.

The brush swished closer to her; she unconsciously shifted along the bench to let it sweep underneath.

"The station closes at eight, love," said the man.

She heard the words; she ought to speak, ought to look at him. She just wanted him to go.

"The main exit gets locked," he persisted. "But you can get out over there—see?"

Her eyes moved to him, to his outstretched hand, then she turned her head to where he was pointing.

"It's the gate to the car park," he said.

She nodded.

"The nine fifty-five to Derby is the last train stopping here," he said. "Meeting someone, are you?"

She didn't reply, and he lifted his shoulders slightly, making a final pass with the brush, and walked off down the platform, crossing the lines where the platform leveled off.

He moved about the opposite platform for a few minutes, locking doors. She saw him pause, look over at her. Then he walked briskly back over the rails, and onto her side. His step slowed as he walked towards her.

"You all right?" he asked.

She interpreted that as an inquiry as to whether or not she was likely to throw herself under the nine fifty-five to Derby. She wouldn't be doing that.

"I'm fine," she said.

"Do you live around here? You'd be better going home and coming back."

She shook her head.

He decided that he'd done his bit for humanity and British Rail, and walked away, over to the other platform, and out of the exit, which he locked behind him.

She had rented one of the cottages she had seen on her daily jogs around the district when she had been at the health farm in April. It was far from people, tucked into the bottom of a gentle, wooded slope. Earlier in the year it had had smoke coming from the chimney, drifting over its backdrop of bare trees, its windows lit comfortingly in the early dusk. Now the trees were thickly leaved, almost crowding it off the hillside. The hearth was hidden discreetly, like a guilty secret, by an embroidered screen perversely showing Paris landmarks. It looked different in the bright summer sunlight; empty, a little sad. There had been a last minute cancellation, she had been told. She had been lucky to get anywhere around here at this time of year. She had been there since Monday, just waiting for today, trying to feel lucky.

Friday, the twelfth of July. Not the thirteenth. It wasn't an unlucky day. Her head came up slightly, as an improbable thought presented itself. It *was* Friday, wasn't it? Had the silence and solitude of the cottage made her lose track? A discarded newspaper lay on another bench; unwillingly, she rose and walked along the platform.

Friday, the twelfth of July. She sat on the new bench, and folded her arms around herself again, physically holding herself together. It was the right day. He knew which station it was. He was on the six-to-two shift. He was going to leave work at two, and catch the four-ten, arriving at five-fifteen.

It had all been arranged. She had planned a meal, the component parts of which sat in the fridge in the cottage. She had had to drive all over the place to get the things she wanted; she had felt like a child choosing Christmas presents. She wasn't sure what he liked, but he had enjoyed the beef, so she had got fillet steak. Everyone liked fillet steak. And she had this wonderful recipe...

Wasn't that what the weekend was supposed to be about? Finding out the normal things about one another that their snatched moments didn't allow? Or was that just what she had been allowed to believe?

The sun was in her eyes now; relentless sun that had shone every day. If she had met anyone on her lonely walks, they had smiled and passed the time of day; sunshine did that. The last time, they had walked past, heads down. But she hadn't wanted the sunlight, achingly beautiful on the unspoiled countryside, when there was no one to share it. All she had wanted was for Friday to come. And now it had.

She turned from the red ball of fire which hung over the roof, and idly read the local paper. Developers had pulled out of a scheme, much to the relief of some and annoyance of others; children had held a jumble sale outside their house to raise money for the local hospital. The usual quotas of accidents and emergencies.

My God. Had he had an accident? But the panic was momentary. She would *know*, she thought illogically. She would know. And perhaps there was just a moment when she would have preferred to think that he *had* had an accident, but she chose to push that from her mind.

The station was in shadow as the sun finally slipped out of sight, and she went back to watching the rails, her mind so full of confused thoughts that it was almost like achieving blankness; she couldn't sort out one fear, one worry from the other, so she emptied herself of everything. No emotion. No thought. No anxiety, no hope. She was simply waiting, instinct triumphing again, like a dog whose master had died.

*   *   *

She had gone, and he had as much time as he needed to get things absolutely right. Rob had been around a couple of times to have a go with the shotgun—he didn't seem all that good, so it might be a real contest after all. Even better. But he had only stayed for about an hour each time. The rest of the time had been entirely his own, once Mrs. Reeves had been and gone.

He had given up on the idea of a silencer; he didn't think you could silence a shotgun. After all, if you could, he would hardly have to be going to all this trouble in the first place.

So he was practicing in the open, which was right. Everything that could be done openly should be. He was practicing for the contest, that was all.

He watched the stopwatch on the calculator readout and raised the gun to his shoulder, trying to hit a plastic bottle propped up on a branch of the oak tree at about head height. The gun went off, the bird-scarer cracked for the second last time of the day.

One last go before the gas-gun went quiet for the night. Always, always, he shot too soon. He couldn't make himself wait the extra few seconds, allowing himself too much time to take his eye off the calculator, and fire the gun. But that was because he was still trying to aim it; it was strange how difficult it was *not* to aim a gun. The whole thing was built for being aimed. But there would be no need to aim, only to press the trigger. He hadn't got it right, but he would. Eventually, he would. He had another seven days to perfect it, and he would. He kept missing the bottle, too, but that didn't matter. The fatal shot would be fired from very close range indeed; he couldn't miss. The timing was the important thing.

He had a Coke to pass the time until the gas-gun was due

again, then threw the empty can in the air, and shot at it. He missed.

He reloaded, his eye on the furiously changing seconds of the stopwatch.

*　　*　　*

The improbable digital clock silently and slowly went from minute to agonizing minute, until the invisible sun had set, and darkness made it impossible to read. On the other side of the station, an orange floodlight came on, lighting a church steeple. The minute hand of its clock edged towards ten o'clock, and the train still didn't come.

When she eventually saw the strip of lights advance, she didn't react; it disappeared for a moment behind the advertising hoardings, then appeared with a slow, rumbling vibration of the rails. She watched it approach with eyes wide with fatigue; she could smell the diesel exhaust that belched from the roof in two streams of black smoke. Three doors opened along its length; and out of one stepped Rob.

There was an instant when she couldn't move, after the body-stiffening hours of tense waiting. Then she jumped up, and ran like a child along the platform, throwing her arms around him, kissing him, almost knocking him backwards as the doors slammed again and once again the train's engines deafened her as she stood in blissful contact with him.

His arms were tight around her. "I rang," he was saying. "I rang about five times. Your phone must be out of order. I had to work. He couldn't get anyone else. I had to go to—"

But she was kissing him, not interested in explanations. They walked, arms around one another, to the stairs, down through the underpass, back up into the warm, soft, dark blue night. She led him to the car-park gate, her head light with relief and happiness. She gave him the keys.

"But I don't know the way," he said.

"I'll tell you."

He smiled, and took the keys, driving under instruction to the cottage. She practically dragged him up the path and into the little house. She pushed the door shut, and they kissed in the darkness. "Do you want to eat anything?" she asked.

"Yes," he said. "You."

She opened what she had thought was a cupboard door on her arrival, and switched on the light to reveal the stairs, steep as a ladder, which led to what had once been the bungalow's roof space. At the top, the length of the sloping roof was uncurtained window, looking out onto dark hills and a moon-bathed sky. It had alarmed her the first night, on her own, that nakedness.

Tonight, it was perfect.

*   *   *

Jeff wasn't getting any better. He beat the gas-gun to it again, and sighed.

It was six-thirty in the morning; even John the Baptist wasn't abroad yet. He had considered the wisdom of such an early start, but given the other aspects of his plan, it really was difficult to see how his actions before the fact could possibly be called to account. Because the beauty of this plan was that it was foolproof. A dozen—a hundred and one—things could go wrong. But if they did, it simply wouldn't happen.

The only thing that he could do wrong on the day was lose his timing. And that was why practice was paramount. All day every day if need be, until he got it right all the time, every time, without fail.

He shot at the plastic bottle between gas-gun blasts, and he hit it. It was torn in two by the bunching of the pellets at that close range. He had to think very carefully about that, too. A murder one intended to get away with wasn't sup- posed to be messy, but this one would be. The very close range necessary would create a lot of blood; he had to be prepared for that. He had to think about the mess; he had to think about where the blood would go.

It had become a problem almost like the ones which had faced him when preparing someone's defense. He had to come up with answers to a given set of circumstances which proved that he had had nothing to do with them.

The deliberate termination of a human life had at first excited him, then worried him, as the enormity of its transition from fantasy to reality had come home to him. Now, he really didn't think of it in those terms at all; it was the plan that excited him now. Making certain that every detail was right, and that nothing had been missed, nothing had been overlooked.

It was complex and simple at one and the same time, like most truly beautiful things. Because it was truly beautiful. It was an exercise in precision. The complexity was all underneath; all that showed on the outside were the pure clean lines of the design. Like the Rolls. Like Fiona, come to that.

Death had nothing to do with it, and would have nothing to do with it except for one split second.

*   *   *

Daylight flooded the room. They had been awake for hours, just talking. Susan sat at the foot of the bed, her legs tucked beneath her, as he lay stretched out, his feet crossed in her lap.

She clasped her hands around his foot. "I thought you had deliberately set me up when you didn't get off the train," she said.

He sat up from the waist, as lithe and supple as the athlete he had been in the army. They would be proud of him at the health farm. "And what would you have done if I had?" he asked.

"Come looking for you," she answered, without hesitation.

He looked at her, frowning slightly. "You must have waited at that Godforsaken place for nearly five hours," he said.

"Yes," she said.

He reached across to the table for his cigarettes, lit one, and lay back down again, cigarette in his mouth, hands behind his head, contemplating her. "Why, for God's sake?"

"I hated this place until last night," she said. "I didn't want to come back here alone."

He freed one hand and removed the cigarette, blowing smoke at the low ceiling.

"I felt like *Greyfriars Bobby*," she said.

She had been thirteen when she had cried over the little Skye terrier's vigil by his master's grave; four years later she had cried over the baby that she didn't want to have. She had still been a child. Perhaps she had never stopped being one.

He laughed, crushing out his barely started cigarette.

She let her legs part slightly, and lay back smiling as his toes explored her. Then he took his feet away, drawing his legs up and falling forward onto his knees, pulling her up onto hers as they kissed. For the first time, they made love in the sunshine; for the first time the quiet moments afterwards were not accompanied by punishing words.

*   *   *

Sunday, and his battle with the gas-gun continued. Again, he smashed the bottle—a full one this time, and orange juice dripped down the trunk of the oak, along the branches, spattering the leaves, even him.

Blood. Blood was a problem. Possibly his next biggest problem to the timing. And yet—providing he could think of an answer—it would give him his next best alibi. Because it would go everywhere, if the orange juice was anything to go by. It was difficult to see how to do that much damage from that close a range and not be within the fallout range. He brushed the orange juice from his shirt, and looked at where the bottle had been. He would be firing from a very much closer range than that.

Yes, he thought, almost pleased to have something to get his teeth into, blood was a problem.

He had never known anyone who had planned a murder. Well, he wasn't *aware* that he knew anyone who had planned a murder—there was always the matter of John the Baptist's woman, and his burgeoning market garden. Most murders were haphazard affairs, brought on by jealousy or drunkenness or—more usually—both. He had had two murders in his time. Both were pleas of manslaughter, and the barrister had been paid a great deal of money for doing practically nothing, since no one was disputing the facts in the first place.

But he couldn't help thinking that most people planned them the other way around, when they did plan them. Worked out what they *could* do, and did it.

His plan had been there all along; it had been entrusted to him. He had to work out how it could be done. Which was tricky, because there was nothing to say that it was even possible.

His shoulder ached, and his hands were getting hot and sweaty inside the leather gloves. Perhaps he should give shooting practice a rest. Now, he was waiting a fraction too long before pulling the trigger.

One more time. He hoisted the gun, and the pain in his shoulder made him wince.

"Don't shoot!" she laughed.

Elsa. Jesus Christ. What was she doing here?

*   *   *

Sunday, and they were out exploring the countryside.

"Bet you can't run all the way to the top."

Susan looked at the gentle slope. "Bet I can," she said.

"Because of two weeks at a health farm three months ago?"

"I was fit before that," she countered.

Rob set off, long legs loping up the hillside, and she ran to catch him. She had to stop less than halfway up to catch her breath and try to persuade shaking legs to carry on. He was almost at the top. She sat down on the grass, laughing at herself. She was forty-two, not fourteen.

"Come on!" he shouted, from the top.

It looked like Everest, and she got to her feet, walking slowly now. She could do aerobics and jog. She could walk for miles without getting tired. But running up hillsides was out.

"How can you do that?" she complained, as he pulled her, panting, up beside him. "You're older than me, and you smoke."

He grinned. "Practice," he said. "Twenty years of sergeant-majors who didn't let you sit down in the middle of it. You can do anything if you practice."

She was still trying to get her breath back as he set off into the woods, walking through dappled sunshine. He turned back towards her, and smiled. "Come and look," he said.

She joined him and looked down at the panorama of English countryside. Gentle hills with patchwork fields in the misty distance, higher ground where they stood, surrounded by trees with shiny leaves sparkling in the sun. The cottage's loft window was visible from this side; she smiled at him. It had been another, gentle, wonderful morning, followed by a long, cholesterol-packed Sunday breakfast, and the sheer luxury of time together. He had been right. This was what she needed.

They walked through the woods; he knew every tree, and spotted animals that she would never have seen.

"How do you know so much about the countryside?" she asked.

"Survival courses," he said. "They don't just teach you

how to shoot and shine your shoes, you know. You have to know what you can eat."

"You mean you spot furry little animals so you can kill them?"

He laughed. "I think the bacon and eggs will keep me going for the moment," he said. "I'll let them live."

Jeff came into her mind, unbidden. On his survival course at home, eating out of the freezer. She didn't feel guilty, not like Rob. But she felt a little afraid. What if he found out?

"Your brother does know you're visiting him, if Jeff should ring him, does he?" she asked anxiously.

"Yes," he said. "But you'll just have to hope he doesn't try to ring you at the health farm."

"Oh, he won't do that," she said.

"What makes you so sure?"

She smiled. "Jeff's much more likely to want to get hold of you than he is of me," she said.

He walked a little way ahead of her, hands pushed down into the back pockets of his jeans. He stopped and turned. "If you know that, then why would it be so terrible to tell him?" he asked.

She walked up to him, her eyes on the ground, her feet unsure of themselves. She looked up at him when she got there. "I don't think he'd care that I was betraying him," she said. "He'd care that you were."

He turned away, and sat on the wide stump of a felled tree, one hand in a fist, the other clasped around it, pressed to his mouth. He was angry, trying not to say whatever had risen to his lips.

She didn't speak, didn't go to him.

"If it's my betrayal," he said at last, "then I should be free to tell him."

Her mouth fell open. "Oh—no, Rob, no. Please. Please don't." She ran to him, kneeling down on the dusty earth. "Promise me," she said, her hands on his knees. "Promise you won't tell him."

He looked at her, his face pale. "Why should you care what he thinks about me?" he asked.

"I don't know what he'll do!" she cried, for the first time admitting the fear aloud.

"*Jeff?*" He stared at her. "You liar," he said slowly. "You want to keep him—you still want to hang on to him, and to hell with what he wants, or what I want. You want to keep him like some sort of hunting trophy, that's all. Falling for me is a bit inconvenient, but you can always make arrangements to see me when you want a bit on the side, can't you?"

"I have never made arrangements to see you!" she shouted. "*You*—you make the arrangements, not me!"

He got up and walked back out of the woods. By the time she got back to the crest of the hill, he was walking towards the cottage.

He wasn't right. Surely he wasn't right?

*   *   *

The American couple were very complimentary about the garden, and about Susan's transformation of the kitchen. They were upstairs now, and Elsa looked at him apologetically.

"Did I come at a bad time?" she asked.

He had been a little startled. There was no reason why he shouldn't be shooting bottles of orange juice out of his own tree in his own garden, but he felt that it had probably looked a little odd.

"I just wasn't expecting you," he said.

"Well, Susan's so keen to sell, and they're looking for somewhere they can move into straight away—I thought I ought to bring them up here before they found somewhere else."

The gas-gun went off, and Elsa's face fell. "Susan said you were going to ask him to turn it off," she said.

"I will," said Jeff. "Provided I get notice. I can hardly ask him to turn it off for the duration, can I?"

Elsa looked a little flustered. "Sorry," she said.

He wasn't. And perhaps he could persuade them that the orange substance dripping from the tree was some sort of creeping entity that would engulf the house. That would put them off.

He heard their footsteps upstairs, and the rise and fall of quiet discussion.

"They need somewhere by the end of the month," said Elsa. "I think we might be lucky."

Might we, thought Jeff, arranging his face into something resembling a smile as he heard the feet come back downstairs.

"It's a lovely house," said the woman.

"Thank you," said Jeff.

"Is shooting popular around here?" asked the man.

Jeff shook his head. "There's only one neighbor," he said. "He doesn't shoot—well, not often. He does have a revolver, but we've asked him not to use it."

"A revolver?" said the man.

"Mm."

Elsa had gone slightly pink.

"But someone else is using a shotgun," the man persisted. "We heard it."

"Oh!" said Jeff, as though the explanation had just presented itself. "No—that's not a shotgun. That's a bird-scarer."

"A bird-scarer?" repeated the woman.

"Yes," said Jeff pleasantly. "For scaring birds."

"How often does it . . . ?"

"Oh, about every twenty minutes or so," said Jeff. He could tell her exactly how often, if she really wanted to know. He could even tell her how many bangs there were in a day at this time of the year. Fifty-four. So many that Susan had run away to her health farm for a fortnight to get away from them. He smiled, but he didn't tell her that. There was

no need; they were heading for their car. He would save that gem of information up for the next lot, if there was a next lot.

*   *   *

She had climbed the narrow steep stairs to find him lying on the bed, still angry. She had looked down at him, and the throbbing intensity of the charge between them was back, as though it needed his animosity to bring it to life. The sex was wild and wordless, and almost fully clothed.

He got up after a while, and began to push clothes into a bag, as she watched, puzzled.

"What are you doing?" she asked.

"Packing. I've got a train to catch," he said. "There's only one on Sunday."

"No!" she shouted, horrified at the thought, scrambling over the bed, pulling the bag away from him. "No—not yet. You can't leave yet! It's too soon!"

"I have to. I've got to be at work at six in the morning."

It hadn't occurred to her; not once. His leaving again hadn't entered her head. Another week of silent, shattering loneliness, made worse by memories of his having been here. She couldn't bear that. They were only just getting into their stride. He couldn't go now. He mustn't.

He picked up the bag and put it back on the bed, but he didn't put any more stuff into it. He looked at her helplessly. "The weekend," he said. "That was the plan."

"No," she said, still breathless with the shock, almost sobbing. "*No*. It's so good, Rob—please. Please stay. Just another few days. Tell them you're sick. Phone in the morning. Tell them you're sick. Please, Rob. Please." She had her arms around him, pulling him back down on top of her, covering him with open-mouthed kisses until his tongue was seeking hers with as much passion as before.

He missed his train.

"You are frightened," he said, when everything was calm,

and quiet, and she hadn't wanted the silence to be broken. "I know you weren't lying."

She didn't want to think about it.

"What's frightening you? Is that why you look so pale?"

She shrugged. "I'm not sleeping," she said.

He grinned his slow grin. "Well, this weekend hasn't done much for you in that direction," he said.

She smiled then. "He's acting so strangely," she said.

Rob raised his eyebrows. "He seems all right to me," he said. "Like you said, he's more cheerful than he's been for a while."

"I know," she said dully. "That's part of it."

He laughed.

"I mean it. Why is he cheerful? Why is he telling me of course I can go away for two weeks if I want to, without a word about having to make his own dinner?"

"Oh, come on, Susan. Can't the man begin to enjoy life again?"

She looked at him. "A woman, you mean?" she asked. "That's just it. He stopped seeing Fiona weeks ago."

"I expect you're just as capable as she is of keeping him cheerful," he said, his voice low.

She shook her head. "He isn't interested," she said. "Not lately."

Rob brightened a little at that. "Perhaps he's discovered the joys of celibacy," he said.

"Jeff?"

"Mm." He thought for a moment. "Didn't you say that Elsa seemed to have something to do with all the drama on your anniversary?"

"Well . . . he seemed angry with her, which was a bit odd, because he hardly knows . . ." Her voice trailed off as she thought about it.

Elsa. She smiled at Rob. It explained everything. The "drives" that he went for in the Rolls; his apparent indifference to Elsa, which she had thought at the time was odd; his trying to talk her out of moving away, when he had seemed so keen on the idea to start with. The gun club—that would be just another excuse, like the garden centers and the nurseries.

"Elsa," she said, giving Rob a kiss.

No woman could ever have been happier to discover that her husband was having an affair.

*   *   *

Again. Fifth time in a row.

Jeff felt a flush of triumph as he laid down the shotgun. Five times in a row, dead on time. He broke the gun, and the cartridges ejected with a strong whiff of another smell that was becoming immensely satisfying. He inhaled it as he put in two new cartridges, and let off shots at the bottle, missing.

"I'll not need the bird-scarer, Ben Kent, if you keep this up," said a voice. "It's no bloody use anyhow. I was better off with the Eyetie gun."

Jeff whirled around, startled by John's voice. "I won't be doing it for long," he said quickly. "Susan will be back in a few days—she won't stand for it."

John nodded. "Why are you doing it at all?" he asked.

He had discarded the white raincoat at last, Jeff noticed; even he couldn't ignore the climbing temperatures.

"I'm going to challenge a friend of mine to a contest," he said.

John looked pointedly at the intact bottle.

"Oh—not shooting bottles off trees," said Jeff. "Clay pigeon shooting."

John frowned, going over that in his mind. "Wouldn't you be best practicing on clay pigeons?" he asked.

"I can't. You need someone to release them."

He shrugged. "I'd do that for you," he said.

Oh God. You would think if you came to live in the back

of beyond that you could plan a murder in peace. He was tempted to ask John if he had had to suffer such an intrusion into his affairs when he laid his woman to rest under the cabbages. What with him and Elsa, this was getting difficult. At least Rob wasn't around. He'd gone to visit his brother in Manchester and hadn't come back yet.

But Elsa had trooped two more lots of people up to the house, giving him the asked-for warning this time. She had been more than a little puzzled about the gas-gun blasting away, but he had told her that John wouldn't cooperate. She was never going to find out any different, because she was scared to death of the harmless old eccentric.

"Oh, that's all right," said Jeff. "I'll lose anyway—he learned to shoot in the army. It's just for fun."

He didn't care if he missed every single one of the damn stupid things. Rob could cover himself with glory. His face fell a little as he thought of yet another possible—even probable—snag.

"Something wrong?"

"Just remembered I left the grill on," he said, walking briskly back to the house, and closing the back door.

How was he going to make sure Rob stayed out in the garden? He'd wander about, come in and talk to Susan, come to see what he was doing...

Snags were part of it, he told himself, as he pulled off the gloves, and got ready to take the car out. He always got ready for the car, with as much care as he would take for a woman.

He'd sort it out, once he was behind the wheel. He always had before.

*　　*　　*

"This time I *am* going," Rob said.

He had gone down with food poisoning, or so his brother had solemnly assured his boss on the Monday morning. It

223

was Wednesday now, and he couldn't stay off any longer than that.

It wasn't so bad this time; she had had time to get used to the idea, and she only had to make it through two more nights alone before she headed for home. She watched him pack, neatly folding shirts and stowing them away.

"You're good at that," she said.

"Learned this in the army, too," he said, zipping up the bag, and sitting beside her on the sofa.

"Do you miss the army?"

He sucked in his breath and moved his shoulders in a noncommittal shrug. "I miss the discipline, in a way," he said. "I miss knowing exactly what I had to do, when I had to do it, and getting into trouble if I didn't."

She thought about the stories he had told her. "You didn't know exactly what you were doing in Northern Ireland," she said.

He smiled. "No," he admitted. "But I knew what not to do. How to behave under fire had been drummed into me. I stayed alive."

"Were you frightened?"

He shook his head, laughing at her. "Of course I was frightened! Anyone who wasn't frightened would have to be daft or dead. Probably both."

She smiled. "How could you stop yourself running away?" That's what she would have done. The minute she saw the car stop and the guns appear. Run like hell.

He shrugged again. "You obey orders," he said.

She took his hand. "I can't imagine you obeying orders," she said.

"Oh, can't you? Then why am I still here, in the middle of the week, when I'm supposed to be at work?"

She held his hand to her mouth. "Because you're loving it," she said. "I wish you weren't going."

"Don't start that again."

"You don't have to get this train," she grumbled gently. "There's one at quarter to eight."

"I know. That's the one I'm getting."

"Why are you all packed, then?"

"Because," he said, getting up from the sofa, and holding out his hand to her, "I want to say goodbye."

She smiled, and allowed herself to be led up the narrow stairs.

But soon, much too soon, she was watching the train leave, and she was alone again. She walked slowly back to the car, sitting in it for a long time before she pulled out and drove back to the cottage.

She had never lived so intensely as she had for the past five days. Swinging wildly from one extreme to the other, from tender, wonderful lovemaking to sheer gratification of sexual desire, to discovering physical pleasures that she had never known. From talking about his army days, and his brothers and mother, to being criticized and condemned, to pleading with him, begging him to stay, instinctively holding on to what she had found, like the first night she was with him, when she couldn't let go of him.

Her senses were reeling still when she got back to the cottage, and she sat on the sofa until it grew dark, then went up the narrow stairs to the wide bed, to sleep alone.

*　　*　　*

Rob was back; Jeff, getting drinks at the bar, waved, and indicated that he would get him one.

"Are you all right now?" asked Neil.

"Yes," said Rob. "I went back to work this morning. Bloody Indian restaurants."

"What's this then?" asked Jeff, as he arrived at the table with two pints and a tomato juice.

"Food poisoning," said Neil. "Rob had the trots in Manchester."

225

"I wondered where you'd got to," said Jeff. "Are you sure you should be having this?"

Rob took the glass. "Nothing wrong with my drinking habits," he said. "Just my eating habits." He looked at the tomato juice. "Have you signed the pledge?"

"No, I'm driving."

He was on his way to London, openly, obviously. That was why he'd come to the golf club. Everything that could be above board should be.

"Anywhere in particular?"

"Thought I'd take her for a spin on the motorway," said Jeff. "It's a while since she was given a long run."

"London?" said Neil, and laughed. "Thought you'd given her up, Jeff."

Jeff looked at him sharply. It was a joke. A barbed joke, but a joke. He didn't know. He didn't know about Fiona; he couldn't. No one must know. She was, after all, blackmailing him. If that was to get out . . . but Neil was just guessing. He suspected that Jeff was going to see a woman, but that was all right, as long as he didn't know who. He was an ex-policeman; he was observant. That was why he was going to be Jeff's star witness.

"Oh—Susan's back tomorrow, isn't she?" Neil went on, to underline the point.

Jeff nodded. He had better be extra nice to her when she got back, he thought. She had to agree to the contest being held. It was, after all, her house. And he had been neglecting her lately.

"I really must see her and thank her for her support for the club," Neil said.

Jeff smiled. "She agreed, did she?" he said, as once again fate took a hand. He had been worried about how to explain Fiona's presence to Susan.

"Yes—a really wonderful donation."

Jeff sipped some tomato juice. "Susan believes in spreading this money around," he said. "She says it's too much for one person."

"I can believe that," said Neil. "But not many people in her position actually put their money where their mouth is."

Jeff finished his tomato juice, and looked at Rob. "How good a shot do you reckon you are, then, Rob?"

Rob waved his glass. "So-so," he said. "I miss more than I hit, I think."

"Think you could beat me?"

"Well, I could beat you with a rifle, but I wouldn't really know about a shotgun," he said. "I haven't seen you shoot."

"Fancy a challenge match?"

Rob grunted into his glass. "Depends on the stakes," he said.

"Nothing extravagant," said Jeff. "Just for fun."

"Sure, if you want."

"Neil—will you be the maid-of-all-work?"

"Doing what?"

"Releasing the clays, keeping score—and making sure no one's cheating," said Jeff.

"How the hell would I know if they were?"

"Releasing the clays and keeping score, then," said Jeff, with a grin at Rob. "We're gentlemen, aren't we? We wouldn't cheat."

"You mean I'd be the chap who sends these things up when someone shouts 'pull'?"

"You've got it. And count how many are hit."

Neil grunted too.

Not a lot of enthusiasm, but no outright refusals. He smiled. "I'll fix it up," he said. "You can thank Susan then, Neil. We'll make a party of it."

Neil looked considerably more interested now, Jeff noticed, as he took his leave, and went cruising happily along the motorway to Fiona.

She wouldn't let him stay, of course, but he asked just to make sure she realized that he was still yearning for her. If

227

he showed as little interest as he felt, she wouldn't agree. And she did, after a considerable amount of cajoling and explanation. All right, she had said reluctantly. She would help him out on the day of the shoot.

It pleased him to think of it like that; it was nicely clinical. The shoot.

He told Fiona a story that she only half believed, but it worked. Rob, he explained, with total truth, was an inveterate chatter-up of women. Susan had never liked him, and would undoubtedly react badly if he annoyed her. But Rob, he told her, in a spectacular divergence from the truth, was possibly going to come in with him on a business project, and he wanted him kept sweet. All Fiona had to do was accept compliments prettily, keep him off guard, as it were, and he'd have the whole thing sewn up. And on that sewing-up depended their future. Because once it was in the bag, he could tell Susan to go to hell, and they could at last be together.

She severely doubted this cock-and-bull story, and who could blame her? But it didn't matter that it was patently a lie; what mattered was that she believed he was doing something—whatever that might be—to get out from under, and set up home with her. That was all that mattered to her, she said.

She was worried, of course. She thought he had got involved in a crooked deal of some sort, and he allowed her to think that while denying it absolutely. He needed her, he had said. That often worked with women, he'd found, and it was bound to work with someone who was prepared to blackmail him into saving himself from himself.

What would Susan think about her suddenly turning up? she asked. Nothing at all, he said, once again grateful to fate, or the gods, or whoever it was that was running the show. She had donated an unspecified but large sum to a local charity—the man in charge of the project was to be there to thank her officially. Fiona could use the same excuse as last time.

Reluctantly, suspiciously, she agreed, then threw him out when he tried it on again.

The long drive home did the trick; he knew how he could cope with the blood. Now he had to perfect the timing inside the house, which was much simpler, and already almost perfect. And then he could set the date.

Of course, somewhere along the line, Susan had to agree to her part in it. Not, he told himself with a smile, her whole part—she probably wouldn't agree to the final act, were she being given a choice about that.

He was almost there. But—the irony of it—he had to visit a garden center on Saturday.

*   *   *

She had been home for just one day, and she was jumpy again. It was Saturday, and the garden center alibi had been trotted out; she was surprised to see it surface again now that he had the gun club.

The knock at the back door made her jump, like every sudden noise did; she was relieved, if puzzled, to see Elsa. "Oh, come in," she said.

"Did I startle you?" asked Elsa.

"I thought you might be someone else," she said, smiling. "I'm glad it's you. Do you want a cup of coffee?"

"Please," said Elsa, sitting down at the breakfast bar.

Susan busied herself with the kettle and mugs for a few moments. "You haven't brought any prospective purchasers with you?" she asked, as the bird-scarer banged.

"Not this time," said Elsa, with an apologetic smile.

"No nibbles, even?"

There was a silence; Susan turned, a little puzzled, to see Elsa looking much the same.

"Well—not today," she said.

Susan frowned. Not today? Was it a public holiday or something? Not that it made much difference to estate agents—they worked all the time, as far as she could see. She dismissed the odd little exchange with a smile. "Oh, well," she said, making the coffee, "it's not been on the market long."

Elsa took her coffee, still looking uncomfortable.

Susan sat opposite her. "You have to admire the garden," she said. "If anyone does come, they won't be put off by that anymore."

"Er. . ." Elsa began, setting down her mug. "You . . . you do know that people have been to see the house?"

"What?"

Elsa spoke to her mug. "While you were away," she said.

Susan half laughed. Oh dear—they should have got their story straight. "Well, I only came back yesterday," she said. "It must have slipped Jeff's mind. They weren't interested, I take it?"

Elsa still addressed her coffee. "I brought three different lots of people," she said, her voice quiet.

Susan shivered; this girl wasn't having an affair with Jeff. Elsa was worried about Jeff, just like she was.

Elsa looked up at last. "Are you sure your husband wants to sell?" she asked.

Susan didn't know, and she didn't care. All she knew was that he hadn't said a word about these people to her, and that something was wrong. Did he know? Had he guessed?

"Only—" Elsa looked more uncomfortable than ever. "He seemed to be deliberately putting people off," she said. "You see, a new factory's opening at the south end of the town, and that makes this place quite handy. They're bringing people in—I really thought we had a good chance of selling, but—"

"But what?"

"Well—he told the first lot that the man next door had a revolver. And he told the next people that the bird-scarer

230

went off fifty times a day, and you'd had to go away because of it."

Susan took that in. All right, presumably he wanted to stay here. Not, it would appear, to be close to Elsa, unless she was wasting a great talent on real estate. But why not just say so? Why promise her that they would leave, if he had no intention of going? Why not tell her about the people coming to see the house?

"You'd better take it off the market," she said.

"Right," said Elsa, looking no happier. "I suppose it's because he's got so interested in shooting," she said, after a moment. "This is the perfect place for that."

Susan's head shot up. "Shooting?" she repeated. "How do you know about that?"

Elsa looked down at her mug again. "Well—he was shooting things," she said. "Every time I came here."

"What do you mean, shooting things?"

"Bottles, I think. Out of the tree. One of them must have been full, because the tree was covered in something." She looked up. "And . . . well, the last time I came, the ground was knee-deep in spent cartridges."

In the oppressive summer heat, Susan went very cold.

*　　*　　*

The garden table and chairs looked very well under the oak, Jeff thought, able now to think about something else altogether while going through his routine in the house. He started the cassette, and turned the speakers to the open patio door. The stopwatch should read three minutes forty-two seconds.

He smiled. Forty-four seconds. Fine. He went into the kitchen, and went through his actions in mime. The gas-gun exploded, and he glanced at the stopwatch. Five minutes dead.

No more rehearsal. It was getting difficult anyway, now

that Susan was back. His final tally with the gas-gun had been thirty times out of thirty, which he had done the Wednesday before Susan came back from the health farm. He had been exhausted by the end of it, but he had done it, so there was no need to worry about that anymore.

Everything else he was having to fit in with her charity committee meetings, and she had been skipping quite a few of them recently. But this evening she had gone to look at what Neil had done with her money; she had expressed a wish not to attend the opening, apparently, so Neil was giving her a preview, bless him.

Now, he had to go over the entire day in his mind, making certain that there were no mistakes, nothing that a forensic pathologist or a scene-of-crime officer could point at as being wrong. They would find exactly what he intended them to find, and nothing else.

It was going to happen on Saturday. Almost three weeks would have elapsed between thirty out of thirty and the actual execution of the plan, and that was quite enough. Rob and Neil were free, and Fiona always was; he'd phone her later to make sure.

*   *   *

"You've done wonders, really you have." Susan was tired of smiling and telling Neil how clever he had been.

"Well—Rob got a lot of people from where he works to come and help out," Neil said.

They were in the newly refurbished boys' club, now called something which Susan couldn't recall offhand. She was being given a special viewing before the opening night.

Rob stood over by the record-selector on the wall, idly reading the titles on offer.

"Do they want a sixties section?" he asked Neil.

"The bloke who put it in said they did," Neil replied. "The sixties are very popular with kids, according to him."

Rob didn't look convinced. He smiled slowly. "What happened to your secret society that you could only join if you were tough enough?" he asked.

Neil laughed. "The Council wouldn't wear it," he said. "But I think with the pool tables and the arcade machines..." He looked at Susan. "Without you it would have been table tennis and a Dansette record player," he said.

"That should have suited them, if they're into the sixties," said Rob.

Susan had come to get away from the house, and to see Rob. It had been two weeks since their holiday together, and it felt like two years. She didn't want to stand around discussing the youth of today's fondness for the sixties.

"Will you be running it?" she asked Neil.

"Oh, God no. They don't want a middle-aged ex-copper around. No—it's a young chap. He has a disco—he's quite well known in the pubs, so I'm hoping he'll bring them in."

"And you don't think you'll have trouble?"

Neil smiled philosophically. "No booze, no trouble. That's the thinking."

"No booze, no customers," said Rob.

Neil smiled at Susan. "I don't think he's as cynical as he makes out," he said.

Susan did.

Neil took a breath, and looked from her to Rob. "Well," he said, trying to sound natural and failing, "I've got another appointment—but finish your drinks." He smiled at Susan again. "Rob can lock up," he said.

Oh God. She didn't like Neil knowing. It wasn't safe.

"Goodnight," Neil said. "And—thank you again, Susan. I wish you'd change your mind and come on Saturday evening—I'd like to acknowledge your contribution."

She shook her head.

He smiled. "Well, I'll thank you properly at High Noon," he said. "'Bye."

Rob locked the door behind him.

"What's he talking about, High Noon?" she asked.

Rob turned. "Hasn't Jeff told you?" he asked, walking back to the record selector. He fed the machine, and pop music belted out.

Her heart sank. What now? What hadn't he told her now?

"He's challenged me to a contest," said Rob. He sat down at the bar and reached over, feeling under the counter for another can of non-alcoholic lager.

She went over to him. "What sort of contest?"

"Shooting," he said.

She stared at him. "What?"

"Clay pigeons," he said. "At lunchtime on Saturday, at your place."

"What?" she gasped. "Why didn't you tell me?"

"I haven't seen you since he mentioned it! I assumed you already knew."

But she hadn't known. And it hadn't been clay pigeons that Elsa had seen Jeff shooting. She sank down onto the stool beside him. "You haven't agreed?" she said.

"Yes—well, I said I'd have a go. It's just a bit of fun."

"Rob—could Neil have told him about us?"

Rob sighed. "He's hardly going to take all that money from you and then run telling tales to Jeff," he said.

"Then why is he challenging you to a contest?" she demanded.

"It's clay pigeon shooting, Susan, not a bloody duel!" He looked at her, his eyes hard. "Or would you like to think that?" he asked.

"Don't be ridiculous!"

"You don't want to tell him—you want him to find out, to fight for you—is that it?"

He pushed himself off the stool, and grabbed her wrist, pulling her towards him. There was a moment when his eyes searched hers for the truth. She might have told him then what she was really afraid of, if he had given her a chance.

* * *

Jeff dialed Fiona's number. "This Saturday," he said, when she answered, in order to keep the call as brief as possible in case Susan came back. "Unless you hear to the contrary. You know what to do?"

There was an audible sigh before she spoke. "Jeff—what are you getting yourself into?" she asked.

"Nothing. Nothing at all. I just don't want him pestering Susan, that's all."

"I thought it was him that you wanted to keep sweet?"

Damn. "Both of them," he said. "There's a lot of money at stake. And I need money if I'm to start up on my own."

"Susan's money?"

"Will you do it?"

Silence. Then, "Yes."

He put down the phone. Now, he wanted Susan to come home. She was the last hurdle.

* * *

Susan tried to get herself back into some semblance of the elegant woman who had arrived at the club. The damn place was still mirrorless. "Do I look all right?" she asked.

Rob smiled a little sadly. "You look great," he said.

They sat down at one of the tables and looked at one another.

"Leave him, Susan," he said. "You're letting your imagination run away with you if you think this contest has anything to do with us."

She wasn't. She shook her head. Rob was in danger, she knew it.

"He's just looking for a chance to show off his skill with a shotgun," he said, putting his hand over hers as it picked at the surface of the table.

"There's more to it than that," she said.

He shook his head. "There's no more to it," he said. "Ask Neil—it was just an idea Jeff had at the golf club."

"Jeff doesn't have ideas," she said. "He makes plans. He always makes plans."

Rob sighed. "Then he's planning to beat me into a cocked hat," he said. "That's all. Look—Susan." He took her hand in his. "Don't take this the wrong way," he warned, "but I probably know Jeff better than you do in some ways. He doesn't know about us. And if you're worried about Neil, don't be. He knows what Jeff's like with other women—he's pleased about us. He wouldn't say a word."

She rubbed the back of her neck, where she could feel the tension turning the muscles into knots. "Rob," she began, "I think he might be—" She stopped herself. It sounded crazy, even to her. But accidents with shotguns were very easy to arrange.

"And I think you should pack your bags," he said, not asking her what she had been going to say. "Before you turn into a nervous wreck."

*　　*　　*

Jeff heard her car crunch over the newly laid gravel. A moment later, the garage door swung open, and a moment after that the back door opened and closed.

He went into the kitchen to find her filling the kettle.

"What have you been doing to yourself?" he asked.

She turned quickly. "What?"

He reached over, smiling. "You're a mess," he said, brushing dust from the light jacket and skirt she was wearing.

She plugged in the kettle. "It's not been cleaned up yet," she said. She reached for mugs. "Do you want coffee?" she asked.

"Why not?"

"It really looks quite good," she said. "It might work."

"Are the kids interested, though?" he asked.

236

"I don't know. Maybe."

"I have yet to find one who is interested in anything," said Jeff.

A silence fell then, as their slightly stagey conversation petered out. He listened to the kettle singing for a moment or two, then decided to plunge in. As so often happens after a silence, they both started speaking at once.

"What's all this about a shooting contest?" she asked, before he could speak.

He laughed. "I was just going to tell you about that," he said.

"Were you?" She looked suspicious, nervous. But then she looked like that all the time these days.

"Yes. I thought maybe this Saturday, if you've got no objections."

She sat down. "Why should I object?" she asked, not looking at him.

"You're not usually too fond of banging," he said.

"What do you mean?" She looked up quickly.

"The gas-gun," he said. "It bothers you, and guns won't be any quieter."

She was very jumpy tonight. Worse than ever. She might not *agree*. That hadn't crossed his mind. She had to agree. He would be charm itself.

"Oh." She picked restlessly at the edge of the Formica with her fingernail. "I don't see what the point is," she said.

He smiled, and spooned coffee into the mugs. "No point," he said. "Just a contest."

"John tells me you've been putting in a lot of practice with the gun," she said. "So does Elsa."

Damn John and Elsa. "Just trying to get my shoulder battle-hardened," he said. "Did Elsa tell you some people were interested in the house?"

"Yes," she said. "Why didn't you?"

He handed her her coffee, and her hand was shaking as she took it. He frowned. "I didn't want to get your hopes up," he said. "I couldn't persuade John to switch off, and I think the regular explosions put them off rather."

"I've taken it off the market," she said.

Good, good. No chance of Elsa turning up with people to view the house on the day of the shoot. That had been a definite worry. Somebody up there was still looking after him.

"We'll wait until winter then?" he asked. "Before we sell?"

She nodded.

"Neil's the adjudicator," he said. "And he wants to thank you properly for your donation." He sat down. "I think you can stand by for chocolates and flowers and a little speech," he said. "I thought it might be nice to lay on a bit of a spread—you know, like you used to do."

She nodded. "If you like," she said.

"Oh good." Could it really be this simple? He had assumed that she would agree; for one thing, she was trying to make it up to him, and for another, she enjoyed preparing food. But just like that? He had thought that he would have to do a bit of persuading.

The last obstacle lay ahead. "I thought Rob and I should each shoot as many clays as we can in ten minutes," he said. "One after the other—we'll draw for who goes first. You really want two guns and a loader for that." He smiled. "Would you load for us?"

Her eyes widened. "I don't know how to load a gun," she said.

"It's easy. I'll show you."

"I don't know, Jeff. I'm not used to guns—neither are you! I don't think it's safe—why do you want to do it?"

He looked down at the floor. "I think I can beat him," he said quietly.

"So what?"

He looked up at her. He knew how to play Susan. "It'll sound crazy," he said.

"Tell me."

This was where he didn't speak, and she would ask him again to tell her. Then, reluctantly, he would.

"Please," she said. "Tell me."

"He's always beaten me," said Jeff. "At everything. Games at school. Sports days. He could always do everything better than I could. And this bloke at the club said that people who are used to powerful weapons aren't so hot with shotguns."

She was frowning slightly.

"I want to beat him," he said. "It's as simple as that."

She didn't speak.

"I'll show you how to load," he said. "Have a go. It's easy."

"I don't want to load, Jeff."

"Let me show you," he said. "Then decide."

She nodded tiredly. "All right," she said.

He had won. He smiled to himself as he went out into the hall, and to the gun cupboard.

*　　*　　*

She waited apprehensively. Leave him before you're a nervous wreck, Rob had said. Of course she should leave him, but she was afraid to. He knew, and all she could do was try not to upset him. She was humoring him now, she knew she was. Because he did know, he must.

She had been covered in dust from the floor of the club. He knew. He knew. Rob was wrong. She simply wasn't good enough at deception. Jeff had it down to a fine art, with alibis and careful planning, and she still always knew when he had been with someone else. So what chance did she have, when she wasn't even competent enough to cover her traces? Damn it, he *knew*, and he was playing with her, dusting her off solicitously.

And that remark about banging. He knew.

He brought her a gun and showed her how to load, then she had a go, but her hands were shaking as she pushed the

239

cartridges home. "No," she said, giving it back to him. "I don't want to do it, Jeff. I don't want you to have this contest at all."

He looked surprised, but again, the surprise was confined to his face. "But you said you didn't object," he pointed out.

"I know I did. But I think it's dangerous."

He laughed. "There's nothing dangerous about it," he said. "But if you're nervous, stay in the house."

Oh, yes, she thought. You'd like that. And then when Neil's filling his pipe or looking in the other direction, your gun goes off by mistake. No—she would be there, watching him.

"I'm going to have a bath," she said abruptly, and left him holding the gun.

She lay in the bath, trying to calm herself down. Rob thought she was overreacting; perhaps she was. Jeff just wanted to beat Rob, who was always taller and faster and stronger than him. Was that why all the practice? He was like that. He was getting as good at it as he could, but he couldn't wait to do it gradually. He was *like* that—he was. That was why she had thought of taking driving lessons the way she had. It was how Jeff did everything, and perhaps the contest wasn't sinister. But if it was that important to him, how would he react to Rob taking *her* from him? Now she was being *silly*, she told herself sternly, and went into the bedroom.

He reached for her, his blank eyes looking into hers, and she wanted to scream.

"No," she said, pushing him away. "I'm sorry. I'm not in the mood."

"You haven't been in the mood since you got back from the health farm," he said. "What's the matter with you? You jump at the least thing, you're uptight—it doesn't seem to have done you much good."

"I'm sorry," she said again, inadequately.

"Come on, Susie," he said. "It might relax you."

She shook her head.

"It's not going to be much of a reconciliation if I can't make love to you," he said.

He had never made love to her. She knew that now. Even if she hadn't just left Rob, she wouldn't want him to touch her. She turned away.

* * *

Jeff sighed silently with relief. He didn't think he could have done anything about it if she had complied.

He had no desire whatever to make love to her, nor, it would appear, she to him. He had had to make the attempt, as he had with Fiona. He had to behave normally. But at least he would have enjoyed it with Fiona.

With Susan, he had had to switch off, to pretend that she wasn't there, as he had the morning that she had told him what she had done to him. Sometimes, he'd had to do that even when they were simply talking; sex was almost impossible. But that was over now; that had been his last show of pretended desire. On Saturday the third of August, the shoot would go ahead as planned.

With that comforting thought, he fell asleep.

August

Saturday the third of August dawned blue and hot. The gas-gun belched with the first rays of light, and began its day's work; every nineteen minutes and seventeen seconds, the birds paid lip-service to it, and shifted their positions on the old man's crop.

His luck had held this far. Jeff glanced across at Susan, whose flickering eyelids indicated that she was dreaming. About what, he wondered? About having him stuck on a pin in a glass case?

He wanted to get up, like a child on Christmas morning, but he mustn't. He must wait until he would normally get up. Nothing must be at all unusual. It was going to work, he could feel it in his bones. It was going to work.

Susan was stirring too, now. He had to pretend to be asleep. She could act as differently as she liked; she was doing half his work for him, behaving like a startled fawn every time he spoke, looking permanently anxious and worried. Perfect. Just perfect.

* * *

Susan got up early, having slept badly, as usual.

But the kitchen, bright and gleaming as it was for about an hour in the early morning sun, made her see things a little more in perspective. Elsa could still be the answer, she told herself. If he had been seeing her, then ditched her, as was his wont, then perhaps her visit had a different aspect. She could have been believing that she was dropping Jeff in it, knowing that he wouldn't have told Susan about the purchasers. If there ever were any.

Yes, all that made sense. Jeff's interest in her had been renewed after she came back from the cottage, and she had had to develop headaches and all sorts of ailments to avoid him. Before that, he hadn't seemed so keen. That would fit with Elsa's having been canceled.

And now he had got it into his head that he was Annie Oakley, and wanted to prove it. That was like him too. Perhaps her problems were of her own making. It would hurt him if she told him about Rob, of course it would. And he had probably been hurt quite enough. But he had never harmed a fly, and she was being irrational and unfair.

* * *

Susan had been up for about an hour when Jeff finally decided it would be all right to start the day. He had a bath, shaved, dressed and went downstairs.

"Perfect day for it," he said. "I was thinking—do you think we should get a barbecue? Or will it pour as soon as we get it home?"

She turned from the cooker, where she had automatically begun to get his breakfast. "You mean today?" she said.

"Yes—it might be fun."

"I've never used a barbecue! Isn't it enough springing this on me in the first place? I'll do sandwiches and cold things."

Which was precisely what he had assumed she would say. If she had taken him up on the barbecue idea, he would have had to alter the plan, and at this late stage that could have caused problems. But it was fun to play her, because he could.

She stiffened at the sound of the car in the drive. "Who's that?" she said. "Surely Neil isn't coming this early?"

Jeff shook his head. "Wouldn't have thought so," he said. He watched as she opened the door.

There was a second of puzzlement, and recognition. "Fiona! What—what a surprise. Come in. What brings you here?" she asked.

"Well, the paper heard about your donation to this boys' club that's opening this evening, and I thought it would be nice to do a piece on it."

"Oh." Susan went to the cooker to turn the bacon, the smell of which was making Jeff's stomach rumble.

"Oh—I'm sorry, I've come in the middle of your breakfast," Fiona said, just as though she hadn't been instructed to do exactly that.

Jeff smiled. "That's all right," he said. "Would you like some?"

"Oh, no, thank you. I've eaten."

"The thing is," said Susan, "I won't be at the opening."

"No, I understand not. But I thought perhaps I could talk to you about it, and the other things I believe you've been doing. A sort of six-months-on piece—you know?"

Susan broke eggs into the pan. "Well—we're a bit busy today," she said.

"That's all right," said Jeff. "Fiona can stay and watch. Maybe the paper would like the shoot, too."

"What's that?" asked Fiona. She was really doing very well for a reluctant actress, thought Jeff.

"A shooting competition," he said. "Here."

"Fiona will hardly be interested in that," said Susan

briskly, dishing up the bacon and eggs, and depositing them in front of him.

"No—it sounds fascinating," said Fiona.

"Right, that settles it. Fiona can stay and watch, and then talk to you."

Susan nodded briefly, which was how she was communicating most of the time these days. "If. . . if you'll excuse me," she said, "there are things I have to get for this afternoon. Sorry, Fiona."

Jeff smiled, and picked up his knife and fork. "Don't worry," he said. "I'll look after Fiona."

Susan went out of the kitchen, coming back with her handbag. "I'll try not to be too long," she said.

Jeff smiled at Fiona as he listened for the garage door, for the car being reversed over the gravel, turning, then roaring off. Susan drove too fast really, he thought. He had been fairly certain that there would be shopping to be done; that was why he had asked Fiona to come early. He wanted to reassure her as to his intentions.

Fiona sat down. "Are you cheating her out of her money?" she asked. "You and this . . . Rob, is it?"

Jeff sighed. "No," he said. "Nothing like that. It's a business deal, that's all. And I don't want anything to go wrong." He touched her hand. "And I want you here with me," he said. "Because if it all works out, you and I can leave here together."

She looked at him, her eyes a little unsure. "Honestly?" she said. "You're leaving her? Today?"

He smiled. "Honestly," he said.

*   *   *

"I'm coming, I'm coming!" Rob's voice was muffled as he called through the closed door. He opened it, startled. "I thought you didn't make house calls," he said.

"Let me in," she said, pushing past him.

He closed the door and followed her into the living room. "What's the matter now?" he said. His hair was tousled; he wore a short, striped bathrobe.

"He's brought that woman here."

Rob rubbed his eyes. "Who's brought what woman here?" he asked, yawning.

"Jeff. Fiona Maxwell."

Rob ran his hands down his face. "I need coffee," he said. "What time is it?"

"Almost half-past ten," she said. "I'll get coffee." She went into the kitchen, pleased to have the familiar routine of something to do while she worked out what she was going to tell him. Everything she thought of made her sound quite mad.

Rob lit a cigarette and followed her, leaning in the doorway. "What do you mean, he's brought her here?" he asked, his voice weary, like an adult trying to talk some sense into a child.

"She turned up this morning saying she wanted to do a story on my donation to the youth club," said Susan.

Rob took a drag of the cigarette, screwing up his eyes against the smoke. "Well, maybe she does," he said, stretching.

"I said it had to be anonymous. Who told her? Neil? You?"

Rob stopped in mid-stretch, and looked an apology at her. "No," he said.

"Jeff's the only other person who knew," she said. "But he's all surprised innocence when she turns up."

Rob ran a hand through his hair. "All right," he said. "He got her here. Are you jealous?"

"No, of course not! I'm *frightened!*"

Jeff turned away with an impatient noise, went back into the living room and flopped down in an armchair. He took a puff of his cigarette, inhaling deeply, releasing all the smoke before he spoke again. "What of?" he said.

"Him. He's set this up for a reason, Rob."

"What reason?"

"I don't know. But why has he brought her here?"

Rob shrugged. "He thinks he can beat me," he said. "He wants her to see him do it. That's all. Maybe he's going to make an announcement—maybe that's why he wants us all there. Thinks he'll humiliate you or something if he walks off with her."

If only it were that simple. If only she could believe that Jeff was going to walk off into the sunset with Fiona. But Rob hadn't seen him, hadn't heard him. Elsa would understand.

"Don't come," she said.

"For God's sake, Susan!"

"Please. Just stay away." She went in to where he sat, and looked down at him. "I think he knows about us," she said. "I think he's found out. I think he's going to try to—" She broke off.

"Say it!" he shouted. "Say it, and hear how damn silly it sounds!"

She went back into the kitchen and made him coffee, but he pursued her, catching her shoulders, turning her to face him.

"Say it," he demanded. "You think he's going to try to what?"

"Kill you."

He let her go and stood back, looking at her. "You know your trouble?" he said. "You *know* you shouldn't be hanging on to him. You know you're hurting everyone. Jeff, and me—and Fiona, come to that. You know you're in the wrong, and you want to lay it all off onto someone else as usual. Onto Jeff, as usual. It was *his* fault you got pregnant. It was *his* fault you got married. It was *his* fault you were a doormat for twenty-five years. Now it's his fault you're in this state. Well, it isn't, Susan! It's your own fault, and it always has been!"

She shook her head. She wasn't denying what he was saying; she wasn't listening to what he was saying. She wasn't imagining this, and he had to understand that he was in danger.

"Listen to yourself! You're driving yourself crazy!"

"I'm not the one who's crazy!"

He sighed, and picked up the coffee, brushing past her as he went back into the living room. "Are you saying Jeff's crazy?"

"Yes."

"And what do you base that on?"

"John said he did nothing but shoot all the time I was away. Day in, day out. For hours."

Rob shrugged, and sat down. "He's always been like that," he said.

She knew that. She'd told herself that last night. But this was different. It was different, she knew it was. She could see the look in his eye. She knew. She knew, and she couldn't make Rob believe her.

"He's planning something," she said, stubbornly.

"What?"

"I don't know! An accident . . ."

"An accident? You don't need to practice all day every day to let a gun off in someone's face, Susan! He wants to beat me, that's all!"

"Please, Rob—please stay away."

He put down his mug, slopping coffee over the side onto the floor, and got up. "I will not stay away," he said. "I'll be there. And I'm going to tell him about us before you end up in a loony-bin."

"No!" she shouted. "No—you can't! You mustn't, Rob, not when there are loaded guns about. You mustn't. Promise me. Promise me."

He stared at her, his head shaking slightly with disbelief. "All right," he said. "All right. I won't tell him."

She felt limp with relief.

"*You* will."

"What?" She didn't understand.

"You'll tell him," he said. "You can pick your time—you can wait until the guns are locked up, and you've hidden all the kitchen knives, if you like. And you can tell him while I'm there, or when you're on your own. But you'll tell him before I leave your house this afternoon, or it'll be the last time you'll see me. Believe me."

Her voice wouldn't come out. She shook her head, trying to speak. "No," she said, when the word finally took shape. "No . . . no, you wouldn't leave me."

"I would, and I will, if this is the alternative."

She stared at him. "But . . . I can't—I *can't* lose you."

"Then tell him. That's your choice."

No choice. She closed her eyes, and nodded, as his arms came around her, holding her close.

"I can't live like this, Susan," he said. "I won't. I know it'll hurt him. But he has to be told. I don't believe he's found out, and I don't want that to be how it happens. I want him to be told. If you won't let me do it, you must do it."

"All right," she said, into his bathrobe. "But you do something for me, then."

He pushed her away so that he could look at her, and smiled. "Anything," he said.

"Take notice of Fiona."

He blinked a little. "How do you mean?"

"Do what comes naturally."

He shook his head, as if to clear it. "You're telling me you think he's murderous, and now you want me to chat up his bird?"

"You're not supposed to know she's his bird," she persisted. "As far as you're concerned, she's fancy-free—and very good-looking. And as far as Jeff's concerned, you're without female companionship at the moment. He'll think it's odd if you *don't* chat her up."

"Why should he think anything?"

"If you're right—if he doesn't know about us—I don't want him worrying about your lack of interest in her."

Rob smiled. "What do you think he's going to do?" he said.

He knew what she thought; she didn't repeat it.

"He's never even swung a punch at anyone," Rob continued. "He'll call me names. Which I deserve. And he'll be hurt and angry. But he's not going to do me physical harm."

"Will you do what I ask?"

He shrugged. "Certainly," he said. "From what I remember of her, it'll be no hardship."

She kissed him, and went to the door.

"But it's only to humor you," he said. "You still have to tell him," he said. "I meant what I said."

She turned. "I know you did," she answered. And she would tell him, once the guns were locked away.

If it wasn't too late by then.

* * *

"Here you are," said Jeff, bringing Fiona the long cool drink she had requested, to where she sat under the oak.

She took it, looking a little more relaxed out in the sunshine.

"There is one other thing," he said.

She tensed up again; really, she was getting as bad as Susan.

"Offer to help Susan, by all means," he said. "But take no for an answer. She hates anyone in the kitchen." That had the merit of being true.

Susan's car came back, stirring up a cloud of dust as it crunched through the dry gravel. She didn't put it away; she pulled into the space beside Fiona's, and got out, reaching back in for a carrier bag.

"Can I help?" Fiona called.

"No, I'm fine. You stay out here."

They all turned as another car was heard; Neil's dusty estate was coming along from the main road. He parked it on the dirt track, and came in, bearing the predicted flowers and chocolates for Susan.

Fiona did an impromptu interview with both of them, until Susan excused herself.

"You won't reconsider about loading for us?" Jeff called after her.

"No," she said. "You know how I feel about guns." And she went into the house, disappearing into the kitchen's murky depths.

Jeff shrugged at Fiona and Neil. "She won't touch guns," he said. It had been a calculated risk. Because if Susan *had* reconsidered, she would have aborted his baby after all. Instead, she had played right into his hands, and only fate could stop it now.

* * *

They tossed a coin, and Rob won. He put Jeff in first. Soon the air was filled with sharp cracks and gunsmoke, the ground littered with ejected cartridges, as the discs spun through the air, occasionally—but not often—shattering as they flew.

They wore ear protection, but the onlookers had to suffer ten minutes of almost incessant noise; Susan's nerves were in shreds before Jeff was halfway through his turn.

He would fire one gun while Rob loaded the next, handing it to him, and so on. Susan had no idea that ten minutes could last so long, or work its way through so much ammunition.

And the last few months had taken their toll; that was why, she told herself, she hadn't realized the implications, didn't realize what was happening, until it was far too late.

It was only after the whistle had gone, and they changed places, only after Jeff had handed Rob the first loaded gun, the whistle had gone again, and the whole thing had started all over again, that she realized what Jeff's plan was.

He had always known exactly how she would react to everything; he knew that she would never want to load for them. She just hadn't taken it the extra step; naturally, they would load for one another. For the next ten minutes, Jeff would be loading a gun—to which he had only very recently been introduced—as fast as he could, and handing it to Rob. And one of those guns—at some point—would go off at the wrong moment.

She could hear him now.

"If only you had loaded for us, Susan . . ."

Perfect. Extinguish the light, and make the moth feel guilty to her dying day.

"Pull," Rob shouted, and Neil sent up two clays, one of which Rob got. The other sailed down to the ground, and he reached for the loaded gun.

Susan couldn't stop it; if she ran to them, Jeff would use that as his excuse for the accident. All she could do was watch and wait for it to happen.

"Pull!"

Two cracks; a loaded gun.

"Pull!"

A loaded gun.

"Pull!"

She couldn't bear it, she couldn't stand it anymore. It was going on forever, like the last few steps in a nightmare journey. Do it, if you're going to! Just do it. Just—

The whistle had gone; the shoot was over. Susan felt like she had when she had drunk too much champagne at the presentation. The unreal people around her were clapping, laughing. Rob was taking off his ear protectors, shaking hands with Jeff.

The guns were checked, and Jeff was holding them, empty, broken, one over each arm.

It hadn't happened.

She was finding it difficult to adjust to that. She had been so sure, so certain, that Jeff was planning something. Something dreadful.

But nothing had happened. Nothing at all.

Jeff smiled. "The adjudicator will now tot up the scores," he said, and handed one gun to Susan as he removed his ear protectors. Then he fell with a sigh onto a chair and pulled off his gloves, throwing them onto the table. "Do me a favor," he said winsomely to Susan. "Put the guns away. I don't think I can walk that far."

"You've got no stamina," Rob said.

Susan picked up the guns with alacrity, feeling more than a little foolish. She could feel Rob's amused eyes on her as she walked back to the house.

She would never hear the end of it, she thought, as she put the guns, innocent of anyone's blood, back into the rack, and locked the door. Never.

* * *

The hot, heavy air was full of the wonderful smell of detonation; Jeff breathed it in as he walked back to the house to get two bottles of wine from the fridge.

Susan came into the kitchen as he was picking them up. "I'll get glasses," she said.

"Good idea," he said, walking back out to his guests.

"Right," said Neil, as he approached the table at which they were now all seated.

"Wait, wait," said Jeff. "Susan's just coming."

"Is she feeling all right?" asked Neil. "She seemed a bit nervous."

Jeff smiled. "She doesn't like guns," he said, then carefully removed the smile and arranged a look of concern. "But she's been very wound up for weeks now," he said. "I am a bit worried about her. She went back to that health farm to see if that would help, but it doesn't seem to have done."

"Maybe she's trying to do too much," said Neil.

"Could be. I think she should see a doctor, but she won't hear of it." Susan emerged from the blackness of the kitchen, and he looked around the table. "Don't mention this," he said urgently. "She'd be furious if she knew I'd said anything."

Rob frowned a little, but then he smiled at Fiona, picking up the corkscrew. "A little wine, m'lady?" he said, as Susan arrived with the glasses.

"Thank you, kind sir," said Fiona, smiling back.

Good girl. Jeff pushed over the papers that he had left on the table, his gloves and calculator on top, as Susan put down the wine glasses.

"Shall I take these away?" she asked.

It was really quite exciting, all the little things that could go wrong, things he hadn't thought of.

"Er...no," he said. "Not yet. I've not quite finished. I'll move them before the food arrives."

They all had some wine when the scores were announced.

"Rob Sheridan—eighteen," said Neil. "Jeff Bentham—twenty-one."

Rob shook Jeff's hand. "That's twenty quid I owe you," he said, as the gas-gun boomed.

"God," said Neil. "How can you put up with that thing doing that all day?"

Susan said she couldn't, and Jeff smiled, having unobtrusively pressed the stopwatch key on the calculator. "You don't really hear it after a while," he said.

Susan stood up. "I'll go and do the finishing touches," she said. "You will move that stuff, won't you, Jeff?"

"I will," he said, and smiled at the people at the table. "We've got some champagne on ice," he said, then frowned a little at something over Rob's shoulder.

Rob twisted around. "What?" he said, turning back.

Jeff inclined his head at the dark patch of earth. "That," he said. "It's been newly dug. Look."

All three turned to look at the little square of damp earth, contrasting with the dusty, dry clay beside it.

"Didn't you do it?" asked Neil.

Jeff shook his head. "Maybe John's decided to give me a hand with this place," he laughed. "Or Elsa thinks I'm not trying hard enough."

They all laughed.

"You'd have weeds encroaching on his vegetable garden," said Neil. "So he decided to do something about it himself."

Jeff nodded, amused. "Must be something like that," he said. "I hope he does the rest while he's about it."

*　　*　　*

Susan began to fill the vol-au-vents and the other things that she would never do ahead of time, on the grounds that they would end up looking like the church hall buffet.

She wondered about the papers that Jeff was working on; he and Fiona had presumably been calculating something. She hoped it was how much he thought he could get out of her.

He could have the lot; she would tell him that. If only Rob was right; if only he was going to announce that he and Fiona were going off together, it would be all right, and she could stop worrying about telling him.

Rob had meant what he had said. And life without him would be unthinkable now.

She glanced out, not sure whether she approved of the wholehearted way in which Rob was carrying out her wishes with regard to Fiona. She had half-expected to be joined by him, so that he could laugh at her, but he was engrossed in conversation, sitting on the actual garden chairs and at the actual garden table that Jeff had bought at an actual garden center. Poor Jeff. She must have been hell to live with, suspecting his every motive.

She felt better now that she was making things to eat, and

the shooting was over. She had been silly. Nothing at all had happened during the shoot; nothing had even looked like happening. The guns were locked away, and she was making everyone good things to eat. Rob would never let her forget it.

*   *   *

Everyone but Jeff was drinking; they had got onto the second bottle with startling rapidity. Fiona was discussing the gas-gun with Rob; Jeff engaged Neil in conversation about golf. That way, Neil would do the talking, and he would be free to let the minutes tick away in his head. Susan's cold buffet always required certain things to be done at the very last minute. They took about half an hour; everything was working perfectly.

And even if it all went wrong here, it wouldn't matter. If she did her finishing touches in five minutes, who would ever know what he had had in mind? If the house caught fire, if her long-lost aunt from Canada turned up, it wouldn't matter, because it simply wouldn't happen.

But nothing was going to go wrong. He took a sneaky look at the stopwatch. Four minutes to go before he too would excuse himself, for the reason that Susan herself had offered to him: to take his papers off the table and back into the house. It seemed like four years, as he steered the conversation towards a natural break which would allow him to leave.

It worked like a dream; picking up the calculator and his papers, he walked casually into the house. Three minutes fifty seconds to go. Placing the calculator and the papers on the breakfast bar, he walked through to the hall, pulling on his gloves as he crossed to the sitting room. He turned the speakers towards the open window and started the tape. Back to the hall, to unlock the gun cupboard. He removed a gun, broke it, and reached back in for a plastic bag, shaking the two items it contained out onto the floor. His gloved hand picked up one, and then the other.

Then, with the end of a pencil, taking the utmost care not to smudge the fingerprints already on them, he pressed the cartridges home.

*   *   *

She had heard Jeff come in as she worked, but he had just walked past her, and she had let him go, still unsure of how to begin. She could hear him in the hall, and she had to tell him now. Getting it over with had to be better than waiting. And there were, as Rob had pointed out, compensations for Jeff in all of this. She didn't want the money, or either of the houses, or either of the cars, come to that. She just wanted Rob, and he had said that it was now or never. Never wasn't an option, so it had to be now. She had to tell him.

"Jeff?" she called, turning.

But he wasn't in the hall; he was standing right behind her, his eyes alive again.

257

Epilogue

A sudden, deafening crack shattered the still air, disturbing the birds, but the people at the table didn't seem to notice. The woman touched the man's wine glass with her own, and took a sip as he stood the empty bottle beside another on the far side of the table, beyond the sharp, barely moving shadows of the leaves. A moment later, in a flurry of flapping wings, birds flew out of the trees, out of the tangled mass by the brook, out of the guttering of the house, and back over the fence. The silence which had followed the report was broken once again by birdsong, as they settled back down.

*　　*　　*

Inside the house Jeff watched, his eyes widening in horror as the dark red stain spread over the pale blue of Susan's shirt.

"Oh, Jeff!" she said.

He shrugged helplessly. "I'm sorry," he said. "I was just

258

trying to get the top off—oh, I'm sorry. Have you got something to change into?"

"Of course I have," she said crossly. "You get the champagne and I'll go and change."

He did as he was told, glancing out at his guests as they soaked up the summer sunshine. He smiled apologetically at Susan as she scraped surplus relish from her shirt.

She didn't smile back. "You'll have to take out the food. I won't be long." But she got to the hall door, and turned. "I'd forget the tomato relish, if I were you," she added with a smile, her good humor restored.

The gods again. She had genuinely startled him, turning and calling for him like that. He had barely had to fake the accident at all.

He waited until he heard her feet on the stairs, then went out into the hall. He picked up the phone, dialed the numbers necessary to make it ring by itself, and replaced it. There was a heartbeat's wait, then it rang out, and he picked it up.

"Hello? Oh, hello—it's been a while since I heard from you." He paused. "What? Really? Well—yes, but I've got people here... well, if you say so. Hang on."

He laid down the receiver, and went to the bottom of the stairs. "Susan?" he called.

"Yes?" she called back.

"I've got the accountant on the phone—do you think you could bring down my bank statements? They're in the safe."

"Right," she called. "I'll be a couple of minutes, though. Is that all right?"

"Fine," said Jeff.

He was talking to his accountant when she came back; he covered the receiver with his hand.

"Can you take out the champagne?" he asked apologetically. "And make my excuses? This is going to take a while."

She frowned. "What's the problem?" she asked.

"Oh—it's about some money I invested months ago. I

have to deal with it now—I'll be out as soon as I can. Oh—don't let them come in, will you? It's a bit sensitive— you know. He doesn't want it broadcast."

She pulled a face, but it was in fun. "All right," she said. "I'll entertain them. But don't be all day."

"I won't." He smiled. "Half an hour," he said. "I promise." This time she did smile back.

He watched from the hall as she picked up the champagne and went out into the bright day. He could hear his guests cheering. A few more trips, and all the food had gone out.

Now he had things to do. Jeff went upstairs, and did the first thing.

There was a lot of blood; ears were like that, of course. Jeff looked at the shirt she had been wearing, and the blood that was mingling with the stains already on it. She had rinsed it out; all the better, he thought, and nodded, holding tissues to his still-bleeding ear. Then he stuffed the stained, wet shirt into the open safe, using the tissue to push it shut and turn the key.

His calculator lay on the bedside table, on top of his bank statements and the other papers. They all had blood on them by the time he'd finished; all he had to do was shake his head like a dog drying itself.

The gun lay on the bed, and he now spent time wiping it free of prints, taking great care; it was, after all, loaded. You could have a nasty accident like that. He smiled to himself. Then he lay on the bed, where he could keep an eye on the stopwatch, and laid aside the tissue with which he had been cleaning the gun.

He would have liked to have taken a last look at his guests, but he couldn't risk going that close to the window. He would have liked to have taken a last look at Fiona. She might guess, he thought, but she would never say. She knew what had happened long before he did.

He would have liked to have taken a last look at John the

Baptist; he *had* taken his last look at the Spirit of Ecstasy that morning.

He grasped the gun awkwardly by the barrel, holding it as far away from himself as he could, with the business end pointing down at his throat, and reached up with his other hand until his thumb could just touch the trigger. He twisted around, half lying on his side, half raised off the bed; his ear bled onto the pillow. The gun pointed down at him from a height of about four feet. He had practiced this so often, it almost seemed a natural way to hold a gun.

His eyes on the calculator, he amused himself by imagining prosecuting counsel's closing speech to the jury.

"We are being asked to believe, ladies and gentlemen of the jury, that Mr. Bentham took his own life. His wife has admitted that her behavior towards her husband since she had won this enormous amount of money had been nothing short of outrageous. She had forced him from his home, from his job—she had caused him to change his name to hers, and to become totally financially dependent upon her. She is asking us to believe that for a man like Jeffrey Bentham, this was too much to bear, and he took his own life. And you may say that that does not seem an unreasonable proposition.

"But consider the facts, ladies and gentlemen. Mr. Bentham had indeed found this behavior inexplicable and bewildering; he was, understandably, upset. But quite clearly—and by the defendant's own admission—he had sought reconciliation with his wife. He sincerely believed in their marriage, and that it could withstand this setback. He was, as you have heard, cheerful and confident of the future. So why take his own life? The evidence which we have heard throughout this trial indicates that he most assuredly did not.

"And so I come to the actual shooting. If I may demonstrate, your honor?"

Jeff could see him hold the gun in exactly the almost impossible position in which he held it; fingerprints, ballistics, forensic medicine would all arrive at a very good approximation.

"Does it seem likely to you that anyone desirous of taking his life would choose to do so by lying down on a bed and holding a gun to his throat in such a very singular fashion?"

There would be laughter in the court; the judge would silence it.

"But it doesn't stop there. In order to have the gun at all, he had to remove it from a gun rack, where it had been placed by Mrs. Bentham herself. He somehow contrived to do this while at no time touching the gun at any point other than the ones at which I am touching it now; a quite remarkable feat, I think you will agree. You may feel that a more likely scenario is that the gun was pointed at his throat as he lay helpless on the bed, was fired, cleaned, and then—and only then—were his fingerprints impressed upon it."

Jeff smiled, watching the time ticking away, though he hardly had to. He knew without looking now exactly when to pull the barrel towards him, and thus push the trigger back.

"But though the gun itself was innocent of fingerprints other than those unlikely impressions, the cartridges were not. And they bore the clear impression of the thumb of Mrs. Bentham's right hand. Mrs. Bentham has offered a possible explanation for this, but you may feel that coincidence is being stretched beyond reasonable limits, should the cartridges Mr. Bentham used to take his life have been the very ones with which she claims to have been practicing loading. And the idea of Mrs. Bentham's practicing loading may in itself seem to you to be at odds with her declared dislike of firearms.

"In Mr. Bentham's safe—also bearing the impression of Mrs. Bentham's fingerprints—was found a lady's shirt, stained with Mr. Bentham's blood. An attempt had been made to wash it; it had been carried, dripping, from the bathroom of the Benthams' bedroom through the bedroom itself and

locked in the safe. Mrs. Bentham has given us an explana-
tion for changing her attire; an accident, she has told us,
with a jar of relish. And indeed relish was found on the
shirt. Perhaps Mrs. Bentham thought that forensic scientists
would be unable to distinguish between tomato relish and
human blood . . ."

More laughter, Jeff was sure. He would have liked to have
been a barrister. But his thoughts of changing direction
within the law had been abandoned when he had found
himself with a wife to support.

". . . or perhaps, rather more pertinently, that was simply
to confuse, should she be unable to dispose of the garment at
some later time, if—as proved to be the case—washing it
failed to remove the stains. She has offered us no explanation
at all for its being in the safe.

"This murder had been very carefully planned. A patch of
ground had been newly dug; Mr. Bentham had not dug it,
though he alone worked on the garden. So who? His next-
door neighbor denies any knowledge of it, as does his wife,
but then . . ."

A knowing look. Jeff could see it. He could see the
courtroom, the judge, the jury. He could see the clerk,
looking disapproving when people laughed. There was quite
a lot of laughter in court; especially the magistrates' court,
which was his more usual stamping ground. But even in
Crown Court. Even at murder trials.

"Newly dug ground immediately following a tragic shoot-
ing would of course raise suspicions; by digging it before-
hand, Mrs. Bentham hoped to escape detection. I think we
can assume that this was where the blood-stained shirt
would have been interred, had there been time.

"But perhaps most damning of all is the cassette tape
found on the hi-fi. A forty-five minute tape, yielding no
fingerprints, blank for almost all of its length until the sound
of one gunshot. The gunshot, ladies and gentlemen, that
everyone in the garden heard, when Mrs. Bentham was

sitting with them. This was to prove beyond a doubt that she could not have fired the gun.

"Mrs. Bentham was alone in the house with her husband, when the regular bang from the next-door bird-scarer was heard. This sound would have masked the sound of a shot fired in the house. Mr. Bentham, who merely left to take some papers inside, never emerged again. Mrs. Bentham did. Having changed her clothes, and explaining her husband's sudden absence by saying that he had been called to the telephone by his accountant, who denies having made any such call.

"It was fortunate indeed that when the recorded shot was heard, Mr. Bentham's guests included the recently retired police superintendent Neil Holder, who could see at a glance that this was not a man who had died only moments previously, but—as was later to be confirmed—some twenty to forty minutes before that shot was ever heard. Thus it was that he ensured that nothing in the house was touched, and directed police attention to the possibility of a recorded shot, and thus it was that vital evidence which would undoubtedly have been removed, remained to be discovered.

"There is no doubt whatever that this was murder, and the forensic, pathological and eyewitness evidence points unerringly at the defendant as its perpetrator."

Downstairs, the tape played silently. Another twenty-five minutes to go before that recorded shot was heard, between gas-gun blasts, and they would come running into the house and find him. And one minute before the next gas-gun blast, and death.

The last minute. The last minute of his life. The realization of his fantasy. Because he had lost his life already; he had lost everything. Money couldn't make up for it.

He had thought that he had a good marriage; oh, he had played around, but that had never mattered. Susan had mattered. They had moved to the flat because she didn't like his mother. They had moved to the semi because she didn't like the flat. He had tried to surprise her with the semi, but she hadn't liked it much either. Still, he had done his best. He had always done his best. He had thought they had a good marriage, and all the time she must have hated him.

Hated him enough to steal his life, to take it as surely as if she *was* about to pull this trigger. And without the life he knew, he hadn't wanted to go on breathing. But that hadn't seemed like enough; no one would have made her pay for what she had done. And that was why he had to murder himself.

He would have much preferred the spiritual and physical comfort of his Rolls Royce, and its gentle, quiet poison sending him to sleep, but they wouldn't have put Susan away for that.

His eye on the seconds, he braced himself against the bed. The gun at his throat, the seconds counting down, Jeff smiled, and looked on the bright side. He had beaten Rob at the clay pigeon shoot.

*   *   *

The gas-gun exploded, but no one took much notice, not even the birds. Four people sat at the table under the tree, two men and two women. They weren't young, they weren't old. They were eating, drinking, talking, as the afternoon glinted dully on the dark glass of the empty champagne bottle, thrust upside down in the melting ice. The ice had turned entirely to water by the time the gas-gun sounded again, making as little impression on the group as it had before.

But then another loud crack echoed through the air, which made all four turn their heads sharply, and look towards the house.

And that was just the beginning.